BROKEN BRIDGES

BROKEN BRIDGES

SID GARDNER

iUniverse LLC
Bloomington

Broken Bridges

iUniverse books may be ordered through booksellers or by contacting:

iUniverse LLC
1663 Liberty Drive
Bloomington, IN 47403
www.iuniverse.com
1-800-Authors (1-800-288-4677)

ISBN: 978-1-4917-0735-7 (sc)
ISBN: 978-1-4917-0736-4 (ebk)

Printed in the United States of America

iUniverse rev. date: 09/16/2013

CHAPTER 1

The world was nothing but pain, and pain was colored light green. Slowly, Joe Brenner opened his eyes, squinting through the sharp ache knifing into his body and his dizzy brain. The green became the walls of what he finally made out to be a hospital room.

He closed his eyes and tried to remember. The spinning began again, and at first, all he could fasten on were flashes, loud flashes in the night. Gunshots, he remembered, there had been gunshots. Lots of them. And aimed at him.

It started to come together and then the fear hit, riding up over his wounds. He jerked his head up to look around the room, almost blacking out with the pain.

A woman's voice came, soft and yet intense. "You're safe. You've been shot. There's a cop outside the door. You're OK."

Joe tried to watch her through the haze, but his eyes could not stay open. As she talked, almost whispering, the nurse reached up and turned a dial on one of the tubes running under the sheet covering his arm. "You need to sleep some more," she said. The last word sounded like *morrrrrrrr*, fading into silence as he slid back down into sleep.

Later, Joe awoke again. The ache was still there, a hundred-pound rock on his shoulder now instead of a hot poker jammed into it. Then he felt the throbbing in his left leg. He saw another nurse talking quietly with a doctor on the far side of the room. When they realized he was awake, they walked over and stood beside his bed. The doctor, a young Asian man with long hair, said, "Welcome back, Joe. How are you feeling?"

"It hurts. Shoulder and leg. Both hurt, a lot." Then he felt how much talking hurt, too.

"You took two rounds, one tore up your shoulder pretty good. You're lucky." He waited, trying to see how much Joe was able to understand. "There's an officer outside and another stopped by an hour ago. They want to talk with you about what happened."

"Not now," Joe mumbled. "Maybe later." *If I'm feeling suicidal.*

"Fine. We'll have him come back tomorrow morning."

By then, Joe was alert enough to realize they would want to know who had shot him. Since he knew, he also knew that if he told the cops, the Vatos would come after him again as soon as he got out. He started to worry, and tried to work out how to get out of the hospital before they found him.

Anticipating, the doctor said, "We're going to have you moved to our rehab facility next door under a different name. You need to work on that leg and make sure you can walk again. We'll check you out of the hospital, and no one will know where you are. Your aunt tried to reach you, but we told her no visitors." He stopped, studying Joe. "You're going to have to talk to the police, Joe. Whoever came after you was serious, and you're still in a lot of danger."

"I know. I'll talk to them. But not now."

But when the detective came the next morning, Joe told him he had no idea who had shot him. The detective, whose name was Facelli, knew he was lying, and only asked one more question. "You were in Vato territory. Someone told us you were dealing for the Valley Muerte family. That puts you across the line. That true?"

"I've heard of them, sure. But I don't deal for them, either one. And I don't know anything about any line."

Facelli just stared at him, then said "OK, Joe. You want to take your chances out there, fine with us. But the line you crossed is a big deal these days, now that things are getting a lot tighter. Everyone's defending their turf now, and the shooters are out enforcing it. You help us, Joe, maybe we can help you stay out of the crossfire."

Joe just shook his head and refused to look at the detective.

"Have it your way for now," Facelli said, disgusted. "But I'd retire if I were you, Joe. You really pissed somebody off."

The rehab building was behind the hospital, connected by a walkway on the third floor. The rehab therapist had told Joe that he needed to walk every day after his physical therapy session in the morning. The therapist, an older Latino guy, said he could walk in the hospital where the corridors were longer, but told him to stay off the first floor where people could see him and he might be recognized.

Joe started out with short supervised walks, a few steps at a time. As he gained strength, they let him go off for longer strolls. His leg had suffered a through-wound, and the calf muscle was painful but not enough to keep him from walking. He began exploring different sections of the hospital, trying to keep his mind off what would happen when he left.

Joe was familiar with hospitals, where his mother had worked as a nurse's aide while she was still alive. She had enrolled him in the employees' child care center and after he started school, he would take the bus to be with his mother after his school let out. His mother would come off shift and they would walk home together. Hospitals didn't scare him the way they did many people, because he knew his mother and later, his sister, worked there. He remembered being proud that his mother had a job where she helped people who were hurt or sick.

As he walked down a new corridor he hadn't explored before, limping and still trying to get his leg to work right, Joe noticed the walls were painted with what seemed to be weird colors. One wall was all blue and the opposite one was pink. He walked past some open doors with signs that said "OB-G."

It seemed quieter in this part of the hospital. Joe realized he hadn't heard any announcements on the public address system, but occasionally, as a door opened, he heard a small squawking sound. To his ear, it sounded as if something had gone wrong with the speakers on the PA system.

He passed through a set of double doors and immediately saw a view he had only seen in movies. In front of him, through a large window, he saw row after row of small plastic containers, each of which held a baby. Nurses were moving slowly through the rows of containers, adjusting the blankets covering each baby—which Joe then saw were either blue or pink.

He took a few hesitant steps down the hall and came to a second window that faced into a smaller room with fewer plastic containers, eight of them in two rows of four. The sign over this window read "NICU."

The nurses in this section were moving rapidly, looking at the dials on monitors that stood by each tiny container and checking the tubing that ran into the containers. Three of the little bins had plastic tents draped over them.

A security desk stood in the corridor outside the section, and a uniformed guard from a private firm was watching Joe from behind the desk.

And then Joe saw two of the nurses and a young girl, maybe fifteen or so, with a big badge that said *Aide*, sitting in the back of the room in rocking chairs, holding impossibly tiny bundles, rocking them back and forth.

As Joe was watching, a nurse came out of the door into the hallway, moving quickly. Joe caught up to her and said, "Excuse me, nurse. Why are those babies in that room?"

"That's intensive care. The Newborn Intensive Care Unit. Most of them were born premature and sick because their moms used drugs while they were pregnant." She said it with a tone of disgust, and hurried past Joe.

And as Joe heard these words and tried to fit them into his view of how the world worked, a memory popped up. Joe, sitting with his mother and sister, putting puzzles together after dinner. As the youngest, Joe often got help from Esther and Dolores, and sometimes one of them would hand him a piece with a smile and say, "Try this one—right there." And he would fit it in, and it would always click right into place.

But this time, what had clicked into place didn't feel so good. Facts he had never wanted to think about were suddenly realities, visible through the windows, tiny bundles under pink and blue blankets.

What happens to customers after they walk away with what I sell them? He had never asked himself that question. He'd never needed to—and he never wanted to. It was a thought he had always been able to push away, until he saw eight little plastic containers surrounded by all those instruments and dials.

Out of the corner of his eye Joe saw that the security guard was still watching him, with a frown now. Joe went back to his room, tired from his short walk, struggling with what he had seen. He knew what he was—he was a drug dealer. Escaping the chaos in his family, he had drifted into a life that kept him apart, making transactions, making a living, reporting back to his supplier, following the rules of the street and the drug trade.

But now, suddenly, with the shooting, those rules were gone and he was on his own, wounded, hunted and isolated. He would have to leave the Valley. To go where, at the moment, he had no idea.

The next day, Joe retraced his steps down to the maternity floor, ending up standing outside the NICU. He watched the babies for a long time. The guard had gotten used to him and left him alone.

As he began to turn away, he saw the door at the back of the room open, and a small woman entered, walking very tentatively with a nurse beside her. The nurse was frowning, and held onto the woman's arm as she took her over to one of the containers. The woman's legs were in shackles—her hands were free but she was shuffling along with the shackles dragging beneath her feet. The nurse led her over to a chair and brought a baby to her, covered in a pink blanket. As the nurse held the baby, Joe saw that the baby was jerking her body back and forth, kicking out and then lying still. The nurse gently handed the baby to the woman, who was crying by now and held the baby as if she had no idea what to do. The nurse spoke to her, angrily, and Joe saw the hurt look on the woman's face. With tears rolling down her cheeks, she took the baby and began to rock slowly while looking down at the small pink bundle in her arms.

And another piece of the puzzle clicked into place. Joe knew, while wanting very much not to know, that the woman was one of his customers, Luisa Contreras, and that he had sold her meth twice in the last few months. Moving over to the corner of the window, he watched the baby continue to convulse and kick out, struggling against her mother.

And then Joe's own struggles began, and he knew that he was no longer a spectator. He'd been making his living selling drugs, selling and moving on to the next sale. But through the window, he had begun to see what his sales meant to other people's lives on the buyer's side of the deal.

Joe continued to stare at the baby from the edge of the window, out of Luisa's line of sight. Then he noticed the security guard walking toward him. He asked Joe, "Can I help you?"

Joe said, "No, thanks. I was just watching them. I'm from the rehab center. I like to watch them." He tried to sound simple, and harmless. It seemed to have worked, because the guard walked back and sat down at his desk, returning to some paper work he'd been doing.

After a few minutes, the woman in the shackles stood up and handed the baby back to a nurse, then shuffled off through the door at the back of the NICU, which opened into another hallway.

Joe turned away and looked down at his hands, which had begun, against his will, to try to wipe themselves clean, wiping each other, wiping again. His hands were clean, but he knew now that he'd left marks on the lives he'd just seen in the small room behind the glass, marks visible in the struggles of a tiny baby girl and the hesitant uncertainties of her mother.

The hallway door into the NICU opened, and a nurse walked out into the hallway. He walked beside her, waiting to speak until she was out of sight of the security guard. "Excuse me, nurse. I was just watching through the window. Could you tell me something about the little girl in the back row? The one whose mother was just here. How's she doing?"

The nurse looked back into the room to make sure she knew which one he meant. "That one's in pretty bad withdrawal. The mother admitted she'd been drinking and using meth in the last few days before she delivered. These women—I don't know how they could be so thoughtless to want to put a baby through that."

"What does withdrawal mean, how long does it last?"

"Usually they get through the worst of it after a hard week or so. But with some, we have to keep them in here longer than that. The convulsions stop, and they get to where they can sleep better. But you can't comfort them, they're really hard to quiet down. And sometimes the effects go on for years. It affects their brains and the way they behave—their whole life. Just because some selfish junkie couldn't kick while she was pregnant."

As she walked away, Joe was still having a hard time putting all the pieces together. He knew the baby was sick, and he knew it was because of the drugs he had sold Luisa, and what Luisa had done while she was pregnant. But now he had to deal with what the nurse had told him. The baby was not going to be sick for just a few days—this could go on for the baby's whole life.

Joe knew that he was in danger—in so much danger now that this part of his life was over. He couldn't go back to dealing, not in his old neighborhood or anywhere else in the Valley. They would find him, his own crew would not protect him, and he was expendable.

And as that certainty sank in, he also knew that the little girl in the NICU, the tiny pink bundle, was also in danger. And those two ideas—the abrupt ending of this part of his life and the painful beginning of hers, began to grow together.

Joe wasn't sure why, but for the first time since his mother had gotten sick, he was worried about himself, and at the same time, about someone else.

The next day, he was back at the window. He watched the baby, comparing her with the other babies in the NICU. Her jerky movements seemed less frequent, and for long moments she rested, but then jerked again, as if she were afraid to stop moving. He continued to look at her, watching her tiny arms and legs, moving, then still, then moving again. *She's getting better*, he thought, *maybe she'll keep getting better. Maybe she'll be all right.*

He turned and began walking back to his room. The nurse he had talked with yesterday passed him in the hall and smiled. "How's that baby?"

"She's doing better," Joe said. "She looks like she's doing a lot better."

"Let's hope so," the nurse said with a frown. "The odds against her are pretty bad." Then she looked at Joe. "Why are you asking? Do you know her mother or something?"

"No, no. I just saw her mother come in when I was watching yesterday and wondered what was going to happen. When does she get to take the baby home?"

The nurse frowned again. "Probably never. The baby's on our watch list of drug-exposed infants, and that means the county will start court action to take custody away. That mom probably isn't going to get that baby back for a long time, if ever. She's back in the county lockup."

"So what happens to the baby?"

"They put her in foster care or an infant shelter, until the mom finally gets TPR'd—that means they take away all her legal rights to be a parent—termination of parental rights. And then the kid gets adopted, probably."

"Oh. Adopted."

"Yes. If all the agencies involved get their act together—the hospital, child welfare, the court—they all get into it. It's a mess, sometimes, and the little kids don't always get the breaks." And then she smiled at Joe, and Joe began to realize that she wasn't bothered by all his questions, and was actually trying to prolong the conversation, and might even have figured out what time of day he was dropping by the NICU.

She was cute, in a Jennifer Lopez kind of way, with pulled-back hair and great teeth setting off a lovely smile. He noticed her name tag, which said Serena Salas, and then she noticed him noticing.

She smiled, put out her hand, and said "I'm Serena—what's your name?"

"Joe, Joe Brenner." He looked at his watch and said "Got to get back to rehab. Thanks for talking to me."

She said, "Yeah. See you."

The next day, back at the window, Serena walked by again and Joe knew now that she was making a real effort to connect with him. He smiled and said "Hi. Good to see you."

Serena asked him if he wanted to join her for lunch out in the employee's patio area. Joe was uneasy, but he didn't want to stop talking to this pretty girl who seemed to want to talk to him. So he got a sandwich and a drink in the cafeteria line and joined her under one of the umbrellas. She had spread out the lunch she had brought from home, and started eating her salad.

She smiled and asked him, "Tell me about yourself. I know . . ." she paused, embarrassed, "I know you were dealing and that you got in trouble doing it. But what did you do before that?"

Reluctantly, he told her a little about his mother and father, enough for her to say when he fell silent, "Wow—a pretty bad dad and a pretty great mom." She laughed, trying to lighten it up a little bit. "Which one do you take after?"

And Joe was unable to answer, until the silence became awkward and he stammered "My mom, I guess. I hope."

After she left, as he walked back to his room in the rehab unit, he replayed her question. *Which one do you take after?* A drunk who thought only of himself, or a music-lover who cared passionately about her kids and the people she took care of in her work? He hoped he could figure out the answer—and he hoped he'd see Serena again. He knew he'd keep going back to the NICU window until he was discharged. And then he wondered again what he would do next.

Walking back to the rehab unit, Joe's leg bothered him more than usual. He was reminded again that being wounded had begun to change his life. He'd been wounded by the Vatos, he'd grown up wounded, and now he knew that another life had been wounded by what he'd done.

And gradually he began to think about someone who could handle the wounded, someone who had been wounded herself, and could bring her great gifts of compassion to the task of handling the wounded.

Joe figured it was time to get in touch with his sister.

CHAPTER 2

Joe Brenner grew up in the San Fernando Valley, not in the heart of the barrios or the endless blocks of low-rent apartments, but not far enough from them to feel he had escaped. His family moved four times while he was in school, so he never formed close ties with any one group. He had learned to be cautious, a loner, always watching out for the explosions at home and those that happened almost daily in the high schools of the Valley. He had become skilled at knowing when a fight was close to breaking out and how to move away from any spillover.

Joe wasn't bad-looking, and a girl who liked him for a while when he was at Grant High told him once he looked like an "early, short John Travolta." He *was* short, 5'7", and thought of himself as a little guy. He had tried lifting weights in high school and had bulked up a bit, but he had never wanted to go the next step, the steroids or huge amounts of vitamin supplements that the coaches sold to the jocks. So he stayed small.

He had dark brown hair that he wore longer than the usual shaved head or buzzed cut of his classmates. He didn't feel the need to look like the rest of them, and later, it helped him seem less threatening to buyers, especially women. He had no tattoos. Lacking tats was another kind of protective camouflage in a neighborhood where all the gangbangers and wannabes had them, along with half the rest of the population under 30.

Guys sometimes made fun of him for his hair and his unmarked skin, but it was a quiet way of saying he was different.

Joe *was* different, stuck between the walls of Anglo and Latino life. His last name wasn't Latino, his face was. And he ended up suspended between the two worlds.

Joe's father Mike was the dominant fact of their family: a veteran who had become an alcoholic bully with no idea of how to be a father to two teenagers and no interest in learning. Mike was angry at his kids, his wife, and his life. He drove and repaired trucks intermittently, but had no steady job. Joe's mother, Esther, had a job as a nurse's assistant at a local hospital, which was the source of the only dependable earned income in the family.

No matter what they did, Joe and Dolores, his sister who was three years older, were verbally abused by Mike. When he was drunk, he would also push them around, grabbing their arms and forcing them into their rooms. As Mike grew fatter and fatter with his drinking and sedentary lifestyle, he was less able to catch them, and they both became adept at moving out of his reach and leaving the house when he lost control. Esther simply stayed in the kitchen, and through some kind of strange, unspoken truce, Mike never hit her, despite hurling curses at her whenever she dared to stand up for Joe or Dolores.

Joe once asked his sister why she thought Esther had ever married Mike. Dolores, then in high school, said "One day Mom told me what he was like when they were in high school together. She said he was big and strong, and he protected her. You've seen the pictures, Joe—she was beautiful when she was in high school. She never finished, she dropped out and had to go to work in the hospital as soon as she got pregnant with me. But Mike was a provider then, working on cars after school and making decent money. And then he went right into the Corps after he graduated, and she lived with Aunt Josie. That lasted four years, and she said when he came back he'd started to drink a lot. The jobs got harder and harder to keep, and the money got scarce. She got pregnant with you when he was on leave. And so she stayed. She told me once she had no idea what any other life would be like, and she wanted us to have a decent life off welfare. So she stayed."

For three years while they were in elementary school, Esther had scraped together enough money to send them to the parish Catholic school, St. Anthony's. The public school in the rundown neighborhood where they were then living was sub-standard, and their mother had for once stood up to Mike and saved money from her small salary to pay the tuition.

The parochial teachers were strict, but generally cared about the children. After they moved away from that neighborhood when Esther got a raise, they returned to the public schools.

What Joe remembered most from his time at St. Anthony's was the idea of an act of atonement. His catechism class had drilled the students on the idea of atonement, and his mother had told him she was proud that he understood what it meant. So Joe had become convinced that he had to perform an act of atonement every time he committed a "sin." When he hurt another child on the playground, or when his mother complained that he had ruined his clothes by getting them dirty, he innocently asked the teacher what acts of atonement he could perform. Usually they smiled and told him to say twenty Hail Marys. Once when he had gotten into a real fistfight with another boy, the teacher made him stay after school and wash the blackboards.

But he never performed an act of atonement involving his father.

One of Joe's strongest memories of his mother was of Esther walking around singing songs in Spanish, singing softly so his father would not wake and strike out at one of them. His mother had the Linda Ronstadt *Canciones* albums, songs Linda had made for her father. Esther sang along with Linda, her tiny voice reaching for the high notes which seemed to go on for longer than anyone could possibly hold a note.

And then Joe had graduated, improbably, from those versions of the extraordinary Ronstadt to finding an old DVD of the film, *Pirates of Penzance*, in which Ronstadt starred. Joe had several fantasies about the rest of his life, but the most active one was about Linda Ronstadt. He had heard that she was half-Mexican, and had half-fallen in love with her—or at least with the Ronstadt in the movies and music she had made in the 80's.

To a kid like Joe, the Gilbert and Sullivan musical was a bit like trying to understand Mandarin, but he watched and listened through the entire video over and over. And when she came walking in her tiny, dainty steps down the cliffside singing *Poor Wandering One*, he melted every time.

And that fake English beach on a sound set in Burbank became, for Joe, an imagined place of escape, where lusty singing and beautiful girls were at the center of daily life, as normal as the sounds of police sirens rising nightly out over the fiercest battlegrounds of the Valley. And forever after, Joe watched all the girls that came across his path through that improbable lens, a musical comedy tradition that would have been utterly incomprehensible to any of his peers—had they ever encountered it.

Soon after Joe entered high school, his mother had gotten a cough that wouldn't leave, and had started to miss work, which enraged his father all the more, since they needed the money. The cough turned into lung cancer. She had never smoked, but Mike's cigarette smoke filled the apartment from the moment he woke up.

She died when Joe was fourteen, and it deadened something within him for a long time. He cut off emotion, went cold, tried to be as tough as his father wanted him to be, feeling nothing. He distanced himself from his friends and from his customers as well, once he began dealing drugs.

But Luisa Contreras had been an exception. Joe knew that she cleaned houses, and he saw how strung out she was when she bought from him. She was thin, and very short, with long, dark hair that she wore in a braid. He had tried making conversation with her once or twice, but she was always in a hurry to get back to her own home. The last time he had sold to her, he wondered why such a skinny girl had become so overweight.

Joe had gotten into selling drugs through a cousin who had persuaded Joe that he could make ridiculously easy money by taking a package across the Valley to "a friend." Joe hadn't realized it was a test, an entry fee he had gladly paid that moved him across the line to a criminal act. Joe liked the money, and he liked the sense of greater control of his life that the money represented. Once he had broken the law, he had carried, he was *involved*. And it got easier for them to ask him to do the next job and easier for him to say yes.

Joe's move into dealing drugs hadn't been all that complicated. His cousin was connected, his father refused to give him any money, and he wanted to buy some of the stuff that other kids had.

Joe had carefully stayed on the outer edge of the dealing business. Twice he had been offered "promotions," which meant the chance to have other dealers reporting to him, a larger territory, and a bigger commission.

But Joe had seen enough from the edges to know that the center of the business was a place of ruthless, random violence, and he had seen enough of random violence growing up. He wanted nothing to do with it. He was aware of all of it: the enforcers who came after anyone who named names when they were arrested, the sellers who were users, and the mysterious Chief of the Muerte crew—*El Jefe*—who controlled one-third of the Valley and was in unending battles to protect that share from the Salvadoreans, the Zeta offshoots, and the new Chinese gangs who had moved into drugs.

After he had been dealing for three years after graduating from high school, Joe was approached by his cousin with a much more dangerous offer. It meant a lot more money, so Joe was uncertain for a few days about how he was going to respond. This time they wanted him to sell across the line, into the Vatos area. The excuse was that it was in a quiet residential area instead of out on one of the main streets where most of the dealing took place. But Joe knew it was a deliberate probe. And even when they offered him double his usual cut of the deal—which meant an extra $250 for a few minutes of work—Joe knew it might end up being a bad idea. He thought about some new music software that he had read about, and then decided to take the risk.

It was definitely a risk. Within an hour of crossing the line, a car drove by the convenience store where Joe was dealing and shots were fired at him.

CHAPTER 3

Two weeks went by, and Joe worked every day on his rehab while his leg got stronger and his shoulder stopped hurting. He went down to the NICU area almost every day, pausing only briefly to look in and see if Luisa's baby was still there. He could tell the security staff was keeping an eye on him.

He had lunch with Serena three times during the two weeks. She didn't work full time, explaining that she was taking classes at the local community college to try to get a promotion on the nursing staff. He enjoyed talking with her, but always held something back, something he felt he couldn't give until he decided what he was going to do after the hospital.

Finally the rehab supervisor told Joe they were going to discharge him on a Friday, which was two days away. He had spent a lot of time in the hospital thinking about his next moves. He was worried about going back to his apartment, because he had no idea where he stood with his own crew or with the gang that had shot him.

And he continued to worry about Luisa's baby.

On the day he was discharged from the rehab facility, Joe called his cousin Charlie. After not getting an answer to four calls, he began to worry that something had gone wrong. Since Charlie had been the one who told him to sell across the line in Vato territory, Joe knew that Charlie knew he'd been shot. Not being able to get in touch with Charlie made Joe wonder if the Muertes had a problem with him.

Joe knew that he had no real problems with the police, as long as he kept quiet about the Vatos. He'd always been careful not to carry drugs when he was dealing, and he had none on him when he was shot. He had worked out an arrangement with the uncle of one of the gang members to stash his drugs in an employee's locker

16

just inside the back door of a restaurant located on one of the strip malls. He'd get an order from a customer, call one of the runners who worked for the gang, get the drugs, and immediately hand them off to one of the kids to deliver to the customer or drop them in a pre-arranged location, usually to a car left open in the parking lot of one of the apartment buildings where most of his customers lived.

Joe checked out of the hospital and headed back to his apartment, after picking up his car at the county impound lot where it had been towed after he'd been shot. He had enough on one of his credit cards to cover the fees. When he got three blocks from his apartment, he called Charlie again, but still there was no answer. He pulled over in a drugstore parking lot, and began planning his moves. He figured that Charlie's not answering meant he had problems with the Valley Muerte organization as well as the Vatos. Just showing up at his apartment was going to be risky.

He waited until it got dark, and then parked his car a block from the apartment. He carefully walked up the back stairs of his building, which weren't visible from the street. He had hidden a key inside a hollow railing on a balcony next to the stairs, and after looking around and seeing no one, quickly used the key to get into the apartment.

He kept the lights off, and moved through the apartment. It was a one-bedroom apartment which Joe had chosen for its location on a quiet side street in Van Nuys. There was a light over the stove in the kitchen which couldn't be seen from the living room windows. After checking the threads he'd placed across the front and back door sills and finding them intact, he sat down in his computer chair and began to think about his options.

He knew he had to leave; the apartment wasn't safe until he got some kind of word from Charlie that he was OK with the Muerte organization. He had no idea if the Vatos would be coming after him again, or if his crossing their line meant they would be going after Muerte higher-ups. But he had to leave.

Joe collected some money he had hidden in the apartment, two credit cards he had never used, and a backup cellphone. He grabbed a suitcase, packed some clothes using a tiny flashlight he kept near his bed, along with his laptop and his guitar. He went back into the kitchen, after picking up a photo album from the living room.

He sat for a moment in the kitchen, looking through the album. Pictures of him and Dolores trick or treating at Halloween, school pictures from St. Anthony's and their high school, pictures of Esther when she was well, and a few, almost too painful to look at, of her in her final months.

And he remembered Serena asking the question: "Which one do you take after?"

His leg was aching again, and he took some painkillers.

Joe drove to a motel in Pasadena which was mid-scale enough for him to feel he would be safe there for a night or two. He settled into the motel room, and then connected with the internet on a secure line through his cell phone. He began trying to access the hospital records. He used an old code number that Dolores had sometimes used from home when she worked at the hospital, which Joe had kept in his contacts list. The code still worked.

After half an hour, he had the latest report on the baby—whose name, he found, was Isabel Contreras. Since he was masquerading as a hospital employee, the privacy safeguards on information going outside the hospital didn't apply. He had to plow though the medical jargon, but was able to find out that her prognosis had improved and that she would be in the hospital for another two days. Then, the record indicated, she would be transferred to the infant group home run by the county Department of Child Welfare.

The hospital record said, tersely, "Mother is not expected to be released from county detention until her court date," which was set a week away.

Joe had taken the photo album from his apartment, and sat looking at it again. He kept looking at the pictures of Esther, remembering the good times with her and Dolores, the times when they were away from Mike and the times before Mike's near-total collapse. And when he looked up from the album, his thoughts went back to the eight little containers in the NICU, zooming in on the little pink blanket in the back row.

He turned a page of the album, and saw a picture of Esther holding him. He was about a year old, and Dolores was standing beside them, with her hand on Joe's shoulder. He sat looking at the picture for a long time. Then he turned out the light and went to bed.

The next morning, Joe grabbed a quick drivethrough breakfast and came back to the motel. He logged on and looked up Department of Child Welfare in the search function on the *LA Times* website. He quickly found more than a dozen stories.

DCW Workers Fired After Children Found Wandering
DCW Sends Children Back Home, Children Beaten
DCW Director Leaves, Temporary Head Appointed
Temporary DCW Head Leaves
Board of Supervisors Report Says DCW Understaffed

He took out the photo album again. On the last page, a picture of Dolores caught his eye. Dolores had just gotten back from her combat medic training and wore her Navy dress whites with the medic's arm band. She was standing with Joe; the picture had been taken by their aunt.

He stared at the picture for several minutes, and then quickly stood up.

CHAPTER 4

Joe had bought his car a year ago on a used car lot in the Valley. It was a five-year-old white Ford Escape, which Joe had bought because it was so nondescript he knew it would never attract attention.

After making enough turns and stops to make sure that no one was following him, Joe drove to the bank in Glendale where he had deposited most of his earnings from drugs, and withdrew it all. It was about $15,000, which he took out over a two-day period to avoid the reporting laws. He stayed overnight in a cheap motel near the bank.

After he picked up the rest of the money, Joe bought a new cellphone using cash for a one-year advance payment, giving a false name and address. At another store, he picked up five one-time phones. His years of selling drugs had taught him some of the cut-out tricks used by dealers, and he knew he'd need them in the days ahead.

He stopped at a Target. He sat in his car for ten minutes, staring ahead at the front of the store. Then, after looking around, he entered the store. He picked up a laundry basket, a baby carrier/ car seat combination, and five towels. He added newborn-sized diapers, formula and bottles, baby wipes, and five outfits—three pink ones, and two yellow ones.

He went back to the motel and checked the hospital records again. Isabel had been moved out of the NICU, but was still in the newborn unit. Then he began thinking about the police. He knew they would come after him once he was on their radar again. His frequent visits to the NICU would be noticed, and his stay in the hospital would lead them to the rehab facility, even though he had been checked in under another name. He realized they would start looking for Dolores, and wondered how well she was hidden.

Then he remembered Uncle Walt.

Walter Brenner lived in Bakersfield. He had visited Joe's family a few times when Joe was growing up, but he and Mike, predictably, didn't get along that well. Joe had gone up to Bakersfield to stay with his uncle's family once, but all he could remember was a big German shepherd that scared him badly when it growled at him every time he came into the room.

But Joe figured that Uncle Walt might be a good way to throw the cops off his trail for a few days. So he sent him a postcard, saying he was planning to come to visit in a few days. Then he sent another postcard to himself at his apartment, with nothing on it except Walt's address. He knew they would eventually find his apartment and search it.

Getting the baby out of the hospital was much easier than it should have been.

Before he checked out, Joe had wandered around the hospital's security setup, after making friends with a hospital security officer who lived in his neighborhood. He studied the banks of cameras and saw which one was looking into the newborn unit. He timed it, and saw that the camera focused on the newborns and the NICU area every two minutes, and then for only about five seconds. On his last visit to the unit, he had noted where the camera was placed and what area it was scanning.

Joe drove to the hospital and parked in the employees' parking lot. He walked in through the visitors' entrance and gave the name of a patient who had been listed in the online register. He located the hospital laundry, which was in the basement. Joe saw quickly that clean uniforms were piled neatly by the door where no one inside the laundry could see when someone picked one up. He quickly placed one in a shopping bag he had brought from the hospital gift store.

The baby had been moved into the area where the other newborns were kept, which Joe assumed meant that she was doing better. But there were still lots of machines beside her crib. And Joe could easily see from the window that she looked smaller than the other babies.

Joe changed into the hospital uniform in the men's room. He walked down to the basement and reached into the storage room for the rolling crib he had gotten from the hallway outside the newborns area. Back in the elevator, he went up to the second floor and walked quickly into the newborn unit. Wheeling the crib over to the nurse who was at a desk in the back of the room, he said, "Dr. Landry asked me to bring her down to the NICU unit—they want to do some tests on the equipment they have in there." He had gotten the doctor's name from the hospital register—Landry headed up the NICU team.

The duty nurse said, "You have to sign for her."

Joe quickly scribbled a name on the clipboard sheet she handed him, turned, and wheeled the baby out. Once he was out of sight, he went into the men's room where he had stashed the baby carrier and lifted her into it, pushing the crib over into a stall and lifting it up onto a toilet where it was out of sight.

He had found two exits to the hospital that were used by staff, and headed for the one that was closest to the parking lot. As he approached the door, the guard stepped forward and looked into the carrier.

"What a cutie," the guard said. "You taking her out?"

"Her mom's car is parked in the back."

"Bye, cutie," the guard said.

And it was done. Joe knew the second, harder part was just beginning—but he had gotten through the first part without a hitch.

Headed east on the 10, Joe looked down at the basket and then up at the road. He had filled a laundry basket with the softest towels he could find in the Target store. Isabel had fussed with the formula he had carefully poured into the small bottles he bought, but she had drunk most of a bottle and then fell back asleep. He had watched carefully how the nurses fed her, and had been able to read the brand names on the bottles of formula they used. Her twitching had lessened, but he still felt her tiny, random kicks sometimes as he drove. He watched carefully for CHP vehicles.

DWFB—driving while feeding baby, he thought. *Just what I need. Highway Patrol would love that.*

He figured it would take the cops a few days to connect him with the baby, and then they would start looking for him and his car. So he had to keep moving, and then hide the car, get new plates—or sell the car.

CHAPTER 5

The road opened up after Beaumont and Banning, and then he took the turn over to Twenty-nine Palms. The route was familiar, since Joe had ridden in the back seat many times as his father took the family on enforced "camping trips" out to where he had been stationed. The trips and the camping left him with a deepened hatred for his father but had not affected his love of the desert. Both Joe and his sister had welcomed the quiet, the empty spaces between the little cities and towns. Getting out on the desert had been an escape from Mike's belligerence as it rose and fell with his drinking.

As he drove, Joe remembered the good parts of those trips. In his memory, sunrises competed with sunsets for color, with only a few clouds needed to explode the dawn or prolong the dusk with ever-changing colors. He and Dolores had learned a few of the names of the desert plants, creosote and Joshua trees and other forms of cacti. The desert, when they could get out away from their camp, was a place of silence, without yelling or arbitrary rules. And at night, when the vast array of stars came into view, they took their canvas chairs out away from the tent and just sat quietly watching the universe going about its own mysterious, faraway business.

At a rest stop, Joe pulled over. He had a number for Luisa Contreras, and hoped that it was working. He figured she'd been released on bail by then, but wasn't sure. He called and listened to the ring. Finally it was picked up.

"Hello?"

"Luisa, this is a friend. I can't tell you my name. I want to help you and your baby. Have they told you what is going to happen? Are you going to get custody back?"

She started crying. "They told me I couldn't get her until I finished rehab. I'm on probation with a thing on my ankle, and I have to get into treatment. But I made some calls and I can't get into any place right away. And they said I only had six months and then they would take her away for good." Then she paused. "Who is this? Your voice sounds familiar. And how do you know about the baby?"

Joe knew then that she hadn't heard yet about the baby being taken from the hospital. "Just a friend." He raised the pitch of his voice, hoping she wouldn't remember him. He started to hang up and then stopped. "You named her Isabel, right?"

"Yes. It's my grandmother's name. Who *is* this?"

Joe hung up. *Isabel.* Now that he was sure that was her name, the immensity of what he was going to do became that much heavier. And so did the urgency he felt.

As he turned onto the 95, headed toward Needles, he thought about the call. The nurse had been right. It might be a long time before Luisa got her baby back—if ever. He looked into the baby carrier again, and saw, with relief, that she was still asleep. Carefully, he tuned the car's CD player to some soft-guitar music that he hoped might be soothing for the baby if she woke up.

Music had been a big part of Joe's life—and Dolores'. After Joe moved out of his father's apartment and got his own place, the small studio apartment in Van Nuys he had just left, he stayed away from most of his high school friends. The only family member he saw was his aunt Josie, who called him every few weeks and invited him over to dinner, which he sometimes accepted.

Unlike most small-time dealers, he saved a lot of what he earned. He wondered sometimes if he would spend the rest of his life selling drugs, but other than the music, he had no clear idea of any other way to make a living.

Joe had other skills than drug dealing, but none of them paid as well. He had lucked into a first-rate computer basics course when he was a freshman at Van Nuys High, and the teacher, seeing his aptitude, had allowed him to take home old parts. Joe had built his own desktop from those parts, and went on to occasionally "borrow" parts from friends who had higher-priced equipment sitting around their houses that they never used. Computers for most of his friends were for video games, and their Xboxes and Playstations were used much more often. Everyone texted with their phones, so computers sat mostly unused.

Except for Joe's. He had added to it and bought new parts once he had gotten into a steady income stream from his dealing. And he was able to combine it with his second love, which was music. He had bought a second-hand guitar with some birthday money Esther had given him when he began high school, and began teaching himself how to play it. He bought and downloaded some music-writing software, and then some audio cards, and ended up with a surprisingly good mini-sound studio.

Joe had written songs in both English and Spanish, songs about women and the boundaries between Anglo and Latino life, and some about drugs, too. Given his bizarre musical history, some of the songs had a Gilbert and Sullivan ring to them, while others were straight out of the *narcocorrido* tradition of the US-Mexico border.

Joe knew he needed Dolores to help with the baby. He drove on, remembering the last time he had seen her.

Joe's sister had graduated, and had gotten a job working in the hospital near their apartment where their mother had worked. One day, she came home and announced that she had enlisted in the Navy as a medic and would be leaving for basic training the next morning. Mike simply grunted when she told them, and went back to the TV and his beer. Esther cried, but she said she was proud that Dolores would be helping others.

That night, Joe had asked her why she had done it. She was quiet for a while and then she smiled, and said, "I liked working in the hospital, thought I might be a good medic. It reminded me of how hard Mom worked and how much she tried to help people. It's good money and I can get a better job when I get out." Then she stopped smiling. "And it was the biggest *Fuck you* I could think of for Dad."

She came home after basic training, and looked terrific in her uniform. She was an incongruous warrior, with a heart-shaped face framed by dark brown hair which she had always kept short. You'd think she was a model until you saw the rest of her. She worked out every day and had an upper body that you'd start to call stocky until you saw how thin her waist was. She told Joe that they had accepted her as a combat medic, and she was headed to eight more weeks of advanced training and then would ship out to Iraq or Afghanistan—she wasn't sure which.

Joe missed Dolores, and wrote to her often after she deployed to southern Iraq. Her letters got shorter and shorter and then completely stopped about three months before she was supposed to rotate home and get discharged.

Finally she arrived home. She had lost a lot of weight, and Joe found it hard to talk with her. The first night she was back, she stayed at his place. She said she had some plans to try to go back to work at the hospital, but had some "health problems" that she needed to take care of first. When Joe asked her what she meant, she refused to answer, and soon left to meet some friends at a bar.

The next day, Dolores called him and said she would be staying with a friend. Her voice was slurred and Joe was sure she had been drinking heavily. After a week or so of not hearing from her, he tracked her down and took her out to dinner. She refused to go inside the restaurant, and so Joe got an order to go and took it out to his car.

Dolores took the food and ate some of it. She looked even worse than she had when she had gotten back. Joe said "Look, Dee, I want to help you out. I know you're hurting. What's going on?"

She glared at him. "Stop trying to nursemaid me, Joe. You've got no idea what I've been through. I can't sleep, I can't focus on anything. So I just want to drink and try to blot it out. So back off!"

"Blot what out?"

"Damn it, Joe, leave it alone!" She was quiet, looking out the window. Then she looked back at him, with the saddest look he had ever seen on her face. "Joe, I saw guys get blown to pieces. I held them while they were dying. Guys I hung out with, guys I thought I loved, guys who never deserved what they got over there. I'm just

27

falling apart, and I've got to get some help. But I can't stay with you, and I sure as hell don't want anything to do with that asshole of a father of ours. So just let it go. I'm going to try the VA and see if they can help." She stopped and then said "And then I don't know what I'll do."

Joe had no idea what to say. So he drove her back to her friend's and hugged her when she got out of the car, and watched her walk into the apartment house.

Two weeks later, he got a call from her. She sounded tired, and told him that she had moved to San Diego to be near the VA treatment center. She said she had visited her aunt before she left and had told her how to contact her in case of an emergency. She asked Joe to leave her alone until she got back in touch with him. Joe asked her where she was going and she gave him a vague answer, saying "I might have to go off the grid for a while, Joe," and then hung up.

CHAPTER 6

Finally Joe arrived at Havasu Lake. He had called his aunt and after some pleading, she gave him the name and location of Dolores' contact. He went straight to the fire station, which was on a small hill in the middle of the little settlement. The Arizona side, visible across the lake in the afternoon sun, had almost 55,000 residents, but the California side had fewer than 5,000, including the tribal population in the Chemehuevi reservation that surrounded and included most of the little town.

Joe had gotten the name of the guy in Havasu that Dolores had given to their aunt. Josie had said he was the only way to get in touch with Dolores. He called the guy, Lee Farmer, and arranged to meet him at the fire station.

Joe remembered that Lee and Dolores had met when Dolores had graduated from high school and was trying to decide what to do with her life. She had been arrested for drinking, and he was part of the LAPD team that took her in. Lee could see that she was troubled, and had referred her to a program in the Valley that a lot of cops had used and that would keep her out of a jail sentence. She lasted a week and then left the program, but he still stayed in touch with her.

He was older, and was just finishing up twenty years with the LAPD. He had gone into the LAPD after graduating from Long Beach State. She had thought of him at first as a kind of father figure, and then it turned into something more.

When Dolores decided to join the Navy as a medic, she had told Joe that Lee had been upset, but saw that she needed to do something to get out of the rut she was in. By then he had moved out to Havasu and was in the firefighting unit out there, working for the county. She had been assigned to a training unit in Kuwait and then rotated into Iraq as the final year of withdrawal was coming to a close. They had written to each other, but once she got into Iraq, she stopped writing.

When he got to the firehouse in Havasu, Joe saw a uniformed firefighter in the inside bay working on one of the fire engines. His name tag said Farmer. He looked to be in his early fifties or so, in good shape, with wavy brown hair that was receding from a high forehead. Farmer was well-tanned, and about six feet tall. Joe had met him once or twice when Dolores was dating him, and had liked him then. Farmer had aged well, and had a natural smile that Joe remembered. But it wasn't there when Joe walked up.

Joe introduced himself, and could see right away that Farmer was going to tell him nothing until Joe established that he needed to see Dolores.

"I'm her brother," he began. "We met several years ago."

"Tell me what she looks like."

He described her.

"What unit was she with?"

Joe named the unit, hoping he had gotten the numbers right.

"Where did she go to high school?"

Correct answer.

"Why do you need to see her? She isn't really seeing anybody right now." Then they both heard a faint cry from Joe's Escape. Joe went over and comforted Isabel as best he could. Farmer had followed him and looked into the back seat.

Surprised, Farmer asked, "That yours—or hers?"

"Neither. But she needs help, and I know Dolores could help her."

Farmer looked into the SUV and something painful went across his face for a moment. Then he asked, "Is your air conditioning strong enough? She shouldn't get hot."

Joe assured him he had had it checked recently and that it had worked fine on the trip out.

It looked as though seeing Isabel had been the final hurdle. Farmer told Joe how to get to the mobile home where Dolores was living. As Joe got back in the SUV, Farmer came around to the driver's side and leaned in. "You tell her anything I can do, she just needs to ask. You tell her, OK? And take good care of that baby."

CHAPTER 7

Joe followed Farmer's directions, which were complicated. He drove out into the desert, back onto the Havasu road, and then back onto Highway 95 headed south.

He drove for half an hour or so, then turned off to the west onto an unmarked dirt road, and followed it for another twenty minutes. He came to some low foothills and then saw a mobile home, fairly new-looking, with random light brown paint patterns on it that camouflaged it into the surrounding desert. He could see that the mobile had been situated up against the foothills so that the afternoon sun was partly blocked by an outcropping at the top of a hill.

Joe stepped out of the car and as he did, he saw the door of the mobile open and his sister walked out, followed by a closely trimmed collie. Dolores motioned to the dog, who sat down in the shade under the stairs coming down from the front door of the mobile.

"Lee told me you were coming. He said you had a surprise, but wouldn't tell me what it was." She frowned. "Look, Joe, I'm glad to see you, but it sucks that you're here. What the hell are you doing here?"

In answer, Joe held up his hand and went back out to the SUV, which he had left running. He reached in and lifted out the baby carrier. Isabel stirred, but then fell back asleep. As he walked up to Dolores, her mouth fell open and she whispered, "I do not believe this." She looked into the carrier and then looked up at Joe, as furious as he had ever seen her.

"What—you knocked somebody up and I'm supposed to raise it—her?!" she angrily corrected when she saw all the hair and the pink blanket.

Then she snapped, "Get inside, we'll talk about this inside."

As Joe walked inside, he was amazed at how much space the mobile had. There were two bedrooms, a sizable kitchen, and a comfortable front room, with a flatscreen TV and a bookcase. There was not a lot of furniture, but Joe recognized some cast off chairs and a table from their family's early days. He assumed that Dolores had "borrowed" them from the stuff his father had put in storage after their mother died.

Once they were settled and had put the baby on the floor next to her table, Joe explained what had happened. As he told her about being shot, her eyes got angrier and her hands tensed up. Then when he said he had taken the baby after he realized that she wasn't going home with her mother, Dolores threw up her hands and said, "You idiot—what were you thinking?! Are you using your own drugs—you must be crazy!" She got up and paced through the kitchen and then turned.

"Joe, look around. I'm as isolated as I can possibly be. I'm off the grid, and I chose to live this way. I'm out here because I can barely be responsible for myself. I don't need anybody in my life right now—not you, and definitely not a baby that may not make it!"

"Don't say that! She's going to make it." He was angry at her dismissal, but kept himself under control. "Dee, I know you had to carry a huge load over there. You told us when you came back, before you . . . you shut down. You said you worried every day about someone shooting at you when you were trying to take care of your guys."

He went on, trying to get through to her. "But Dee, no one is shooting at her. You're in no danger if you help her. I've got plenty of money with me, and I can cover all our expenses."

She looked at him and said "No danger? Five to ten years locked up as an accessory to kidnapping? Joe, you're a fool. And you're dangerous. Because that would kill me. It would flat out kill me to be behind bars. You're asking a lot, Joe."

"I know that. I wouldn't have brought her here if I had any other choice. But I just felt—I felt I had to do something or they were going to take her away and give her to someone else."

She threw up her hands. "Joe, let's face it. Almost anyone else would be better equipped than you to take care of a baby."

"That's why I'm here. You're a medic, you know about kids. You wrote and told us about the civic action stuff you did with the Iraqi women and their kids."

She scoffed. "Sure, I know about kids. But dealing with a little malnutrition and heat rashes isn't the same as handling a baby withdrawing from drugs. What was the mother on—do you know?"

Embarrassed, he answered, "Meth and booze, I think."

"Shit, Joe. That baby may never come out of this. Even after the withdrawal is over, she may be messed up forever. How is she doing on that formula?" Joe had brought in the supplies he had bought at Target and had fixed up a bottle for Isabel, who was starting to whimper. He gave it to her and held it, and she greedily began to suck on the bottle.

"See, she takes it fine. Seems to like it."

"Well, you lucked out on that one. Some kids who don't get nursed take a long time to get used to the bottle." She looked down at the baby. She smiled for the first time and said "I don't believe this. You've got a *baby*, Joe. And you brought her out here."

Trying to change the subject for a while, Joe asked, "What's the dog's name?"

"Sancho." As she said his name, the dog's ears rose and he lifted his head, watching her. "I got him from a friend of Lee's. He really likes it here." She snapped her fingers and the dog came over and then lay down at her feet. "He's been very good for me. Joe, I talk a lot to Sancho. He's great company, he never argues with me, and when I wake up in the night screaming, he doesn't run away. He comes over and puts his head on the end of the bed and waits until I come out of it."

"How often does that happen?"

She smiled sadly. "I've got it down to maybe once or twice a night. Depends on what I've drunk—or haven't drunk. I can stop drinking any time, Joe—like Mark Twain said about smoking, I do it all the time."

She looked at the baby. "But now you've really screwed up, Joe. She can't stay here. You can't stay here, either. Hang out for a few days—but you can't stay here. And they're going to catch up with you."

Joe remembered how she was when she had first gotten home, and he knew she was still messed up. She obviously didn't want him to stay, and wanted nothing to do with another problem in her life. But he had thought through what he would say when he was planning to take Isabel, and had rehearsed it all the way out on the drive.

"I need a week, Dee. Just a week. Sure, they're going to know she's gone, and they'll try to find me. But you told us when you left for San Diego that you might come out here and go off the grid." He looked around. "Seems like you've got that covered. No phone lines, no power lines, no neighbors. Place looks like an abandoned mobile. And you've got your car out of sight over behind those rocks."

"That's what I wanted."

"Where'd you get the solar?"

"I met this professor in Basra who was experimenting with high-efficiency solar panels for houses. He said it worked, but only on small buildings. They couldn't take it up to scale. He told me where to get some samples at their factory out in Lancaster. They make it so it looks just like the top of the mobile, no big black panels. Works great—keeps the A/C going when I need it and keeps the power on the radio." She gestured over to the large satellite receiver on the bookshelf beside her bed. "I have a subscription that Lee pays for—gets 200 stations. The receiver is only a few inches wide, it's up on top of the mobile. No one could see it."

"Gotta have your music, huh."

"Yeah."

"That guy Lee really put me through the wringer before he would tell me where you were."

"Yeah. I thought a long time about how I could disappear, and who would help me. Lee and I had a big thing after high school. We were going to get married, a couple of years before I joined up.

But first he wasn't ready—he's older and wasn't sure he wanted to get married. And then I wasn't ready, and then I was over there. Timing was never right, and now he's with someone who is really good for him. But he's one of the best men I've ever known. He put in twenty for the LAPD and then got disability pay and came out here and started working as a firefighter. There's something in him that makes him want to work hard and want to help people. Hell of a good guy."

Joe looked around at the inside of the mobile. "You've fixed this up pretty good."

"Yeah. I've even got the Internet."

"Can't they trace you?"

"No. I got to know some of the telecomm people over there. They showed me how to do cut-outs so a wireless signal goes to a server they can't trace. The wireless bill goes to Lee."

"He really protects you."

"Yeah, he does. He's so damned loyal—I wish I could see him more often. He is so solid and so loyal. But he knows I have a problem and told me I needed to get help for it."

She began pacing into the kitchen and back to the living room. "So I did. I went to the VA when I first got back, before I moved out here and went off the grid. The VA program was a joke. They do an intake and then they tell you to come back. I had to go all the way to San Diego, and they acted like I was trying to cheat somebody out of disability pay. I never asked for it, I just wanted some pills or someone to talk to about the nightmares. But they kept asking me to come back and would make appointments two months later. After three months of that BS, I gave up."

"I remember—you just disappeared."

"Yeah. I felt bad leaving you, but you were all wrapped up in dealing and I tried to tell you to stop, and you just laughed at me. I told you that you were going to get messed up. And so they shot you, Joe. What the hell? Do you know who did it?"

"Yeah. My crew wanted to try to push into someone else's territory, so they sent me. I thought I could do a quick run and not be noticed."

"Didn't work out so good."

"No."

Dolores went into the kitchen. She was silent for a long time, putting some dishes away. Then she walked back over and looked into the baby carrier. Isabel had gone back to sleep.

Dolores sat on the couch and said, in a softer tone, "Joe, do you remember when mom took in that foster kid? You must have been six or seven. The little girl had only stayed with us for a few weeks. The birth mother 'got well' or something, but I remember watching Mom take care of her." She laughed, but unhappily. "I wish I could forget it, but I just can't."

Joe said, "I sort of remember it. She was a scared little kid, I remember. I wondered why she would go back with her mother if she was that scared."

"Don't think she had much choice." She looked at Isabel. "Like this one."

She shook her head, frowning. "Joe, I think this is a very bad idea, and I wish you hadn't come here. But no way am I going to throw you and her out." She laughed, softly. "Mom would come back and haunt me, probably. A few days won't solve anything. Let's give it a month, and see if she comes through the withdrawal OK. Let's see how she is in 30 days, and whether anyone finds us out here. I don't really care if they find me, I'm not going back. But they'll put you away for a long time, Joe."

"I know." He looked over at the little bed. "And they'll take her away, too. OK—a month. We'll see how a month goes."

CHAPTER 8

Sometimes, during the days that followed, Joe would walk over and pull a chair up next to the baby carrier and just watch Isabel. She was tiny, impossibly small, a miniature human with fingers and nose and lips like a human's, but on a scale Joe had never seen up close.

From tiny his mind went to *fragile*, and from there he got to *perishable*, and then he had to work hard to push away the real meaning of perishable. He failed, and he struggled, knowing that to perish meant to die, to fade away into a state of death, no longer alive. Flowers were perishable, and food was perishable, and so, Joe grasped for the first time, was Isabel.

She had a full head of dark brown hair, and her skin was a very light brown. Whatever the color is at the edge of brown and pink and white, Joe thought—that was her color. One night, searching the internet on Dolores' laptop for the meanings of the name Isabel, Joe was amazed to learn that there was a color called *isabelline*, a color described as fawn-brown, light cream brown. Isabel's skin was isabelline.

And then he realized that it was almost certain that her father was white.

The dog was a big part of Dolores' life, Joe soon saw. And soon, he realized, the dog caught on that Isabel was different from Joe and Dolores, and needed more attention. He dozed by the cradle during the day, and could quickly sense when Isabel was stirring, wanting food, or changing. When she started moving, Sancho would stand up to make sure that Joe and Dolores knew she needed some kind of help. If they didn't come right away, he would begin to make a soft, high-pitched sound back in his throat, quiet enough not to disturb Isabel but with an urgency that they always recognized.

At one point, Joe, joking, said "That dog is so smart, he could probably raise her by himself."

Dolores laughed and said "You wish." She went on. "He really is amazing. I had to trim him up because it gets so hot out here. But I wanted a collie, because I remembered watching Lassie with you on reruns when we were growing up. He barks when coyotes wander by, and he barked when you drove up. Cheaper than an alarm system, and much better company."

It was night, and Joe was just dozing off in his small bedroom. Gunshots, then glass breaking. Joe was showered with fragments, as he jerked out of sleep, grasped what was happening, and rolled onto the floor. Automatic weapon fire crackled and Joe saw with horror the wall of the mobile stitched open with bullet holes, whining metallic sounds zipping through the far side of his room.

He heard himself shouting *get the baby* over and over—and then he felt Dolores shaking him, waking him. "Joe, you're OK. It was a dream. Come on, you're OK, wake up."

He came out of it then. Feeling himself in bed, covered with sweat and breathing in gasps, with Dolores leaning over him and patting his face. She waited until he was fully awake and calmed, and then sat down on his bed, with a half-smile. "Welcome to PTSD-land, man. Looks like you've got the entry fee covered—you got shot at. And now you have to take the ride. It sucks, huh?"

"Wow. I was sure they'd found us." He looked around, "Isabel OK?"

"Sleeping like a log. A tiny log."

CHAPTER 9

Law office

The headlines screamed "Baby Kidnapped as Child Welfare Crisis Deepens." In her office, Nicole Larwin spread out the paper and re-read the article for the fourth time that morning, yellow marker in hand and a legal pad filling up with her notes.

Nicole Larwin was a senior lawyer in a firm that had existed in the downtown area for over a century. After ten years of working for the county District Attorney's office, Nicole had finally admitted to herself that she wanted more freedom to take cases involving children—cases that might not make sense for a DA but that needed an advocate who was able to press for damages wherever the case led.

The DA, Reggie Dempsey, had recognized her talent and her tenacity early in her work, and protected her when he got occasional calls from county or state officials who had come into range of her continuous pushing for results. He had been elected and re-elected by wide enough margins to feel secure in his office, and he had backed Nicole several times when one of her crusades had resulted in complaining calls to the DA.

But after a case in which Nicole had rocked some county agency boats even more than usual, the DA had taken her aside and said she might want to look for a *pro bono* slot in a law firm that would give her more freedom.

She looked for a long time before she was certain she had found a firm that would allow her to do what she wanted to do. It helped that she had gone through law school with the grandson of the firm's founder, and it also helped that the firm was a long-time contributor to progressive causes. Nicole had been selected as a *pro bono* partner—one of only two in the firm. The deal was that she was able to work on cases that "didn't pay" as long as she spent a quarter of her time on the cases that did.

Nicole seemed aloof, distant, and then she would smile, usually when she wanted something from someone or when she thought her team had made progress in nailing someone. She had carefully recruited a group of paralegals and interns from area law schools who reported to her. They all adored her and worked long hours. She had a plaque on her wall, from a Japanese quotation her father had borrowed decades before: *Work is a Ceremony.*

Her features were softer than her manner, in a round face with blue eyes set off by her nearly black hair. She wore it in a tapered cut that framed her face. She was about 5'6", but looked taller because of her long legs and thin waist.

Money wasn't important to Nicole. Her parents were comfortable, and she made enough to dress well and live in a decent condo in a safe part of Pasadena. When she wanted to travel, her father gave her some miles from the endless accounts in his travel agency, his second career after teaching school for thirty years. She took fewer and fewer trips as she went up the ladder—both because the work got more intense and because her relationships got less intense, ending up with her not really wanting to be with anyone for more than a few days at a time.

Nicole had started out on child endangerment cases, usually kids who had been caught up in their parents' arrests for drug charges. But as she continued working on these cases, she found herself wondering what actually happened to the children. After some poking around, she learned that the kids were usually removed from the house where the arrest had taken place and put into foster care. In following up on a case where a family of three children were all removed and placed in a group home, Nicole had gotten to know one of the protective services workers, who asked her to come along on a visit to the children.

When Nicole saw the conditions in the group home, she asked the staff what services the children had received, and whether the youngest one had been sent for developmental screening, as legally required. The blank look on the face of the overworked staff member shocked Nicole, but helped her begin to understand the system that lay behind the children's "case." She began to shift her attention from the misdeeds of parents to the misdeeds of the agencies that were supposed to be serving them and protecting their kids.

And gradually, she began to realize that there was another layer behind the agencies' flaws: the elected officials who set the boundaries on the level of resources the agencies would get and the level of results that were politically acceptable—defined by what happened in the media. That layer was more difficult and more dangerous to probe, but Nicole quickly saw that it would be a lot more challenging to take on headline-grabbing elected officials than low-level bureaucrats or neglectful parents.

And that was the filter through which she was reading about the little girl who had come to be known as Baby Isabel.

As she read the story, Nicole began to plan a way to use the tragedy to turn another spotlight on agencies and politicians who were too quick to blame each other and too slow to act. She had learned early that it often took tragedies to move the sluggish machinery of government, especially when it came to the problems of poor and abused children. Whoever was to blame for what had led to the baby being kidnapped—from drug dealers to drug buyers to hospitals and other agencies—Nicole had looked into the problem of drug-exposed infants enough to know that there was plenty of blame to go around, extending far beyond the kidnapper and Isabel's mother.

One of her interns, Steven Wong, had been assigned to dig into the story behind the kidnapping of Isabel Contreras. When he came back to her with a carefully assembled description of what had happened, Nicole's antenna went up even higher.

She decided to call in her staff, two paralegals and three interns, and brief them on the issue.

"It's even worse than we thought." She looked at a pile of papers and emails on her desk. "Listen to this. A CPS worker was supposed to be on her way to take the baby to a shelter that is set up for infant care for babies who had a positive tox test at birth. But she didn't get the message about when she was supposed to pick up the baby—because her PDA wasn't networked into the cell system. It only works when she is at headquarters. So she finally got to the hospital four hours after the baby was taken."

"Four hours—so she just missed getting her," said Deborah Gordon, one of the interns.

"It gets worse. We talked off the record with a worker who had access to the prenatal screening records for the clinics in the area where the baby's mother lived. It turns out that the mother tested positive on a screening that was done when she was six months pregnant. So the clinic gives her a referral to a treatment program. But she never showed up. No one at the clinic followed up. And the treatment program, which got a fax saying she had been referred, never followed up to see why she didn't show." She shook her head. "We knew three months before this baby was born that she was in danger—and nothing happened."

She went on. "So seven agencies were involved before the baby was a week old: the hospital, the cops who got the call about the drugs in her apartment, the prenatal clinic, CPS, the treatment agency she got referred to, the paramedics, and now she's got a criminal case in Superior Court."

She paused and looked at her team, trying to see if they were following her. "Whoever took her had a reason for doing it, and we need to figure out what that was."

"Could it have been the baby's father?" asked Rachel Jacobsen, her lead paralegal.

Nicole looked at the notes. "They asked the mother who he was and she isn't talking. Birth certificate says unknown. Detectives are trying to get more information from her and from her mother, but no luck so far. I suppose it could have been the father, but chances are mom had no real relationship with him. They said there were no signs of anybody else living in the apartment except her. Supposedly it was a real bare-bones place."

Gordon asked, "Does she even want the baby back?"

"That's the thing. Detectives and the social worker at the women's jail said she talked about the baby all the time, and wanted to know what she had to do to get her back when they find her. She's really worried about her—not acting at all like one of the moms who drops and runs."

As the team filed out of her office, Nicole thought about all the pieces of the case that were emerging. The police had begun an investigation of the kidnapping, and the media attention meant they were going to be under tremendous pressure to find the baby. But they were going to focus on the kidnapper, and not the agencies that were involved. So she decided that would be her job.

She knew she wouldn't have the time, with all her other cases, to get into the nuts and bolts of all the agencies that were involved in Isabel Contreras' brief life. She decided to look for an investigator who could help her assemble the facts she'd need to go after the agencies that had bungled the Isabel case.

She had accumulated a fund from two settlements that she had arranged in cases representing trafficked women against corporations who had supported the smugglers behind large prostitution rings in Southern California. The partners had agreed that these funds could be used to advance her continuing work on children's rights, and Nicole had tapped the fund several times to supplement her own staff.

As she mentally reviewed the list of investigators that she had used on recent cases, none seemed to her to have the skill to gather the information and tell the story she wanted to have told.

Then she remembered hearing about a journalist, Sam Leonard, who was a friend of a young woman she knew, Rosa Flores. Nicole had been a mentor for Rosa while Rosa was in law school, and had heard her talk about Sam.

When she was in college, Nicole had heard Leonard's coverage on National Public Radio of The March, a human rights demonstration that had brought roughly a million Mexicans to the California border. Sam had gone back and forth between the woman who led The March, Maria Sanchez, and the Governor, and had been with Maria when she was shot near San Clemente. He had won a Peabody award for the radio stories, which Sam had later turned into a book that was awarded a Pulitzer.

She called Rosa and after exchanging greetings, asked her how to get in touch with Sam Leonard. Rosa said he was doing some free-lancing and the last she heard was living in Orange, over in the old section of the picturesque city in the middle of Orange County.

CHAPTER 10

Nicole tried the number that Rosa had given her, and the phone was answered on the first ring.

"Leonard here." The voice was soft and business-like. Rosa explained that she wanted to hire an investigator and that Rosa had said he might be available. She told him a little about the case and that it had to do with the news stories about the kidnapping.

"Sounds interesting. Might stave off some of my early-onset dementia. When can I get together with you?"

Nicole made an appointment and hung up, wondering what she had gotten herself into, but looking forward to meeting him. *Early-onset dementia?* she thought, assuming he just had a weird sense of humor.

The next day, Sam came into Nicole's office, admiring the décor which was upscale legal-professional, bookcases full of law books and degrees on the wall, with personal touches that said Southern California female. She had pastels of the ocean on her wall, and two oils of the Sierra, one with a roseate sunset behind the jagged peaks. A picture of an older couple with Nicole's features stood on the credenza behind her desk.

Nicole motioned him to a chair beside her office table and thanked him for coming in. She watched him for a moment as he settled in. He had an older man's gravity, but a continuous, low-wattage smile seemed to promise that he didn't take himself all that seriously. He wore hearing aids, and she hoped he wasn't going to be too handicapped by them. His thinning hair was a mix of gray and dark brown, and he had a mustache that was nearly all white.

"Sam, you come highly recommended by Rosa Flores."

"She's very special. She's living with the son of one of my oldest friends."

"She's told me a bit about your adventures in Mexico. Must have been fascinating."

"It was that, and more." He paused, and then asked her, "So how did you get into this work? Why not the hot corporate fast track?"

Nicole laughed and said, "Mr. Leonard, are you interviewing *me?*"

"Sort of." He leaned forward, smiling his faint smile. "I figure I'm going to bust my ass if I end up working for you, and I already know from Rosa that you're one of the good guys. But I need to know more about who you are to make sure I can do this job right—right for me and right for you. I have a hunch, based on what I've been reading in the *Times,* that down at the end of this thing you're going to have to make some tough calls. And I want to make sure that my work gets handled right by you when that happens."

Nicole was partly surprised at his boldness and partly pleased that he was thinking three steps ahead, instead of just trying to get the contract as most other investigators would have done.

"OK. Fair question: why do I do this work?" She leaned back in her chair, looking at Sam, gauging his value as a possible employee but somehow unable to lose sight of his appeal as a man. "Here's the short answer. I grew up with a nurse and a teacher." She gestured at the photograph of her parents. "Both my mom and dad worked hard, and their work was about helping other people. Unlike some kids these days, I liked my parents a lot, and I liked how they did their work. Once I decided I couldn't stand the sight of blood and I didn't want to be a school teacher, that left law or psychiatry. Law seemed less depressing." She paused, watching Sam.

"But why this kind of law?"

"I worked at a law school clinic when I was second year. Same one our friend Rosa worked at. I saw third year students and clerks make a big difference in the lives of some kids who were on their way to foster care—and I never looked back. I'm very good at it, Sam. So good it fills up all my time."

She wondered why she had veered into the personal part of her work, and shifted back to the content. "So they kept promoting me, and I kept working harder. I won some big cases, and the DA liked my work and backed me a few times when I went after some political and agency people who were talking big about kids' needs but never followed through."

"I read about that." Nicole assumed he had Googled her before the interview—just as she had done to him. He went on. "So you're willing to put pressure on these agencies if we find that they're screwing up?"

"Putting pressure on those agencies and corporations who hurt kids is what I do. It's why I left the DA's office to continue the work here in the firm."

She thought about what he had said. "But what we've never done, what I've never done, is to put pressure on all of them at once. We've been going after them one at a time, whenever they mess up enough that it becomes visible. But what I want you to find out is how much the problem is about the way they work together—or don't." She paused, then added, "As I read about what happened in the Baby Isabel case so far, there's a lot of blame to go around."

Sam said, "When I was doing beat work for the *Times* a century ago, we did it the way you've been doing it. One at a time, after they screw up. There would occasionally be investigative reporting on a bunch of agencies, but usually it was LAPD or the Sheriff or County Parks and Rec, Social Services—one at a time. But I'll bet you're right—what happened to that little girl may be about more than one agency. It may be about a bunch of them."

Nicole nodded, seeing that he got it. "That's pretty much what I heard when we went to talk to the hospital. They blamed child welfare, and I just knew that child welfare would blame somebody else." She stopped and pointed at him. "Sam, I want you to wade into that pile of blame and figure out what the hell is really going on. I've got fifteen cases right now, and I just can't spare the time to get into the depth of this kidnapping and everything that lies behind it. Do you want to do that?"

"Hell, yes. Now that I know where you're coming from, I'd love to do it. Beats hell out of sitting around writing my memoirs." He laughed, and added, "But I'm going to need some help. I have a line on a younger guy who could help me. He just graduated from USC in journalism and is hot to trot."

"Hire whoever you want. The firm has given me a budget for this project and I think we're fine for an additional staff person."

They talked about Sam's rates and how long he thought the project would take. Sam said he thought he could wrap it up in a month, delaying some free-lance writing that had no deadlines.

Nicole gave him a list of agency contacts to start with, and asked him how soon he could begin.

"Is Monday soon enough?"

"Monday is good. Give me a summary report at the end of each week so I can see what you're doing, and then we'll get together again at the end. Let me know if you have any trouble getting to people. I still have some contacts in the county, and they'll help us."

Joshua Bronson was Ernie Scott's nephew, and he had just graduated from journalism school at USC. Ernie had called Sam and asked him to have lunch with Joshua and give him some advice about where to look for a job. Sam agreed and asked Ernie to drop by and have dinner with him. Ernie was on a trip south to see his son, Jim Scott, who was living with his girlfriend, Rosa Flores, and working at an aerospace plant in the San Fernando Valley.

Ernie lived up in the Owens Valley, and he and Sam had first met in Vietnam. They had worked together as informal advisors to the Owens County Sheriff on a serial murder case in the Valley two years before, and had a fine time recalling old stories about their exploits, some true and some embellished and aging well over time.

After finishing dinner, Ernie said, "Sam, this Joshua is a good kid. My sister tells me he had some problems in high school, but it was mostly about him wanting to study what he wanted to study and not what the teachers wanted him to study."

"So he's really smart, but headstrong?"

"He's smart as hell, but I wouldn't call it headstrong. He has a thing about people—well, I'll let you see for yourself. Don't want to bias you. But he's very smart. And he's a really good kid, Sam."

After the first half hour of a lunch arranged by Ernie, Sam thought he had figured out what Joshua's "condition" was. He was obviously bright, but Sam soon picked up something else: he had sky-high emotional intelligence. Joshua was so attuned to other people, it was eerie. When the waiter came over, Joshua gracefully made conversation with him, asking what food was good, how much he liked his work, and how long he had been working there. He thanked Sam for meeting with him several times before the order even came.

Sam had explained the project with Nicole Larwin, and when Sam started talking about all the meetings with agencies that they had planned, Joshua frowned a little and then said, "The work they do in those agencies must be very hard. With budget cuts and the work affecting kids' lives so much—it must be very hard for them right now."

Sam hadn't seen that much empathy from social workers and ministers he'd known for a long time. *This kid has antennas the rest of us never turn on*, he thought to himself.

So he made Joshua an offer, and the kid accepted it immediately. Then he said, "I need to tell you, Mr. Leonard . . ."

"Sam."

"OK, Sam. I need to tell you that Uncle Ernie has told me a lot about you—the work you did as a journalist, and you personally. I'm honored to be able to work with you. I hope you'll give me feedback on how I'm doing."

Sam was struck at the formal tone Joshua used, and that he would immediately ask for feedback. Joshua, he realized, was an odd mixture of self-confidence and respect for his elders. In Sam's experience, the first was common among Joshua's generation, though not always justified. The second was mostly absent.

"I'd be glad to, kid. And I'll warn you in advance, I'm probably going to call you 'kid.' I don't mean to put you down in any way; it's just the age thing. I think we'll both probably get something out of this."

Joshua smiled and said, "No problem, Mr. Leonard."

"Sam, Josh. Is Josh OK?"

"Josh is fine. I'll work on the Sam part."

As he left, Sam found himself thinking that the kid was going to be fun to get to know. He was tall, a little over six feet, with sandy colored hair that he wore medium length. His face easily broke into a natural smile when he was listening, his light hazel eyes watching intently.

An audience, Sam thought, *just what I need—an audience.*

CHAPTER 11

Two detectives had been assigned to track down leads on the baby's disappearance. They had started at the hospital the day after Isabel disappeared. Both of them had worked on missing child cases before, and both had been detailed to work with the county child welfare agency, so they knew the ropes on cases like the Baby Isabel kidnapping. The older, Bill McQueen, was seven years from retiring. His partner, Joanne Alarcon, had only made detective four years ago and was already hungry for a promotion.

McQueen and Alarcon had been called in to meet with the Chief of Detectives in the Valley, Burke Connelly. Connelly was famous in the LAPD for his record in solving cold cases and his connections with the media. He had been an advisor on several Hollywood movies about cops, and had won most of the awards given out by the LAPD.

Connelly's office was nondescript, and to McQueen's and Alarcon's surprise, none of the predictable photos of him with movie stars and none of his awards were on the walls. The walls were covered with detailed electronic maps of the Valley where active cases were open—all marked with a red light. Cold cases were marked with blue lights. A large flat computer screen showed the assignments of cases to all detectives in the Valley division.

Connelly started in as soon as they sat down. "You two are lead on the Baby Isabel case, but there's a lot of backup. Maybe a lot of second-guessing, too. The media is all over this, and you need to check in daily with the PR people downtown at Parker. Don't talk to any press about this unless the PR guys clear it first. Now tell me what you've got going."

McQueen said, "Captain, we've got a meeting with the hospital security people this afternoon. Then we thought we'd see the baby's mother, who got bailed out and is waiting trial on a child endangerment charge."

"Good. Look into the father—that's obvious. See who else with a record might have been in the hospital while the baby was there. Maybe somebody got the idea of snatching the kid and selling her. The black market in adoptions is still active. Work the mother on her criminal charges—see if she will give us anything if we can get child welfare to give her a shot at getting the kid back or if the DA will reduce the charges."

McQueen said, "Yes, sir."

The nurse told the detectives, "There was a guy who stood for a long time, several days, every day and looked into the NICU. He asked me questions about the babies in there."

"What did he look like?"

She thought about it. "He was maybe mid-20s, sort of Latino, regular length hair, not buzzed the way they do." She meant gang members but would not say it. "He was short, maybe 5'7' or so. I'm 5'5'. I saw him talking to one of the other nurses, but she's off today."

"What's her name?"

"Serena Salas."

Alarcon made a note. "Thanks. We'll give her a call when she's back."

They stood at the end of the hallway as the nurse nervously watched them. McQueen said to the nurse, "We checked the hospital logs, but no one close to that description was logged in when the baby was taken." He turned and looked out the window. "What's that building?"

"That's rehab," she answered.

"Does it have the same log as the hospital?"

"No, I think it's separate."

McQueen motioned to Alarcon and said, "Let's check it."

They did, and they found that Joe Brenner had moved from the hospital to the rehab unit and had checked himself out two days before the baby was taken. By then they had interviewed the guard at the back door of the hospital, and his description of the man who had taken the baby out of the hospital matched the nurse's.

"Interesting. This guy's in the hospital because of a drug deal that went bad. He crosssed a line and got shot. So why would a drug dealer take a baby?"

"Maybe we should go talk to the mother again. Maybe she knew him."

But Luisa Contreras told them nothing, although they could see in her face when they asked about Joe Brenner that she knew something about him. Then they went to the address that Joe had given the hospital. It was a vacant lot in Van Nuys. His bill had been paid from a credit account that was closed a week later. So they went to the narcotics unit in the Valley, and came back and showed the hospital guard some pictures of dealers who had been arrested previously. None of them looked familiar to him.

Then they got a break. Two mid-level gang members in the Valley had been arrested in a take-down that had resulted from one gang dropping a tip on another one. When they showed the two dealers a composite sketch taken from the descriptions of the nurse and the guard, the dealer with the most to lose told them it looked like a low-level dealer named Joe Brenner who had done some work for them.

They found an old address for a Joe Brenner who had attended the high school mentioned by the gang members. They found Mike Brenner at that address, and interviewed him, with zero results. He said he hadn't seen or talked to his son in two years. Then they found the deceased mother had a sister. They interviewed her, and she said her sister, Joe's mother, had died several years before and she had no contact with Joe's father. She said she had no idea where Joe was. She mentioned Joe's sister, but told them she didn't know how to reach her. She said she hadn't heard from Joe for several months and denied knowing that he was dealing drugs.

When they ran the sister's records, they found that she had been a Navy combat medic in Iraq with the Marines. The file also noted that she had gotten a Silver Star for actions under fire with her unit.

She had gotten back a year ago, but had disappeared. The VA had an old record from a San Diego health unit, but the address was a vacant apartment in San Diego.

Then they got a hit from the DMV, with Brenner's license, a description of his car, and an address for an apartment in Van Nuys. McQueen asked Alarcon to get a warrant to search the apartment. When they did, they found a postcard shoved under the door with an address in Bakersfield.

McQueen and Alarcon sat facing each other in their side by side cubicles in the Valley headquarters. McQueen summed up. "We've got an address in Bakersfield that looks like it's a relative, a Walter Brenner. We've got the baby's mother, who says she knows nothing, but definitely knows something. And we've got Brenner's sister who has disappeared."

So they decided to go back to the mother. They found Luisa Contreras on probation, cleaning houses with her mother, and then they got another break. Luisa was higher than a kite on marijuana, and once they had probable cause based on her condition, they searched her car and found ten ounces of marijuana.

They took her down to the detention center, let her wait for a while, and then went into the interrogation room. Alarcon agreed to take the harder approach.

Luisa was in bad shape. She was coming down from the high, but was terrified about what would happen next. Alarcon began the interrogation on a soft note, asking her, "Luisa, do you have any pictures of Isabel?"

Startled, Luisa stammered, "No. They took her away too fast. I never got any."

Alarcon reached into a manila folder. She handed Luisa a photo. "Here's one they took when she was moved out of the NICU, the day before she was kidnapped." She handed it to Luisa, who began crying, clutching the picture.

"*Ay, Dios mio, mi hija, querida hija.*"

"Do you want to see her again?"

"Oh yes, of course I do," she said, wiping her eyes, but never taking them off the picture.

"Then tell us what you know." Alarcon paused, and then asked Luisa, "Do you know Joe Brenner?"

"No. I mean yes, I met him, maybe once or twice." Then she stopped. Alarcon could see she was trying to figure out how much more to tell. So she clamped down harder.

"Luisa, you know you need to get into treatment to have any chance of ever getting your baby back. They told you that while the baby was still in the hospital. But let me tell you something else. If you are not telling us the truth about Joe, you will probably end up with criminal charges, and you are going to do time. You got arrested and then we caught you with dope again. So your chances of seeing Isabel are getting close to zero unless you cooperate."

She paused, then delivered the clincher. "Do you think Joe took the baby from the hospital?"

Luisa dissolved into tears, then looked up and said, "Yes. I got a call from someone who said he had the baby. Later, I thought about it, and I thought it might be Joe."

"Do you know where to find him?"

"I have no idea. I just got the one call. I never heard from him again."

"Where do you know him from?"

"He . . . he was my dealer. I bought drugs from him."

She knew more than what she was telling them, and the detectives were sure they could squeeze her, but she had confirmed what they had already suspected. Joe Brenner was who they were looking for. They had no motive yet, and they spent an hour after Luisa was taken back to her cell trying to figure out why a drug dealer would steal his customer's newborn baby.

Finally they gave up trying to discover a motive. They called Connolly to check in, and he quickly said, "Go back to the aunt—the sister may be the best way to run him down. Everyone told you he's a loner, with few friends. He must have taken the baby to the sister's place—wherever that is."

So they did. They told Joe's aunt that she would be an accessory to kidnapping and to possession of drugs with an intent to sell. She was very frightened, and told them she would make calls to everyone she knew who might have an idea where Dolores was. She asked them to check back with her the next morning, and they agreed. In the meantime, they went back to the three friends from high school who seemed most likely to have been in touch with Dolores. One of them said Dolores had stayed with her after she got back from Iraq, but she was so strung out and drinking so heavily she had asked her to leave after a few days.

Then they asked her if she knew any friends that Dolores might be staying with. The woman Dolores had stayed with remembered that she had a boy friend when she was in high school, an older guy who was in the LAPD. Surprised, they asked his name. But she couldn't remember it. They pressed, and she remembered that the guy had taken Dolores to her senior prom. She said she would go through her yearbook, which she had loaned to a friend. She promised to get it back that night, and asked them to call the next morning. They quickly agreed.

The next day, they returned and she gave them the yearbook, pointing to a picture of Dolores with an older man. They borrowed the yearbook, promising to return it.

When they took the yearbook to LAPD personnel, the techs said they would have to run the picture through their face recognition software to see if they could get a match. That afternoon, McQueen got a call.

"It's a guy named Lee Farmer. He served twenty and retired. Last address we have for his pension check is out in Havasu."

They arrived in Havasu the next morning. They found Farmer at the fire station. He obviously knew what they had come for, and was ready for them.

"I know what you want, and I appreciate that you're just doing your job. I've done the same thing, many times. But this is different." His face was closed, his arms folded across his uniform.

"You need to understand this: I would lie for her. I would steal for her. I would do anything for her."

McQueen snarled, "All because she was your main squeeze a long time ago?"

They were trying to provoke him, trying to get him to lose it and end up in custody where they would have a better shot at breaking him and getting the information they needed to break the case open.

He looked at them scornfully, knowing what they were doing and knowing there was zero chance it would work. "No. Because she is who she is and because of what she went through for this country. She's broken right now, and she's trying to put the pieces together. And I'm going to do all that I can to make sure she's left alone so she can do that. She deserves everything the rest of us can give her. And if you don't get that, then you have no idea who she is."

McQueen said, "We may not know where she is, but we know where you are. And I can assure you that your pension will be in jeopardy—and your job here, too, pal, if you are named an accessory to a felony kidnapping."

Farmer smiled. "You mean I won't be allowed any more to go out there in 110 degrees and peel some guy out of an burnt-up accordion that used to be a car? Wow—what a threat."

Then he leaned forward, finger jabbing, smile gone. "You weren't listening. I would do anything for her. She deserves it. And that's the end of it." And then he refused to say anything more to them.

McQueen said to Alarcon as they drove away, "We're going to have to take him in."

Alarcon shook her head. "I don't know about that, Bill. She's a decorated war hero and he served twenty honorably—you really want that headline?"

"He's our only lead to the baby at this point. You saying we should just give up?"

Alarcon said, "No. But I don't think this kid is going to keep the baby out here forever. She's still sick, probably, and if he cares about her, he's going to have to bring her in."

McQueen drove on, quiet, thinking. "We should call the base at 29 Palms. Maybe she's been in touch with some of her buddies."

Trying now to placate him, Alarcon answered, "Good idea."

McQueen made the call, reached the base security, and was told they had no record of a Dolores Brenner.

McQueen hung up, and said "Dead end. For now." He pounded the steering wheel, frustrated. "Who the hell is this broad that she just disappears and this guy is protecting her?"

"You read the file. She went through some heavy shit over there. My brother was in Mosul for a year. Seems like those guys deserve some peace for now." She was quiet for a minute, then said, "Maybe we should check out the lead in Bakersfield."

CHAPTER 12

The Desert

Joe had taken his guitar out to Dolores' place, thinking vaguely that it would fill up some of the time. The first time he had played it, Dolores frowned and said "Only the soft stuff, Joe. None of that hard rock crap." So he confined himself to ballads and some re-working of the quieter songs from the Ronstadt *Canciones* albums.

He was playing one day when Dolores was rocking Isabel. The baby had been very fidgety all morning long, and Dolores was having a hard time calming her. But a few seconds into Joe's playing, Isabel stopped moving and was quiet. They both realized that the music had done something to her, and after a while, Joe stopped playing. Immediately she started jerking against Dolores' arms, thrusting her legs out over and over. Joe resumed playing, and she fell still again.

Joe and Dolores looked at each other in shared surprise. "She loves it—she quiets right down when you play!" Dolores exclaimed.

"Yeah. Guess I'd better keep playing." Out of his love for anything Ronstadtian, Joe had thought to bring along the album of lullabies that Ronstadt had made for her own children, a revision of rock songs sung softly and called *Dedicated to You*. He played some of them on the guitar, and then quickly moved over and put the CD on Dolores' stereo setup. Again, as soon as she heard the singing, Isabel was quiet.

Dolores laughed and said, "She's a connoisseur of music."

"Of Ronstadt music," Joe clarified.

Isabel was sleeping better, and her crying for a bottle had settled into a routine of feeding her every three or four hours. She would fall asleep some of the time when they were rocking her.

At Dolores' suggestion, Joe had driven over to a used furniture store in Needles and had bought a rocking chair, which they used frequently to calm Isabel, and get some rest for themselves. He had also bought a used cradle that sat on the floor.

As the weeks went by, Joe and Dolores spent more and more time arguing about what to do at the end of the month they had set as a deadline, which was fast approaching. The rest of the time they spent checking on Isabel and feeding, diapering and rocking her.

After feeding her and putting her down in the cradle, Joe said to Dolores, "This isn't hard work—taking care of her—but it's constant. It's always there."

Dolores gave him a disgusted look and said "Welcome to momsworld, Joe. How do you think we were raised—how does any baby get raised, if it has decent parents? The work just goes on and on during the first few years. It's a 24-7 job."

"Yeah, but if you're spaced out on drugs, how can you do all that? I never understood any of that before."

"You just sold them the stuff." She said it accusingly, and then stopped, seeing that he took her comment seriously.

"Yeah. I never thought about what it did to them—or to their kids. I just made the sale, took the money back to the crew, and got my share."

"You finally done with all that, Joe?"

He took a long time answering. He didn't want to give her a glib, easy answer. He knew he could make money in other ways, but dealing was a way of life he had settled into, and knowing that part of his life was over wasn't the same as knowing what he would do next. He didn't yet want to think about the consequences of taking Isabel. So he said, "I think so. I've just got to figure out what happens next."

Dolores asked him, "Whatever happened to your friend Tina? She seemed like a great girl—why did you let her get away?"

Remembering, Joe frowned. "She told me she was pregnant, and that she had to decide what to do about it. She was pushing me hard to quit dealing, and we just broke up."

"She told you she got rid of it?"

"I guess so. She said she had a decision to make about me, and I got the impression that she wasn't going to keep it if we couldn't be together. And I didn't like her telling me what to do, so we just broke up."

Dolores gave him a slight smile and changed the subject.

Joe had one serious girl friend after high school—and a lot of girls he spent time with who weren't at all serious. The one that was, Tina McGowan, had been special. He had met her in his senior year, and had looked her up after he graduated. She was a year behind him, and they had been together for most of the year after she graduated. Tina had flowing, curly black hair, green eyes, and was short, with dancer's legs from her classes and work at a local dance studio. They spent time at the beach, and often went camping in the Big Bear mountains. Tina loved the outdoors, and Joe had enjoyed taking her to places that he had gone with his family before his father fell apart.

After being together a few months, Tina pressed Joe to tell her exactly what he did for a living. He had told her he was "in sales," but she knew there was more to it than that. Finally he told her he sold drugs, but didn't use them. She was quiet for a while, and then asked him "And that's all you want to do—just sell drugs?"

Joe said no, and told her that he planned to get out of the business after a while, but that he was making too much money to stop just then. She dropped the subject. They spent some very passionate time together in the mountains and at his apartment. She was energetic, and Joe found that he was able to let down his guard and become a different person with Tina, excited by the wilder forms of sex they had together.

Joe had been introduced to sex by a very willing cousin, but found that with Tina, sex with someone you cared about was completely different, far more enjoyable and much more moving. Tina introduced him to variations on a theme that included no words sex, sex watching favorite movies, and sex after walking around his apartment naked for most of a day. Joe's customary no-emotion exterior disappeared quickly when he was with Tina. She was able to bring him to a state of mind—and body—where he was less in control than he usually wanted to be. When he wasn't with her, Joe wasn't sure how he felt about that loss of control; when he was, he didn't care.

Then after a year of being together, one day she came to his apartment and sat down with a very serious look on her face. She asked him again when he was going to quit selling drugs and get a real job. Joe could tell something had changed, because Tina was much more insistent. She asked him if he had plans to get more education and to continue with his music. Joe had written some songs for her, and had even recorded two of them and given her a CD with the songs.

She kept on, pressing him harder than she ever had before. "You can do so much more, Joe. You don't want to be a drug dealer all your life—so why not quit now? Why not go on to college—you can do it. Go with the music, Joe. Do what you love."

She was pleading at this point, and Joe asked, "Why are you pushing this so hard?"

She gave him a very sad smile, and said "Because I found out yesterday that I'm pregnant, and I need to decide what to do about it. I am not raising a drug dealer's baby, Joe. That's not who I am, and I hope that's not who you are. But you have a decision to make—and so do I. If I don't hear from you, I'll make it by myself."

And then she left. Joe had been speechless, knowing his world would change one way or the other, with Tina out of it or with him needing to find new work. For a few days, once he realized that Tina was serious and wouldn't be calling him anymore, he had a fantasy about being a father. And then he began to think about his own father, and how bad it had been at the end. Joe knew he could be a better father than his own father had been, but he had little reason to believe that he could be a really good father. And so, like many young people in their twenties, he allowed the power of doing nothing to win out.

He never heard from Tina again.

A year later, he ran into her on the street with some friends of hers, and she smiled at him but walked on by without saying anything. She was thin, and with some friends whom Joe knew to be party girls, and Joe realized that she had gotten rid of the baby. He felt a twinge of regret, but he was late for a pick-up of merchandise, and moved on past her to his car.

And then Joe looked over into the cradle and saw that Isabel was not moving.

Sancho had already risen, and was whimpering. Joe quickly went over and picked her up, and heard her gasp.

"What's happening? She isn't breathing right!"

Dolores said, as she moved quickly toward him, taking Isabel from him, "You have to watch out for it, drug-exposed babies have a tendency to SIDS—sudden infant death syndrome. Their brain and breathing aren't completely hooked up yet, and sometimes they just don't breathe." She began walking with Isabel, patting her on the back gently. "It's coming back OK now, she's breathing. We've got to watch for that, Joe."

They sat back down, Dolores in the rocker with Isabel, and Dolores said, "This is just one more reminder that we can't keep her out here forever. She needs to be getting regular pediatric care, Joe—and they need to know her history, that she was born into withdrawal."

She paused, and then said, "Joe, I've been thinking about this. They have this program now where people can drop newborns off at fire stations and other places, no questions asked. It's sort of an anti-abortion thing, to get newborns into adoption if their parents can't take care of them, trying to keep them alive and get them into good medical care as early as possible. You could do that, Joe, you could pick a fire station in some quiet suburban area and drop her off late at night and then call right away so they would take care of her. No muss, no fuss, and she's in good hands. Joe—you've got to do it. We can't keep her here. I told you a month, and it's almost up. It's time to do something about this."

She was pleading now, for Joe's sake as much as the baby's. "Joe—if you care about Isabel, you have to get her into safe hands and good medical care. I've done all I can. And there's something else—something I'm really worried about. It's June. It's going to get hotter than hell out here, and I haven't used the solar all through the summer yet. We would need to keep the AC on all the time, and if it went off, it could be very dangerous for her. I've got a backup generator, but I only have storage for a hundred gallons of gas. After that—we're toast."

Then she added the clincher. "And Joe—if you take her back, they'll eventually stop looking for you. And for me."

It was a long speech, and Joe knew that Dolores had been thinking about it for a long time. He knew that Dolores was still worried about prison for her role in taking care of the baby, and he knew that the risk to Dolores was a big factor in what he needed to decide.

But all Joe could think of was loss—the loss forever of the child who had become the most important person in the world to him. He mumbled "Let me think about it. I know you're right, it makes a lot of sense. But let me think about it."

And then he walked out into the desert, trying to forget Serena's question.

Which one do you take after?

CHAPTER 13

As Joe began walking, he thought about Isabel, and he thought about where he was. He and Dolores loved the desolation, but at the same time he knew it was hardly the best place to raise a sick baby. He admitted to himself that desolation was not the first thing that would come to mind when responsible parents were considering where to move with a baby.

A few nights after he arrived with Isabel, Dolores explained to Joe how she had ended up where she was. "It was the emptiest place in California," she said. She had used maps of the southeastern corner, the least known, least populated section of the state, and had then drawn a line between the 40 on the north, the 95 on the east, the Marine Corps training areas on the west, and the 62 and Joshua Tree National Park on the south. In the middle of all those boundaries, nothing showed on the map. Nothing. More than 3000 square miles, more than half the size of Massachusetts—and nothing marking human habitation within those boundaries.

To the east lay the Whipple Mountains Wilderness area. It is where the Mojave Desert shades into the Sonoran Desert from the south and east. Volcanic craters, lava flows, miles and miles of dunes, narrow washes that run ten feet deep in monsoon season and dry the rest of the year. A stark landscape—like the "surface of the moon," the trite phrase-makers say, sooner or later.

There were roads, a few of them, oddly named: Telephone Pole Line Road, Cadiz Road, Nations Road, the Heritage Trail. But they were either straight as an arrow across open spaces or winding around natural features of the landscape, not well maintained—and mostly unpaved once you got off the main highways.

Along the northern boundaries of the desolation ran one of the most famous roads in the nation's history—old Route 66, now feebly called "National Trails Highway." It had once been called

"The Mother Road," and John Steinbeck made it famous in *Grapes of Wrath* as the Joads' road to California from the Dust Bowl.

Ghost towns lined the road now, some once famous: Siberia, Ludlow, and the ironically named Bagdad. There was a road in the desert that led to Bagdad—not the one in Iraq but a little ghost town on old Highway 66 in the desert north of the Marine training base, where most of the inhabitants had eventually been on the road to the real Baghdad, or the real Kandahar—or had just gotten back.

Dolores summed it all up. "So it's no man's land, and no woman's land, Joe—and it seemed like a fine place to set up quarters."

And Joe thought, as he walked aimlessly north, it was probably no baby's land either.

And yet the desolation had its compensations.

The routine that Joe, Dolores, and Isabel had settled into included the peace and quiet of the desert's isolation. Joe woke first, shortly before Isabel began crying for her first bottle or diaper change. He moved the rocker out to the front deck, facing east into the mountains that rose between them and the Colorado River.

This was Joe's favorite hour, when he had the dual blessings of Isabel and the sunrise to ease him into the day. At first, the dark dissipated, but no hint of sunrise yet revealed its site. It was still the cool of the day, before the sun began to heat up the desert. Then the glow began over the Whipple peaks. Slowly, the glow widened as the sky lightened, and then, minutes later, the breakthrough point was visible where the sun would first rise over the tops of the mountains. The point shifted a few yards each day, and after his first week, Joe had watched the sunrise so carefully he could pinpoint exactly where the sun was going to breach the mountains.

The first tip of sun was just that—a yellow tip poking above the jagged top of the mountain's edge. Second by second, the tip widened into a sword point of pure light, then a crescent, turning into a half-circle, then finally the full orb of sun. When clouds provided an accompaniment to the sun's breakthrough, the colors varied widely, from coral to pink to Homer's "rosy-fingered dawn," and on to a full palette of the colors from yellow to red and back again.

Watching the sun rise. Joe could make these four words last more than an hour every day of his time in the desert, looking down from time to time to watch Isabel sleep or picking her up and rocking her if she was fussing. Sunlight slowly brightening the beginnings of her day and his, showing the desert's perpetual changes and expanse, viewed off the front deck of their isolated enclave.

As he walked, Joe thought about the cops looking for him. He knew that by now they had figured out who he was and that he'd taken Isabel. He worried about not being able to reach Charlie and thought that might mean the gang had problems with him as well as the cops. And he was certain that the detectives had been in contact with Lee Farmer, whom he knew would protect Dolores, but who might have made a mistake that allowed them to trace his contacts with her.

Sooner or later, one of these groups would be successful. As vast as the desert was, he knew he could not hide there forever. Dolores' safety was at risk as well as Isabel's, and he was unsure that even her military honors would be able to protect her from an accessory charge.

Joe gradually shifted his thoughts from Isabel to her mother. When he had last talked to Luisa, she was in bad shape. But to make a decision about Isabel that he could live with, he needed to know how Luisa was doing, and whether there was any chance Isabel would end up with her, rather than a stranger. Joe knew in his head that an adoptive parent might be much better for Isabel if Luisa was still messed up. But in his heart, he wanted to know Luisa's chances. He wanted to believe that the harm he had done to Luisa and Isabel could be atoned for, somehow. But he knew he could not turn Isabel over to the random workings of a network of public and private agencies he had no reason to trust. So he needed to see if Luisa was headed in the right direction.

And the only way to do that was to talk to Luisa.

CHAPTER 14

So Joe came back to the mobile and took one of his throwaway phones. He told Dolores what he was going to do, and drove an hour into Arizona to try to hide their location. He knew that if they were tapping her phone, they could locate his phone, even if they didn't know who was using it.

She answered on the first ring. "Hello?"

"This is your friend. The one who is trying to help your baby, I wanted . . ."

She broke in. "Joe—is this Joe Brenner?" Her voice was rushed, nervous.

He was silent. Then, realizing she still had no idea where he was and that the cops knew by now that he was the one who had taken the baby, he answered. "Yeah. It's me. Isabel is fine. She's doing well. I can't tell you where we are, but she's doing very well. I needed to talk to you about how you're doing."

She was sobbing by then, saying over and over "Thank you, thank you. I wanted to know she was OK. I thought you might call, after you called me that first time."

Until he heard her voice, Joe was not sure whether he was going to try to probe her condition over the phone or risk a much more dangerous face-to-face meeting. He had thought carefully about how he could do it, but he knew it would be risky.

"Luisa, listen. Do you have a car? And do you know if the cops are watching your house?"

"I can borrow my sister's car. I don't think they are—they came and talked to me for a long time, and a guy came last week to see if I had heard anything. They knew you had taken her, Joe. They're looking for you. But I don't think they're watching the house. They took the ankle thing off a few days ago."

Joe thought for a minute and then decided to take the risk. "I need to talk with you face to face, Luisa. I'm going to explain how we can do that. I'm not bringing Isabel, she'll be safe with some friends of mine."

She agreed, quickly, and Joe explained where he wanted to meet her and what she should do to lose any tails. He cautioned her about being obvious that she was leaving. They agreed to meet in Palm Desert in two days.

Two days later, Joe arrived an hour early at the coffee shop where he had set the meeting. He parked where he could see any car that followed her.

She drove up in an older Toyota Corolla, and walked into the coffee shop. Joe sat for fifteen minutes, watching to see if any suspicious cars turned up. He knew that if they were really keeping an eye on her, they could have put a GPS tracer on the car. But he was far enough from Dolores' place to feel confident that they couldn't track him out into the desert without him knowing it.

He walked into the coffee shop, and Luisa immediately stood up from the booth where she had been sitting. He motioned her to sit down, looked around the booths and tables, and saw nothing that seemed to be a problem.

He slid into the booth, and smiled at her. For a moment, he flashed back on all the times he had met her to sell her drugs. Again, he felt guilt at the memories.

She looked better than she had the last time he saw her. She had lost all the baby weight, but had not returned to being as thin as she was before. He looked at her eyes carefully, trying to see if she was on anything. Then he watched her hands for a tremor. She seemed clean to him.

She was waiting for him to speak first. "Thanks for coming, Luisa." Then he looked around, and pulled out his cellphone. He had two pictures of Isabel, with the background concealed.

Tears began running down her face as she looked at the photos. "Oh, she is so beautiful. Thank you for taking care of her. I know you are in trouble for it, but she looks wonderful."

"Luisa," he said as gently as he could, "I have to ask you some questions, so that I can make some decisions about Isabel. I don't want to upset you, but I need answers."

"I'll try." She watched him, nervous and wanting to please him.

"Who's the father?"

She jerked back, and frowned. "He's nobody I'm with or ever would be with. It was a young guy whose house we were cleaning. After I had cleaned his place a couple of times, he started giving me big tips. Like a hundred bucks. He tried to talk to me, too." She looked down. "It wasn't like I was selling myself, you know, but I sort of felt obligated. We did it a few times, but then it was a bad scene at the end, and I never went back. He really knew nothing about sex, and had no idea how to do it. He tried to reach me several times after that, and I finally blocked his number on my cell phone so he couldn't get in touch with me."

"You're sure it was him."

"Yeah. I wasn't with anybody else then. He never used anything, and I thought I was OK with the timing. I must have messed up." She paused, and he knew what was coming would be even more embarrassing. "I was high on pot—we smoke sometimes before we clean houses. It makes it go smoother—it's dirty work, so we get high to make the time go faster. By the time I realized he didn't have anything, it was too late. I was stupid."

"Why do you get high when you work?"

She glared at him. "Funny question for a dealer to ask!"

"I know, I know." He stopped and tried to get his own head straight about what he wanted to say to her. "I know I sold you the stuff, and I'm sorry about that. Now I'm sorry. I wasn't then."

"Why now?" Then she gave a short laugh. "Because you got shot, huh?"

"That's part of it. But now that I've seen what it did to Isabel, it's different." Then he pushed back, wanting to keep the initiative. "But you would have gotten it from someone else, right?"

"Yeah. Probably." He saw her anger, mixed in with her guilt, and knew he had to be careful not to lose her.

He asked Luisa what drugs she had used when she was pregnant. He'd started to read on the Internet about drug-exposed babies, and just like it said, using abstract, clinical language, she was a "polydrug user." For Luisa, that meant alcohol, marijuana, "a little meth," and a lot of tobacco—a pack or more a day. As Joe had thought, she'd used whatever she could get.

Briefly, Joe had tried to convince himself that the meth he'd sold her was the least of the problem. But then he remembered an article he'd read about the effects of meth on infants—and that put an end to any relief he'd wanted to feel.

He asked Luisa how often she'd gone to the prenatal visits that had been scheduled for her by the ob-gyn who diagnosed her pregnancy. She told him she'd been "three or four times." Then he asked her if anyone had ever asked her about drinking or using drugs when she was being seen at the clinic. Luisa said no, no one had ever mentioned it.

"Did they ever give you blood tests?"

"Yes, and I worried about that." She told him that on her last visit, the nurse doing the preparation had looked at her closely and told her, "If you're on anything, you'd better get off of it unless you want your kid to come out deformed, or have it taken away."

The bluntness of the warning scared Luisa, and she finally stopped using in her eighth month. And she began to worry that it might be too late.

"What did they tell you about your chances of getting her back after you got arrested?"

"They said I had a chance. This worker who used to be on meth and lost her kids and now works in the court said I could get her back if I went to treatment and stayed clean. But I can't find a program, and I . . . I don't know if I can do it."

"You don't want her back?"

"It's not that. I don't want to stop. I can't—I tried and I keep going back to it, over and over. I just keep going back." She looked down, embarrassed. "I haven't used for a few days—I didn't want you to see me high."

She went on, wanting to talk about the baby rather than her addiction. "They told me that when they find you and Isabel, they'll bring her back and put her in foster care. And then I've got six months or something like that to get clean, and at the end of that time they put her up for adoption if I'm not on track."

Joe had deliberately left the cellphone on with the pictures of Isabel showing, and kept nudging the phone so the pictures would stay on. She looked down at the pictures, and began to cry again, softly.

"I knew it was you, Joe. They told me you were shot, and then I wondered, because the paper said you were in the same hospital where she was born. I worked out the days—we were there at the same time. I didn't tell anyone, until the cops came and started pressuring me and threatening me."

She leaned over and said, "But you weren't a bad guy, Joe. You were a dealer, sure, but you never treated me like trash, the way some of the dealers do. I tried your old cell number, but I knew you'd gotten rid of it in case the guys who shot you were still looking for you. And then when you called, I was so happy that I knew who she was with, and it wasn't somebody who would sell her or some big institution where they'd just give her a number and no one would care about her. I can tell by looking at the pictures that you've taken good care of her."

Joe thanked her for coming, and said that he would call her soon and tell her what would happen next, His final words to her were as blunt as he could make them: "Get into a good program as fast as you can—and stay in it. If you want this baby to come back to you," he said as he showed her the pictures a final time, "you have to do that work. She's worth it—you can deserve her if you do the work."

He waited for a half hour, still half-expecting the door to burst open and cops to surround him. When he thought it was safe, he left, driving around in circles for long enough to be sure no one was following him.

Driving back to Dolores, Joe re-assembled the pieces of his puzzle. Dolores was right: Isabel needed better care than they could provide her. As much progress as they had made and as hard as they had worked to give her what she needed, she was going to need more help than they could give her. And sooner or later someone would find him.

But Luisa was not yet to the point where she was going to have good odds of being allowed to take care of Isabel any time soon—if ever.

So Joe had to decide to take Isabel back and run the risk of her being placed in an institution or, at best, with foster parents who might well become her adoptive parents. He briefly wondered if they would be able to find a doctor in one of the small towns in Arizona who would be able to check on Isabel regularly, allowing them to keep her until Luisa's fate was known. But he assumed the criminal charges of baby kidnapping meant that a wide network would be fully alerted to watch for Isabel. And he knew now that he'd been identified as her kidnapper.

Which one do you take after?

CHAPTER 15

Dolores had improved as Isabel began taking up more and more of her time. She didn't fake sobriety, but Joe could tell she was more in control of her drinking than before they had arrived. Yet he heard her cry out from her bedroom at the back of the mobile home nearly every night. As Sancho padded quietly into her room to comfort her, returning to lie beside Isabel's cradle, Joe knew Dolores was a long way from ridding herself of the demons she had brought back from the Middle East.

Joe finally decided to talk with her about it. "Dee, tell me what happened in Basra."

She looked at him, eyes full of pain. "I can't, Joe." She reached over into her desk, pulled out a large white folder, and tossed it to him. "It's in there—at least what some officer wrote up." And then she left the mobile and walked outside with Sancho.

Joe opened the folder, which contained a large certificate with the heading, "Commendation for Corpsman Dolores Brenner." And Joe read,

Commendation for Corpsman Dolores M. Brenner, USN

On July 2, 2010, during the withdrawal of USMC forces from Southern Iraq as part of Operation New Dawn, Corpsman Dolores Brenner was serving as a combat medic attached to the 7th Regimental Team, which was assigned to protect a large convoy removing materiel from two Coalition bases in southern Iraq. The convoy came under fire, and while attending to two wounded Marines, Corpsman Brenner observed a group of insurgents advancing on her position. At considerable risk to herself, she secured the weapons of the wounded and fired two full magazines into the advancing enemy. She killed or wounded at least five of them, and was then reinforced by a squad of Marines. She then stood up and carried each of the wounded Marines to safety while under fire. Once assured of their safety, she returned to the battle and took up a firing position on the extreme right flank of the unit, in the most exposed position, firing until the enemy completely withdrew from the attack, While engaged, the Marines on her immediate left received RPG rounds, killing one of them and wounding Corpsman Brenner with shrapnel.

For this action, she has been awarded a Purple Heart and a Silver Star, for her wounds and her bravery under fire that posed extreme danger to herself. Corpsman Brenner is one of the bravest warriors this officer has ever had the honor to command. She richly deserves the Silver Star, and the honor due to her for being only the tenth woman to win this award since World War I.

Signed, Colonel J.L. Chamberlain, USMC

Joe decided that Dolores was going to need professional help, and that it wouldn't do much good for him to try to talk to her. But he understood a little better, after reading the citation, what she had gone through, and he was very proud of her. While he was sneaking around the back streets of the Valley selling drugs, Dolores had been saving lives—and taking some when she needed to protect her Marines.

Isabel had only gotten sick once. She started having diarrhea, and after three days of a low fever and her being unable to keep any food inside her, they decided to try a tea made out of local plants that Dolores had cultivated.

Dolores explained, "When I was over in Iraq I got close to some of the local doctors. A few of them were women, and they were an amazing blend of modern science and thousand-year old herbal cures. They knew things about plants in the desert that I had never heard of in our training, so I started reading a lot of stuff online about desert plants. There's this great book by a guy at UC Berkeley, Jepson, who describes all the plants and has great pictures.

"Joe, there's dozens of plants out here, but the most common one is creosote. Some people call it chapparal. *Larrea tridentate*. It's like a pharmacy in a bush. You can use it as an analgesic, a diuretic, for sunscreen, as a disinfectant even. FDA put out a warning about using it, but if you know what you're doing, it's fine. I'm going to give Isabel a tiny bit of the extract from the leaves and see if it helps her. Just a tiny bit—this drugstore stuff isn't working worth a damn."

And it worked. Isabel made a terrible face when she tasted the mixture of a teaspoon with a few drops of the extract mixed in with her formula, but she kept it down and the diarrhea eased after another day.

Both Dolores and Joe read report after report on drug-exposed infants, until Dolores' printer had a four-inch stack of paper piled up beside it. They had found studies on the effects of prenatal exposure, the different drugs used by pregnant women, and screening programs that had successfully cut drug and alcohol use in half among pregnant women who had been screened and referred to brief treatment. They pored over reports about infant development and early mental health, and they had downloaded assessment tools that they eagerly used as benchmarks while they watched Isabel move from a baby with erratic movements to a nearly three-month old with an emerging personality.

Her sleep problems were still with her, and they were up with her at least twice a night for feeding and calming. They traded off, with Joe and Dolores each having their own routines. Joe used the music, and Dolores combined gentle rocking of Isabel with her exercise program, taking a few steps, then lowering herself and the baby in a half-squat movement that Isabel seemed to enjoy. Rocking side by side, then bending toward the floor was repetitive enough to keep her content, while giving Dolores a workout that left her muscles strained and her heart filled as she watched Isabel's smiles.

They had noticed that she was fascinated by the overhead fans and would watch the circling movements for a long time. Then they read that this fixation might be a symptom of the baby's inclination to repetitive movements, and tried to vary her environment a little bit with a slow-moving mobile Dolores had bought in Needles.

They had also read that strange textures bothered some drug-exposed babies, so they experimented with different blankets until they found one that Isabel would clutch close to her when she fell asleep. There was a velour-like surface on two of the blankets that Isabel seemed to like, and they used only those blankets for her bedding, using the rest for Sancho's nest beside a crib they had bought when she outgrew the cradle.

Joe was fascinated by what the literature said about bonding and attachment. While some researchers said there was no such thing, others traced the devastating effects in the lives of infants who found out the hard way that there was no one they could trust, no one who consistently came when they cried out, who would hold them and comfort them when they were upset. Being unable to count on people, Joe realized, was often fatal to a child's emotional development, and could be tracked far into their adult life. And it made him all the more grateful for what he knew his mother had given him and Dolores as they grew up.

And he struggled with his decision every time he thought about an institutional "home" or a new, unfamiliar home where Isabel would spend her first few months after he took her back.

With time on his hands while Isabel was sleeping, Joe tried to clear his head about what he would do next. He knew that he would probably have to serve some jail time if he took her back, unless he could figure out a way to do what Dolores had suggested—just drop her off somewhere and disappear. But then he would have no idea what would happen to her, or what would happen to Luisa's chances of getting her back.

He tried to explain this to Dolores one day when they were eating breakfast. But she had little patience with his problem.

Dolores said, "Sometimes you think too much, Joe. I figured out a long time ago that you go through this one day at a time, and you try to forget the bad ones and hang onto the good ones. After that, all the thinking is just getting you stuck inside your own head."

Then she motioned to his plate, saying, "Eat your eggs. And then see if Isabel needs changing."

CHAPTER 16

Sam and Joshua prepared carefully for their agency interviews. They knew some would be brief, those held with "checkoff" people—officials who had to be interviewed for protocol or political reasons. And then there would be those who were worth as much time as Sam and Joshua could get from them, those who were most likely to be substantive and candid, rather than superficial.

Joshua had prepared a folder with the names of each of the interviews and the times and locations of the meetings. They had decided to use Sam's Highlander for transportation. They developed a standard list of questions, but Sam encouraged Joshua to improvise when it seemed useful or to let the conversation go wherever it seemed to be heading.

The Department of Mental Health

Sam and Joshua began their interviews with the mental health agency's program director, a fiftyish Asian man who had been promoted up through the ranks over a lengthy career. He began by explaining the different types of funding his agency provided to private and nonprofit organizations.

Sam said, "So you make these grants, to dozens of agencies."

"Right."

"And presumably some of them work, and some don't."

"Well, yes. Some have better outcomes."

"So you keep funding the ones that are ranked highest?"

"Oh, we couldn't *rank* them. There are too many variables to do that. And the legislators who give us the funds wouldn't like us pointing fingers at agencies that weren't ranked at the top if they were located in their own districts."

"So you just keep that information buried."

"We don't publish it, that's right."

"Have any legislators or auditors or anybody else ever asked you for those rankings?"

"No. That's never happened."

Sam shifted direction. "You work with women with maternal depression, post-partum depression?"

"Yes."

"Do any of those women have drug and alcohol problems, too?"

"Well, yes, some do. We have some programs that work on what we call co-occurring problems."

"Some programs do that—but others are just mental health?"

"Yes."

"But when new mothers are depressed, what do they do?"

"Well, I suppose your point is that some of them drink and use drugs."

"Isn't that likely?"

"Yes, it is. But these programs are usually specialized."

"You specialize. Even though the moms have more than one problem."

"Yes."

The Department of Child Welfare

Next they met with one of the unit supervisors in the child welfare agency. Sam began by asking how widespread substance abuse was among the agency's clients.

The supervisor was an older woman who had been with the agency for thirty years. Her demeanor suggested she was too busy to meet with Sam and Joshua. She seemed irritated by Sam's question. "Frankly, Mr. Leonard, we see substance abuse as one of many issues our clients are dealing with."

"So it's just one more thing."

"Well, yes. It's one of many things they face."

"But how many of the clients of your agency have drug or alcohol problems?"

"Well, the workers say it's a large majority. But we only record about 20% of those."

"Do you think the workers are right—or your statistics?"

"I'm really not sure. We just add up the data that is given to us. You see, recording a substance abuse issue is voluntary—the state and federal data systems don't require us to indicate whether substance abuse is a problem."

Sam followed up. "So it could be a lot more than 20%, but that's all your workers have actually recorded in the file?"

"Yes."

"Would it surprise you to know that the state reports to the feds that only 4% of all foster care cases involve parents who use drugs and alcohol?"

"That seems low to me. But it's a voluntary field—the workers don't have to fill it out. The feds don't require it."

Then Sam asked, "How does your agency work with a mother like the young woman who gave birth to Isabel? How do you put pressure on her to get into treatment? Isn't that the problem—they won't get into treatment when they should?"

She frowned. "No, that would be blaming the victims—that would be deficit thinking, to blame the parents for their addiction."

"But aren't the real victims the children?" He reached into his stack of folders and pulled one out. "Here's a report from the federal government that said there were almost 700,000 children who were victims of proven child abuse or neglect in 2012. Aren't these the real victims?"

"Yes. But if we blamed their parents for their addiction, we would be ignoring the fact that they have a disease, just like hypertension or diabetes."

"But people with hypertension or diabetes have to take their medicine or they get sicker, right?"

"Yes."

"So why don't you work to get these parents into treatment—treatment that would help them with what you call their disease?"

"We do. We refer many of these parents to treatment."

"You refer them? How many enroll in treatment?"

"We don't have that information."

"You don't? So we shouldn't blame the parents—but who should we blame if you don't follow up on the referrals you make?"

"We are not responsible for the decisions these parents make. Some of them get into treatment and get their kids back—and some don't. We are not responsible for their choices."

Sam looked at Joshua, remained silent for a while, and then said, softly, "Sounds a bit like blaming the victim to me."

Valley Hospital

Sam and Joshua had asked to speak with the administrator of the hospital where Isabel had been born, and the administrator, Dr. Ramon Soltero, agreed to meet.

When they arrived, Soltero had set up several charts on the conference room adjoining his office. The charts showed the total number of births and those that spent time in the NICU.

Sam began, "Could you explain to us how you screen for drug or alcohol effects on newborns, Dr. Soltero?"

"We have a standard procedure if we suspect drug exposure." He hastily added, "We did this one right—we reported it to child welfare. That baby had obvious withdrawal symptoms, and we sent the report over right away."

"How many reports like that do you do a year?"

Looked embarrassed, Soltero answered, "About thirty last year."

"And how any births did you have here?"

"2,035."

"Are you familiar with the statewide prenatal screening results on the state Health Department website?" Seeing Soltero shake his head, Sam said, "It estimates that as many as 15% of all births are prenatally exposed to drugs or alcohol. So that would be about 300 births here, right?"

"Well, we don't screen all of them. We only screen if there is an obvious problem that we think might be caused by drugs."

"Do you think that you should screen all of them? You screen, by state law, for over twenty different birth defects. Why not for one as prevalent as prenatal substance exposure?"

Soltero was looking very uncomfortable. "We have been relying on prenatal screening for that. We are only able to screen when there is reason to suspect that drugs affected the newborn."

"Do you screen for alcohol?"

"No, that's more difficult."

They talked further, but Soltero did not budge from his position that they had done what they should in Isabel Contreras' case, and couldn't screen all babies.

The Early Childhood Agency

The person who came out to meet with Sam and Joshua from the early childhood coordination agency was a short, wiry man in a well-fitting suit and long, carefully trimmed hair. He introduced himself as Rob Ryan.

Sam had done some background work on Ryan. He was a campaign consultant who had been hired by the agency for his public relations skills.

"How can I help you?"

"We're doing some work for a law firm on the child welfare problems the county has been having."

"We'd be glad to help in any way we can. We don't work very much with child welfare, though. Our primary work is with child care and health agencies."

"That's good. We're concerned about the newborns in the county who were prenatally exposed to drugs or alcohol."

"Well, you understand we're funded from the tobacco tax. So our primary concern would be with the effects of tobacco on children under 5."

"You're concerned about children affected by tobacco prenatally?"

"Yes."

"But not alcohol?"

"Well, primarily tobacco. That's where the funding comes from."

By this time Ryan had pulled out his PDA and began looking at messages. Sam had ignored it at first, but it was becoming a distraction. And so Sam just stopped talking. After a few moments, Ryan looked up, and Sam said with a smile, "I'll wait for you to finish."

"Oh no, just dealing with a crisis. What were you saying?" He put the PDA down, reluctantly.

"Tobacco and alcohol. Did anyone suggest taxing alcohol, too, since a lot of babies are affected by alcohol as well as tobacco?"

Looking uncomfortable, Ryan said, "The sponsors felt that it would be easier to convince the public that tobacco should be taxed to help young children."

"Do you think that had anything to do with the strength of the alcohol lobby in California?"

Ryan looked even more uncomfortable. "I don't know. Possibly."

"But don't a lot of women who use alcohol also smoke? Do you have data on how much overlap there is between the two?"

"Our research people might have that. I don't."

Later, Josh asked Sam why he had handled the PDA interruption in the way he had. Sam smiled and said, "The Blackberry nod, they call it. They call them PDAs—which I finally figured out meant pricks driven by automation. He shifts his attention away from our conversation, shows us something else is more important—so I just stop talking. At least I don't have to be part of the pretense that the bastard is paying attention to the conversation."

For once, Joshua's empathy quotient for the interviewees was at zero, and he nodded agreement.

The Department of Public Health

They met next with the public health agency. Nicole had suggested they talk to the vital statistics unit, so they had made an appointment with the head of the unit. She was a tall brunette, working in a office with three separate monitors showing charts and spreadsheets of data.

Sam began. "There are about 135,000 births in the county each year."

"Yes. That's approximately the number."

"And of them how many are reported as born exposed to drugs or alcohol?"

"Well, we don't really have that number. We're not required to compile that number. And the hospitals really don't report it very often."

Sam reached over and pulled out another folder. "This is the federal legislation from which the county gets several million dollars each year for child abuse prevention. The state signs a plan that promises that all drug-affected births will be reported to child protective services." He looked quizzical. "But you don't have that number, even though the state promised the federal government that a plan for safe care would be developed for every baby born drug-affected?"

"No, that would be the hospitals' responsibility—and DCW's."

"But you run the vital statistics unit—you count the number of births."

"Yes."

"Do you have any information *estimating* the number of those births that are drug-affected?"

"No, I don't believe so."

Another folder. "This is a study of 17 counties published by the State in 2009. It says about 15% of all births are babies who were prenatally exposed to drugs or alcohol."

"That's interesting."

"Do you have any reason to think that the rate in this county is higher or lower?"

"No, not really."

"So that would mean that about 20,000 births each year in this county were drug—or alcohol-exposed."

"Yes, I suppose that's right."

"And that would mean that a total of 365,000 kids under 18 were drug and alcohol-exposed at birth, and today they are all walking around this county or somewhere else with whatever effects prenatal exposure caused in their lives."

By now she could see where Sam was going, and she obviously thought it was time to try to head him off. "We are not responsible for those numbers, and we have no way of getting that information. You really would have to ask maternal and child health or the child welfare agency about that."

Joshua could see a Columbo question coming. Sam had explained that there was once a TV show about a detective named Columbo who would finish questioning a witness, or possible murderer, and then turn at the door and say "Just one more question" and then ask the toughest question that could be asked— the clincher that the guilty person hadn't prepared for.

"Just one more question. What would it cost to collect that information?"

"I have no idea. No one has ever asked us to do that."

After each interview and at the end of the day, Sam and Joshua wrote up their notes. Sam relied on his ancient laptop, while Joshua dictated, using Dragon voice recognition software. After the first thirty minutes of their note-writing together, Sam banished Joshua from his study to the living room. "You want to talk to yourself and call it work, kid, fine—but do it out of earshot of my fading hearing."

CHAPTER 17

The Desert

Dolores had gone into Needles to get supplies and had said she would be back by dark. When it got to be eight and the sun had disappeared over the desert, Joe called her.

She answered the second time he called. When he heard her voice, he could tell that she had been drinking. "Dee, are you all right? You sound like you've been drinking. The CHP picks you up, and you're going to be in a world of trouble. Do you need me to come and get you?"

"I'm fine, li'l brother. I just stopped off and had a few brews. I'm 'bout an hour out, and I'll be fine to get home. I've driven a hell of a lot drunker than I am right now. Be sure to feed Sancho, OK?"

She got home two hours later, and she was far from fine. She had an empty six-pack in the car—her old Honda Civic that she had kept from before she went to Iraq. As she stepped out of the car, Joe watched her from the front door of the mobile. She was walking, but with difficulty.

"Hey Joe, told you I'd make it. How's the kid?" She staggered up the steps and came inside, falling onto the couch. The dog came over and nuzzled her hand, trying to get a reaction. But she was too far out of it to do more than stare blankly at him.

"Why'd you take a risk like that, Dee? If the CHP catches up with you and follows you back here, we're all screwed."

"Back off, Joe. You're not my fooking nursemaid." She giggled. "Fooking—there was an Irish guy with our company, had just gotten citizenship and got into the Corps. Everything was fooking this and fooking that. We all picked it up after a while." She got up and went into the kitchen, swallowing down a glass of ice water out of the refrigerator.

She stood in the doorway, swaying. The bravado was gone, and she was frowning, looking at Joe with unfocused eyes. "I'm so tired."

Joe had seen it hundreds of times before, hearing the echoes of Mike's slurred mumbling. It scared him more than anything that had happened since he took Isabel.

"Joe, it's so hard. I try to forget it, but it's everywhere. When I try to sleep, when I wake up—I keep seeing it. All those beautiful boys, blown up all over that fucking desert." Then she looked at him and said, "I'm going to go try to sleep this off, Joe. Catch you in the early." As she staggered off to her bedroom, Joe watched her, wondering how much longer their luck was going to hold out.

The next morning, Joe was feeding Isabel when Dolores came out of her room. She groaned and said, "I must be losing it. Time was I could have drunk that much and bounced back at oh-dark thirty the next morning like nothing had happened."

Joe was quiet, continuing to hold Isabel and give her the bottle. When she realized he wasn't going to say anything, Dolores snapped "Don't give me the lecture, Joe. And don't give me the silent BS either. I got lonely for some beer and found a bar where nobody bothered me." She was silent, watching Isabel for a while. Then she said, softer, "I thought I was getting better, Joe. But it looks like it isn't working."

"I know you're still hurting, Dee. But this isn't going to help. I may go to jail sooner or later, but I'd rather do it for trying to do something good instead of because you led the cops here."

"I know, I know. I just got so thirsty out there. And then I couldn't stop, I didn't want to stop. It wasn't hurting any more, I could think about the good times, and the rest of it went away for a while." She shook her head. "Maybe it's time for you to take off, Joe. They're going to find us sooner or later, whether I get squared away or not."

Joe knew she was right, and he kept thinking about how to get Isabel back without messing Dolores up any more than she already was.

CHAPTER 18

The man called himself The Watcher, and he had been watching Luisa Contreras for several months, off and on. She had never come back to his condo in Altadena after It happened. But he had found an old tax form that he had filled out that had Luisa's mother's address. He went there and sat in his car until she came out. Then he got her phone number from an Internet service, using her address. He called twice but hung up both times, unsure of what to say. *Hi, this is the guy who banged you a few times and wants to do it again? Hi, you used to clean my condo—where did you go?*

She had gotten fatter than when he had been with her, and he didn't like her looks as much. But he still followed her and tried to figure out a way of talking with her. He couldn't forget the sex—it was the only time he had had sex with anyone, and he had been excited in a way he had never felt before, an experience he knew he could never learn in a book or access on the Internet. For once, he hadn't been watching—he had been swept up in something himself, and he wanted more of it.

He was following her into a strip shopping mall in Glendale when he saw her stop and slowly walk over to a guy who was standing in front of Albertson's. He parked where he could watch them. The guy handed her something and then quickly walked away.

The Watcher, whose name was Bryan Sorenson, had inherited a sizable trust fund left him by his parents, who were in the movie business and had been killed in a car accident when he was in high school. While they were alive, they were often away on location, and spent very little time with him, leaving him with a male nanny who was mostly into watching pornography and smoking pot. Bryan was left to amuse himself on the Internet, and became very skilled at manipulating various websites where he played video games.

His grades were good, and as a full-pay student, he attended colleges on the trust fund, trying Cal Tech, Pomona, and other colleges in Southern California, but never staying at any one of them. He had tried to get into Occidental, where the President and other luminaries had attended college, but wasn't able to get admitted.

While he was at Cal Tech, he had gotten interested in computer science, and had figured out a way to manipulate search engines to screen out fake entries. The big search engines had been having increasing problems with firms that hyped their Internet status so that they could move up the list of preferred sites, and he got in touch with three of the biggest ones. Once they verified that his software was effective, the largest of the firms bought his software for an amount that left him with a bank account that dwarfed his original trust fund.

Sorenson had bought a large condo in Altadena, which was where Luisa and her mother had been cleaning houses when he met her. Once he was out of college, he became even more of a recluse. But he liked to work in a clean office, and that meant he needed a cleaning crew for the rest of the condo.

Sorenson read the articles about the Baby Isabel kidnapping with mild interest, wondering why the mother's name was never mentioned. Curious, he got in touch with a contact in the IT section of the LAPD, a software contractor who worked for the IT unit who had given him access to the internal files on police cases several times in exchange for software that Sorenson had pirated for him.

Sorenson almost fell out of his computer chair when he opened the file. *Luisa Contreras?! That was her baby?* Then he began to wonder who the father was. Quickly, he accessed the birth record, and saw the telltale designation: *No father identified.* He sat unmoving, his brain doing the arithmetic.

Then he turned back to the computer, and quickly found the names of the detectives assigned to the Baby Isabel case. It was a few minutes' work to access their home computers, where he found a good deal of the case files which they had, against all regulations, transferred to their home email so they could work on reports from home and then transfer them back to their desktops at the station.

Once he had read the files and counted back from when he last saw Luisa, he had to face the fact that Baby Isabel was probably his child. Sorenson lacked the emotional depth to understand what that meant, but he absolutely understood one thing—if that was his baby, and someone had kidnapped her, he might be able to get back in touch with Luisa if he could find the baby and bring her back.

Going back to his computer, he read in the police files that the primary suspect was a guy named Joe Brenner, a low-level drug dealer who had been in the hospital when Luisa gave birth. He realized that this might have been the guy he saw Luisa meeting with in Glendale. Then he read that the detectives had interviewed a guy in Havasu who probably knew where Brenner's sister was— and that they suspected that the baby was somewhere out in the desert.

The hardest part of his hacking challenge still lay ahead; now he had to find the place where Joe Brenner was hiding out. But Sorenson had spent some of his time recently hacking into the Air Force base in Las Vegas where the Predator drones were controlled. He enjoyed watching the drones circle around over Afghanistan and Yemen and then drop down to obliterate people and houses. But he had also realized as he watched the live footage that the drones and the electronic systems they accessed could search many square miles of desert for signs of life.

It took him three days, but he was finally able to access the infrared frequencies that detected signs of humans in the deserts and mountains of the Middle East. He searched and found that several recon drones were being used by the Marines in joint training exercises with the Air Force at 29 Palms. It took him only two hours of hacking into their search programs to isolate three locations west of Havasu where Joe and his sister might be located, based on the heat signatures he could see on the photos that were stored online.

Now he had to figure out how to get there and take the baby—his baby. And then use her to get back in touch with Luisa.

Sorenson had very few friends, but he had driven by a bar in South Pasadena that was often full of motorcycle riders. With more resolve than common sense, he walked into the bar and simply asked the bartender if he knew anybody who could do a job for him that might involve "a little rough play."

The bartender laughed and pointed him to a group in the corner that had full biker vests and bandannas. Sorenson walked over and asked them if they would be willing to do a job for him. They laughed at him, too, but quickly fell silent when he tossed ten one hundred-dollar bills on the table and said "I can pay well for what I want."

The negotiations resembled attempts to communicate across several galaxies, but Sorenson finally succeeded in making them understand that he wanted them to pick someone up from an address "out by the River." They agreed on a price, and Sorenson told them he would meet them at a junction near the three locations, which were all within a ten mile radius. He would pay them when they located the target, which he finally explained was a baby, taken in a custody battle with his wife. The bikers weren't avid newspaper readers and their idea of television was raunchy reality shows, so they had no idea that the baby was Baby Isabel. They asked for another thousand up front, which Sorenson quickly pulled out of his jacket pocket and handed to the head biker.

The deal was made. Sorenson said he wanted to try to get the baby in a week, and they made plans to meet at Vidal Junction where he would give them the locations to check out.

CHAPTER 19

USC Medical School Department of Pediatrics

At Nicole's suggestion, Sam and Joshua drove over to USC to meet with Irena Chervoussian, a pediatrician who had specialized in fetal alcohol effects. They arrived in her office and found a short, vivacious woman with long dark hair and Middle Eastern features, who was dressed in medical whites and greeted them in an office with Persian carpets and paintings on the walls.

"Please, gentlemen, sit down." She gestured them to a small conference table on which her assistant had set out tea. As she poured for them, she began talking. "I am very glad you asked to see me. I gather you are doing a very thorough set of interviews about the events triggered by the taking of that unfortunate little girl."

"What are her odds of success, Doctor?"

She frowned, and steepled her fingers with a slow, thoughtful movement of her body and hands. "It depends on so much. How soon they find her, how she has been cared for, what her mother was using, where she ends up in placement—so many things."

She went on. "As much as we have learned about prenatal exposure, we simply do not know yet where prenatal exposure crosses over into mental illness. A nine-year-old who was prenatally exposed is diagnosed with pediatric bipolar disorder when she starts hearing voices and falls into manic night terrors and fear of being touched by anyone. Was it the drugs and alcohol ten years ago, or was it the three generations of mental illness that she unluckily inherited?

"These kids are like the old maps that used to have a legend out at the edge of the maps: *terra incognita*. Unknown territory. We diagnose them with all kinds of disorders, and we prescribe therapy, and train the parents, and load the kids up with medications when we think that will help. And sometimes the kid pulls out of it and makes a heroic recovery—and sometimes nothing works. They get obsessed with sex and with drugs and with computer games and all kinds of terrible distractions. And then, sometimes, a single teacher or a parent or grandparent who really believes in them helps the kid turn their life around."

Sam asked "How much is it the parenting and how much is it the exposure that makes the difference?"

Chervoussian smiled. "Ah, the classic nature vs nurture question. The answer, of course is both. But I must tell you that after three decades in this field, I have learned never to under-estimate the power of the organic deficits. Parenting can help greatly, but parenting starts where the child's brain starts.

"Adoptive parents have the hardest time, it seems to me. Some of them know in their heads what they are getting into, and yet they're never prepared for the heartache. And others are simply good human beings who wanted to open their lives to a child, and make a better life for that child. And then, unknowing, they inherit the worst excesses of the generations of biogenetic history and dysfunction that child carries in her cells, and it scars the lives of that entire family—the parents and the children alike. I see these families in our clinic, and it can be so sad. And yet when it succeeds—or brings moments of success along with the pain of coping endlessly with all these effects—it can be truly glorious.

"I've worked with these kids and it's heartbreaking to see how hard it is for the ones that are really trying to lick it. They get to where they can read other kids reacting to them, they know they are being weird, and they try to calm themselves. The fancy word is self-regulation; the real word is *brakes*—what stops the rest of us, most of the time, from doing or saying things that are goofy, strange, or life-threatening."

She reached over and motioned with her fingers in front of Joshua's forehead. "It's right there, the prefrontal cerebral cortex, which developed last in the species, so it develops last in the individual. Adolescents don't have it fully developed, which is why teenagers do dumb things and take risks. Many prenatally exposed kids are, in effect, teenagers for life, because that over-ride is just not functional in their brains. The brakes, the over-ride, the second-guesser just doesn't work. Some would say it's the conscience or the internal gyroscope that keeps us balanced."

She stopped and looked at one of the paintings on her wall. It was obviously children's art, and she began telling them about it, as if to take a break from the intensity of her remarks. "Several years ago someone who had an international exhibit of children's art from all over the world realized there was nothing from Iran." She pronounced the word carefully, as if to say *I will use that word but you know I mean Persia.* "And so the exhibit organizers got some art work from an international firm that worked with Iranian suppliers, and this was one of the ones that won a prize. I love it."

After a suitable pause, Sam asked, "You've worked in this area of medicine for a long time. Where do you see the leadership coming from? Who's responding to these problems? Are there any political leaders who focus in this area?"

"Politics is so useless on these issues." She waved her hands, dismissing those she was talking about. "You get idiots like the libertarians, who essentially agree with those so-called feminist groups that say a woman has the right to put anything into her body that she wants to—and both of them basically write off the kid. Then you get the pro-lifers who say the baby is a person before it's born, and so the mom should be prosecuted and thrown in jail instead of put into treatment. What they conveniently leave out are the miscarriages."

"Miscarriages?" Joshua asked.

"Yes. About one million pregnancies a year in this country terminate by themselves. Sometimes it's because the body knows the fetus won't live. And sometimes, a lot of research says, it's because prenatal substance exposure compromised the birth. If you really thought the fetus was a person, you'd think that they'd insist on prenatal screening. I mean, think about it. Medicaid funds almost half of all births now, and so it's obvious that Medicaid should be paying for universal prenatal screening.

"Gentlemen, I don't know your religious or philosophical views on these issues. But you have come to ask me mine. And I will tell you that the harm being done to children and women by the religions of the world is the greatest scandal on the face of the planet."

Josh glanced over at Sam, realizing that he had never thought to ask Sam how his Franciscan origins squared with this part of their mandate to address the problems embodied by Baby Isabel. Sam clarified matters with a chuckle and the slow statement, "I've never heard anyone improve on the old Italian's response when someone asked him about the Pope's latest statement on birth control: *You no playa the game, you no maka the rules.*"

Dr. Chervoussian laughed, a clear, tinkling sound that was like a soft bell ringing. "I've never heard that one before. That's delightful—and even more apt in my part of the world than in Italy, I suspect."

She frowned and went on. "Part of the problem is what we call it, and how we classify it.

"It isn't in the DSM, you know. So it can't be real—except for the scars it leaves on millions of children. The DSM gap—millions of kids and no pigeonhole to put them in. So they call it 'other health impairment' or something like that. Something that covers over a mother's thoughtlessness, the tragic brain chemistry that caused it, and the damages it does for years after. 'Other health impairment.' Yes, you could say that."

Joshua asked, "Sorry, but what's the DSM?"

"Diagnostic and Statistical Manual of Mental Disorders. It's the big book the health insurance companies use to decide what treatment services they will reimburse. They don't list prenatal exposure, but for a long time they listed homosexuality as a mental disorder." She laughed. "It's not exactly pure science.

"And some of these ob-gyns and pediatricians who just don't get it know nothing about the real science. Older men, mostly, who insist that alcohol is no problem, despite all the evidence. Why, I heard just the other day about a doctor who sends pregnant women a bottle of champagne when they get into their third trimester. The man should be horsewhipped! That's why universal prenatal screening is the only answer."

"Does anybody do that?" Sam asked.

"Washington State used to, some California counties come close, a few other States try, but Medicaid cuts all over the country are going after prenatal screening as not 'medically necessary.' And insurance companies don't insist on it either. California law now requires screening for more than two dozen birth disorders, but substance exposure isn't one of them, even though it affects more than 15% of all births, compared to much smaller rates for the other disorders."

Then she became very serious. "This whole thing is not about a baby that was kidnapped, gentlemen. It's about a baby that was poisoned." She spat the word out like a curse, as if she felt the pain herself. "It's about what could have prevented that—what could have made a difference for that baby."

Her face now was almost beseeching, trying to get them to understand what could have been, what should have been for Isabel. "We could have known before she was born, and we could have been there for her from the moment she was born—from long before, if we had done the screening right. Five questions, taking five minutes. That baby's life was jeopardized because we couldn't get our act together enough to get somebody to ask her mother five questions when she showed up for prenatal care."

She paused, and then added, "It's the old Howard Baker line from your Watergate scandal: what did we know and when did we know it? Except this time the answer is crystal clear—we knew she was greatly at risk, and we knew it—or could have—before she was born."

Sam asked, "So what does that say about the mother's rights?"

Chervoussian nodded, and said, "She has rights, definitely. And she also has responsibilities. Once we're doing serious prenatal screening, we can give her a chance to get into treatment— short-term intervention, longer-term help—whatever she needs.

Half of women stop using or cut down when they know they're pregnant. And half don't. I don't want to punish anyone as a first response. But some women won't take the second chance, or the third, or more. We owe her that second chance—and we owe her baby very careful watching to see if she takes it."

She went on. "Here's how I see it: You have a right to put whatever you want into your body when you are pregnant. But if you use a substance that harms your child, you do not have an automatic right to raise that child. You harmed her before she was born, and the chances are pretty good that you will continue to harm and neglect her after she is born—unless you check yourself into first-rate treatment and take it seriously. And the job of the system is to worry about her safety, both before she is born and after."

Then she said something that made Sam wonder how she really felt about Isabel's kidnapping. "Whoever took that baby must have had an idea about what had already happened to her, and what was about to happen to her. I suspect he, or she, wanted somehow to try to make it better. However misguided, however wrong—I think the kidnapper was trying to make it better for that baby."

She glanced at the clock, and moved briskly to her summation. "If you want to know what I would do about the problems that led to Baby Isabel's birth and kidnapping—although I have no idea who took her or why—I would tell you that we need three things: universal prenatal screening using a validated screening tool, we need an absolute priority for pregnant women to get admission to the best possible treatment we can find and fund, and we need developmental screening every six months for every baby we know to have been prenatally exposed."

She began striking the table with her index finger. "And we need to end our frenzy of over-reaction whenever a new drug comes out. I have been through coke babies, and meth babies, and now prescription drug babies. And I will tell you it is the alcohol and tobacco babies—the babies affected by the *legal* drugs—who are the most damaged and the largest group by far." She paused.

"And that, gentlemen, should keep the politicians busy, if you succeed in getting their attention for more than a few minutes."

As they drove to their next appointment, Sam asked Joshua, "So what did you think?"

"She's amazing. You just want to tape her and play it before every TV program that pregnant women might be watching, or in doctor's offices. She needs to talk more often to politicians—though I guess she'd piss them off by being so blunt."

"I suspect so."

CHAPTER 20

The Department of Substance Abuse Treatment

Their next interview was with the operations supervisor from the drug and alcohol treatment agency. Sam began by asking, "Are there enough treatment slots to take care of the parents who need treatment for drugs or alcohol?"

Alice Palmer, a fortyish, narrow-faced woman with reddish hair tinged with gray, answered, "We admitted about 40,000 clients to treatment programs last year. About 65% of those admissions were parents. I don't have any information available to me about prenatal exposure, though."

"You don't? One estimate based on statewide data is that about 21,000 babies were born each year in this county who were prenatally exposed to drugs or alcohol."

"I don't have any reason to agree or disagree with that number."

"But you try to get pregnant and parenting women into treatment."

"Yes, we have an entire unit that works on that."

"And how many women were admitted last year?"

"We referred 1200 women."

Sam looked over at Joshua, his face saying *we've heard this song before*. "Referred, OK, but how many got enrolled and completed the program?"

"We don't have that information. You would need to ask the analysis unit for that."

"You're the program office?"

"Yes."

"And you don't have information on the program outcomes?"

Highly irritated by now, the program supervisor snapped, "We have it, but it's not at my fingertips, Mr. Leonard."

Joshua, by now used to sometimes playing the softer interrogator, asked "Is the analysis unit supposed to give you that information?"

"Yes they are, but they're short-staffed, the way we all are now, and so we don't get regular reports any more."

Sam came back in. "We noticed that the last report on your website was five years old."

Through gritted teeth, she said "I'm not responsible for the website. Will that be all?"

Sam pressed on. "Just a few more questions. If I've got the numbers right, there are more than enough slots to provide care for all the women who gave birth to these babies. So is there some kind of policy that tries to connect these women with the treatment they need?"

"We have many priorities that we have to pay attention to—services for these women, but also for prisoners in the county jail system, for DUI offenders, for intravenous drug users."

"Who sets these priorities?"

"Some are set by the federal government, some by the state, and some by the county Board of Supervisors."

Sam was quiet for a while. Then he asked, "And none of them said that these 21,000 babies were a priority?"

Palmer glared at him, obviously trying to keep herself under control. "I assume that's rhetorical, Mr. Leonard, and I'm afraid I'm out of time."

Sam and Joshua made a coffee shop stop on their way out of the county office building. After they sat down with their coffees, Joshua said "Not a happy camper."

"No, nor a data-using camper either, it would seem." He looked off through the front window of the shop at the pedestrians hurrying by on the sidewalk outside. "How can you run a program unit that has responsibility for over a thousand women and not want to know what really happens to them in your program? How can you take money for a program and not want to tell the people that gave it to you what happened? And how can the idiots who gave it to you not demand that information every year when the budget rolls around?"

Joshua smiled, "I assume that's rhetorical, Mr. Leonard."

The Department of Public Health

In scheduling a meeting with the health department, Sam and Joshua had gotten their wires crossed with the agency scheduler, and they ended up seeing two senior managers at the same time. They assumed they could just do a group interview, but what they had not bargained for was the wide variance in the outlooks of the two officials—who seemed like they were from different planets.

Both made clear in the first few minutes of the interview that they were very close to retirement, and that they felt very comfortable being candid. They were a bit of a Mutt and Jeff routine; one was over six feet tall and the other was nearly as wide as he was tall. Their names were Dexter and Vaughn.

Dexter, the tall one, began by referring to the investigation Nicole's firm had launched.

"My attitude is that we should just ignore it. It's just more trouble. Agencies have always been like that, and they always will."

Vaughn spoke up. "I don't see it that way. The kids who fall between the cracks—those are the kids you really need to worry about."

Dexter scoffed, "It'll eat up all your time, and no one will thank you."

Vaughn smiled. "If you want gratitude, as Harry Truman said, get a dog. And get out of social work. Some of what you'll need to do to check on the ones who get sent back home is work you'll never get paid for. That's the saddest thing, to me—a call on the way home, or a drop-by after work. Stuff that takes a little extra effort."

"Right. Stuff some supervisor will chew your ass out for doing because you're working off-hours and it makes everybody else look bad."

Vaughn went on. "I had a case a while ago. This may sound like I am making it up—but it happened. Woman was reported for apparent abuse of her two-year-old. We investigated, and it turned out that she had nine previous children—*nine*—and eight of them had been reported and had been removed. Case goes to disposition hearing and the judge, based on what the worker told her, leaves the kid in the home.

"You know what happens next, right? Kid gets brought to an emergency room and ends up dying of malnutrition compounded by broken bones. Big investigation then happens—records are all confidential and closed to media, but someone talked to the paper and the judge handling the case tells someone that she reviewed the case very carefully when it came before her and actually spent thirty minutes talking with the worker in the hallway. Now that's very unusual. So they were arguing about something, or at least the worker and the judge disagreed about something. My bet is the worker wanted the kid removed and placed in care, but the judge said no."

Sam and Joshua had sat watching the two agency officials disagree, swinging their heads back and forth as if they were at a tennis match. Sam started to speak, but Vaughn was quicker.

"So you guys are going to do a report—and it'll be good. Someone in the county will decide to have a trial, or a hearing, or something to justify all the work. And a lot of finger-pointing will go on, and some headlines will follow. And then it'll all die down."

He paused, and looked as sad as anyone Sam had ever seen in the whole three weeks of interviews. And then he added, "Until the next one."

As they walked to their car in the parking garage, Sam said to Joshua, "Two very different guys."

"Yeah. But they both know a hell of a lot about what goes on inside the cubicles and the directors' offices."

Driving from meeting to meeting, some in the downtown area, and some in regional offices around the county, Sam and Joshua gradually got to know each other better. Joshua's curiosity helped greatly.

That day he asked Sam as they headed out to the San Gabriel Valley for their next meetings, "Why do you still work, Sam? You've got the Pulitzer, you're OK financially. So why not retire?"

Sam smiled. "Watch that R-word, kid. This only looks like work. It's really medicine. Doing stuff I care about is—what's the phrase the lousy insurance companies use—'medically necessary.'" He laughed. "It's medically necessary that I do some of this work, instead of just sitting around, Josh. I'd start rotting and be gone in six months. I'm 72 years old, and this keeps me going. As long as I don't do too much of it, and as long as I can get up to the Sierra every summer and do some fishing on the Owens River and in the lakes."

At first, Joshua had some trouble getting past Sam's age. The hardest thing, Sam realized, was what Joshua was going to call him. The fourth time he called him Mr. Leonard, Sam interrupted and said, "Look kid, you've got to start calling me Sam. Mr. Leonard sounds a hundred years old, and I don't like it."

Then Sam got an inspiration.

While driving in Sam's beat-up Toyota Highlander, Sam usually listened to his satellite radio. He had the stations set on classical music, 50's music, and a Willie Nelson station. Joshua had made clear that he could tolerate classical, but the other two were really painful for him.

So Sam said, "Here's how it's going to be, kid. Every time you call me Mr. Leonard instead of Sam, I'm turning on the 50's station for an hour. I mean it. Think that will cure you?"

Joshua responded with a small smile, "You mean I have to listen to doo-flop music?"

"Doo-*wop*, kid, it's doo-*wop*. Have some respect. Yeah, that's exactly what I mean."

Joshua said, "OK, Sam, I get you. That's perfectly clear, Sam. Got it, Sam."

CHAPTER 21

The Desert

Joe was out on the front porch taking a break from feeding Isabel when he heard the sound of approaching motorcycles. He quickly stuck his head inside the front door and yelled at Dolores, "We've got company. Get Isabel to a safe place."

As he walked back out onto the porch, he saw four bikers riding up, wearing leather vests and imitation Nazi helmets. They stopped about twenty yards from the front of the mobile. Joe leaned up against the porch and tried to look calm.

The biker in the front of the pack dropped his kick stand and said, "We saw your tire tracks. Looks like you've got a nice setup here. We're thirsty and we'd like some beer. And then we're going to see what you've got inside that nice mobile."

"I don't think so," Joe said. "We've got no beer, and you've got no business here."

Then Dolores opened the door and walked out, standing next to Joe. She left the door propped half-open, and made sure they could see the .357 magnum she had in a shoulder holster. "We're doing fine here. And we'd appreciate your turning around and heading back the way you came."

"Well, well. A little lady with a big gun. Is she your protector, little man?"

Joe smiled and said "You'd better believe it. Don't mess with her."

At that, the lead biker reached into his saddlebag and pulled out a .45, setting it on top of his gas tank.

As soon as Dolores saw the gun, she drew the magnum and calmly placed a shot two feet to the right of the bike. "The next one goes into your gas tank and the one after that goes into you. It's a long walk back. Leave us alone and you'll be fine."

Frowning, but not moving, the biker said, "Now that's just not friendly." He motioned to the other three who moved their bikes further apart in a semi-circle. As they moved, Dolores handed Joe a shotgun she had concealed behind the door.

The biker growled, "Unless you think you can beat all four of us, you got a big problem." He nodded to the biker on the far left and the biker quickly raised a concealed Uzi 9mm and laid down a line of bullets along the top of the mobile. The leader said "That's just a taste of what you've got coming, bitch. Now get us that beer, or . . ." He stopped, because there was a strange whooshing sound coming from the west.

Joe looked up to see one of the strangest sights he had ever seen: four camouflage-clad Marines—he assumed they were from the 29 Palms base—hovering about fifty feet off the ground, with automatic rifles trained on the bikers. Each of the Marines had a tank on their back which looked like a scuba tank. A cloud of dust swirled under each of them, which Joe could see was being kicked up by the steady streams of air coming from the tanks.

Dolores had raised her magnum, training it on the head biker. Then a loudspeaker boomed out, "Drop your weapons. Drop them now or we will fire. Leave these people alone and ride on."

But then, in the final moments of his life, one of the bikers made a huge mistake, and got off a shot at the closest of the moving Marines. Within seconds he was riddled with automatic rifle fire, his vest torn open with rounds that blew out his back and whined off into the desert. As he fell off the bike backward, his bike exploded.

The other bikers froze, then raised their hands and dropped the handguns they had pulled out seconds before.

The loudspeaker boomed again. "Ride!" And with that, the bikers kicked their cycles into gear and wheeled out of the area, stopping only to toss the lifeless body of their friend onto the back of the last cycle to leave.

The Marines slowly glided to the ground, and one of them walked up to the mobile as the others formed a line facing the road where the bikers had left. "Hi, folks. We were on maneuvers out here and heard shots over this way—wind must have been blowing west. Thought we'd check it out because no one is usually out here." He lifted up his goggles and said, "I'm Staff Sergeant Lassiter. Ma'am, is everything OK?"

Dolores said, "Dolores Brenner, and this is my brother Joe. You came along at just the right time, Staff Sergeant. Thanks."

Lassiter gave her a strange look and said "Dolores Brenner? Dee Brenner? I know you. You're the medic that got a Silver Star for saving those guys' asses outside Basra last year during the withdrawals. You're a real warrior, woman."

Dolores grimaced and said "I got a lot more than the decoration out there. I got seriously fucked up. That's why I'm out here, trying to get over it."

Lassiter nodded and said with a wry smile, "Happens to lots of us. Glad you found a place to chill out." He handed her a card. "Look, here's my cell number. You have any more problems over here, give me a call. We've got special cell towers all over the place out here—they look just like Joshua trees, but they work great. You need anything, just call." He smiled. "We'll just hop over."

Joe finally found his voice and asked "What the hell are those things on your backs?"

"We're testing these things in live fire exercises over on the base. We'd appreciate your not mentioning them—they're supposed to be secret. For desert ops."

Dolores said "Definitely. And thanks."

"Anything for a Devil Doc. Semper Fi, Dee," he said. Then he turned and motioned upward with his hands. Within five seconds, all four were airborne and headed west.

Joe was having trouble closing his mouth. "Ohmigod. What timing. They fly in, blow that guy away, and fly out. Wow." He turned to Dolores. "He knew you. Looks like a Silver Star is one hell of a calling card."

She frowned, and shook her head. "Cost me too much—I'd give it back in a second. Let's go check on Isabel."

CHAPTER 22

Bryan Sorenson heard the sounds of the bikers before he saw them out of the front window of the restaurant in Vidal Junction. The bikers pulled up as Sorenson walked out of the restaurant, and he saw that one of the bikers was missing.

"What happened? Where's the other guy?"

The head biker answered, angrily, "What happened was that we got fucking ambushed by some flying Marines, man. Didn't you check that fucking place out? This was supposed to be a quick in and out, asshole. Instead Dog got vaporized by some fucking Marines." He leaned into Sorenson, glaring. "Give us our fucking money—we're out of here."

With very little experience dealing with bikers, Sorenson then made his first mistake. "You didn't get the baby? Then you didn't do what I paid you to do—I'm not giving you the rest of the money."

"Oh no, friend. You promised us a payoff and now you're going to give us the money or we'll kick the crap out of you and your fancy car."

Then Sorenson made his second mistake. He reached over with his wireless key and locked the doors on the Escalade. The head biker walked slowly over to the car and saw a large briefcase on the seat. He reached back into his saddlebag, pulled out his backup automatic and casually used it to break the window, ignoring the car alarm and lifting the briefcase off of the front seat.

Sorenson then made his final mistake, grabbing for the briefcase. Two fast shots from the biker's automatic put him on the ground beside the car.

And all the restaurant owner saw as he walked cautiously out the front door after hearing the shots was Sorenson's body, a pool of blood beneath it, and a dust cloud as the three bikers rode off.

His call to 911 went straight to Lee Farmer at Havasu.

CHAPTER 23

LAPD Valley Headquarters

The detectives McQueen and Alarcon got the call about a shooting at Vidal Junction, which somebody in the San Bernardino County Sheriff's office had connected to the search for Baby Isabel. They found out that the 911 call had gone to Lee Farmer, who had rolled with the paramedic unit. Farmer's name had turned up as a person of interest in the Baby Isabel investigation, and that had triggered the call to the LAPD. The guy who had been killed, Bryan Sorenson, was a computer guy who lived in Altadena.

As they tried to put the pieces together, McQueen asked Alarcon to see if they had gotten DNA from Sorenson's body. She called and found out that it was being processed in the lab shared by San Bernardino and Riverside County. When she called them, they said they would have results in three days.

McQueen asked Alarcon, "So what's the connection? This guy gets wasted by some bikers—what does that have to do with the baby? Farmer got the call, but that's just because it happened out there. So maybe she's hiding out there somewhere."

"The Marines do training out there. Maybe they saw something. Want to call the base?"

They eventually got connected with the head of the MP unit at the base, who was unwilling to give them any details, but said one of his training units had gotten into a scrape with some bikers east of the training area. He claimed that the incident was covered by "national security" regulations and he would have to get authorization to give them any more information. McQueen told him that he would have the LAPD get in touch with the base commander.

Then Alarcon got a brainstorm. "Maybe this guy was the father. Maybe he was out there looking for her. We have Isabel's DNA, right? Have the lab run it."

When they got the call two days later, they were elated to find out that Sorenson was almost certainly the baby's father. They headed back to Luisa's house to re-interview her. She admitted within the first five minutes of the interview that Sorenson was the baby's father. But she said she hadn't seen him for over a year.

They waited impatiently for the connection with the Marine base commander to come through. In the meantime, they tried to reach Farmer, but was told he had taken a month's leave and was somewhere in the Eastern Sierra, without a contact number.

They had followed the Bakersfield lead, which had cost them a week, waiting to make contact with Walt Brenner, who was out of town on a construction job. His family had left him two years ago, and he lived alone. When he finally came back, he told the Bakersfield police that he hadn't seen Joe for a long time and had no idea where he was.

McQueen dreaded his weekly session with Connolly, who he knew was going to ream them out for making no progress. The shooting was their best lead, and so they decided to head out to the base at 29 Palms and see if they could speed things up with the Marines.

CHAPTER 24

Public Communications, Inc.

Sam and Joshua arrived at a contractor's office in Pomona. Nicole had suggested they talk with a former classmate of hers from college who was co-owner of a private firm that had done some public relations work for the county. Nicole said that her friend would have an interesting story about interagency relations, but refused to tell Sam and Joshua any more about the issue.

The friend was a very attractive Asian woman named Bessie Wong. She welcomed them, telling them Nicole had urged her to speak frankly and that she would do so, with the understanding that her name and her agency's name would not be used. Sam agreed, and she began.

"They called it the logo war. One of the agencies that was part of an interagency group on child abuse prevention had proposed sending out a guidance memo to all staff explaining how to handle cases that involved more than one agency. The fancy name for these things was 'protocols,' but it was really an interagency agreement about who would do intake and who would do referrals and what was supposed to happen after one agency referred a kid or a family to another agency. They wrote it, with our help, and then they sent it to the Agency Review and Revisions Group—the ARRG. Good name." She smiled. "And then all the problems began."

"What's the agency review group supposed to do?"

"You're going to think I'm making this up." Sam could see that Wong had a wonderful sense of irony and a fully-developed sense of humor as well. It looked as though both were essential in the work she did. She went on. "There's a unit in this agency— and in most of them in a county this big—that spends all of its time reviewing all materials that are going to be sent outside the agency for public use. They spend their time reviewing formats, type size and fonts, colors for brochures, what pictures and charts can be used. And one of their responsibilities is deciding where the agency's logo goes on the document. The logo itself took two years and two separate design contracts to complete before this unit signed off on it. We worked on it as a contractor, internal staff worked on it, lots of input."

"I suppose these people never see real clients or anything like that?"

"God forbid. They're communications types, they know nothing about kids or families." She paused and said, "I guess I should add that I'm a CASA volunteer and spend at least a half-day a week in court with kids. I'm a capitalist with a heart."

"I see," Sam responded. "Those are the best kind, I guess."

"So anyway, they finished this guidance memo, and they decided that the two agencies both had to review it. That took another several months, and finally both agencies agreed. The only remaining detail was where to put the logo."

"Let me guess—they both wanted their logo on top."

"Bingo. So that led to another blizzard of memos, and then they said they would put the logos on the bottom of the first page. But they could never agree which one would go on the left—which was supposed to be the prime position. And finally, after all these memos and meetings going back and forth, they decided not to issue the thing after all because they couldn't agree on whose logo should be first."

Sam and Joshua sat there, trying to include what they had just heard in the larger frame of all the human pain they had seen and heard in their interviews. Finally Joshua said, "But what about the kids?"

"What about the kids, indeed?" She paused and looked at them, wanting to make sure they got her message. "I'm a private contractor. But I got into this field because I wanted to work with agencies that helped children. That's what I thought they did, anyway." She paused, and they could see how angry she was. "There's a stock phrase they use all the time in these agencies. You hear it all the time. 'In the best interests of the child.' It's supposed to be how they decide difficult cases—in the best interests of the child."

She stopped, and blinked hard, several times, and Sam could see that she was so angry she was trying not to cry with her frustration. "But from what I've seen, they've changed that a little. It's really in the best interests of the *system*."

CHAPTER 25

Joshua and Sam were talking at a Mexican restaurant around the corner from Nicole's office after their session with Bessie Wong. They had gotten into a pattern of having late afternoon coffee or a beer after their interviews. They had two more agency interviews to do and then they were going to report back to Nicole.

Joshua sipped his coffee and then said, "You know that 'blame the victims' speech we got the other day?"

"Yeah—from the woman who ended up blaming the victims."

"Yes. I was thinking, maybe it would be a good idea if we went and talked to some of them—to the kids and parents, I mean." He was watching Sam carefully for his reaction.

Sam was quiet, just looking at Joshua. Then smiling, he said, "Sometimes you really piss me off, kid."

Joshua could see that Sam wasn't serious, and asked, "Why, Sam?"

"Because thirty years ago my first instinct would have been to talk to the kids and the parents. Of course we should do that—nice work bringing it up, Josh. Let's figure out how we could do it."

So Joshua made an appointment with a treatment agency that Nicole had told them was one of the two best treatment programs in the county. They drove out on a Friday morning to meet with the staff director of the agency, who had agreed to put them in touch with some of the women who were enrolled in the program with their babies.

Recovery, Inc.

The director, whose name was Brooke Sanders, was a fiftyish woman who greeted Sam and Joshua in her office. She studied them for a moment, and said "So you guys are looking into the drug-exposed baby problem?

Sam answered, "That's part of what we're reviewing, yes."

Sanders looked at Sam and Joshua and sighed. "I don't mean any disrespect, but it may be hard for two white guys to understand what goes on here."

Sam said, "We appreciate your skepticism, but we're pretty good listeners. We're really trying to understand how well all these agencies work together—when they do,"

"*When* they do is right. A lot of the time they don't. OK, you say you're good listeners. Nicole Larwin's recommendation counts for a lot around here—she's come through for us before. Let me tell you about a woman we're working with right now." She reached over a pulled a file out of her desk drawer, saying "Classic case of interagency FUBAR."

Sam chuckled and then saw the puzzled look on Joshua's face. "It's an old military phrase, Josh. FUBAR—means fucked up beyond all recognition."

She laughed. "Right. My ex was Special Forces. Seemed like a phrase that applied just as well to our work as to his." She glanced at the file, then looked up. "Did they get you guys to sign a confidentiality form when you checked in?"

Sam nodded.

"Fine. Here's the story. This woman came to us from Riverside County. She gets referred to us because she got arrested for possession and her 3 day old baby and her 4 year old were with her in the motel room. The guy she was with disappears, not sure who the father is." She paused. "See, what sometimes happens is that they try to kick their habit while they're pregnant, do fairly well with that, and then binge after they have the baby.

"So you've got a criminal case for possession, a possible child endangerment or neglect case, and two kids in foster care because mom is in jail. No overt signs of withdrawal with baby, but you never know. The backlog in developmental screening is a few weeks, so we don't know yet about any effects of the drugs—or the alcohol she probably drank if she was using illegal drugs. So baby is in a nursery group home and 4 year old goes to a live-in program for preschoolers."

Sam asked "And who's coordinating all of this?"

She looked at him with amusement. "That's a rhetorical question, right? Of course no one is. So far we've got only five agencies: the Sheriff, the Superior Court, the child welfare agency, the two group homes. Each of them would say they are coordinating with the others—but that means they send email back and forth and place a lot of phone calls that get left on answering machines.

"Then the mom comes to arraignment and it starts to get really complicated." She looked at the file again, turned a page. "She pleads not guilty, because if she pleads guilty the kids are gone. She makes bail—grandpa or some boyfriend acting through grandpa comes through. At that point, our worker, who's stationed there in the court thanks to a federal grant, approaches her and tells her four simple things: there is a place for you today in the best treatment program in Southern California, I'll take you there now, I've been through this whole thing and I got my kids back, and if you don't do this, your kids are going to grow up and call someone else Mommy."

Joshua couldn't help himself from saying, "Wow. How often does that work?"

She looked at him with a very sad expression, and then said, "There are some weird statistics in our business. Some programs claim 80% success rate, some are more honest. When we approach women in court, about half of them take the offer to enroll. Of those that enroll, about half make it to the end of a six month program. The others get something out of it, but positive completes, as they call it, are about 25-30% of those that need it. Others come back to us later, and make it on the second or third try. But by then, especially when the kids are under 3 or newborns when they first come in, the kids are gone. Unless a family member steps up with a lot of time and a lot of patience."

She went back to the file. "So this mom gets to our program, starts detoxing—turns out she's on heroin—and a week later she's as clean as she's been for a long time, and she wants to see her kids. Her court case is coming up in a week, so she's in legal limbo until the criminal case and the child neglect cases are resolved. She may still do jail time."

She stopped and read the file for a few moments. Then she grimaced. "File says at one point the kids' lawyer—mom has a lawyer, baby has a lawyer, county agencies have lawyers, *we've* got lawyers—it's full employment time for all the lawyers you could ever want to work with. And some of them even know what they're doing. But one who definitely doesn't, in this case the baby's lawyer, asks our worker when mom comes back to court, 'what difference would it make that she's in treatment?' *What difference would it make?* This 26 year-old lawyerette says she doesn't see what difference first-rate treatment would make in the lives of the mom and the two kids.

"Then it gets even more complicated. We've got a criminal case. But now we've got a bunch of what they call 'collaborative courts,' which are actually a great idea if they ever got their act together and served more than a few clients at a time. Instead of doing jail time, some people get into these little, token-sized programs. But each of them is coming in a different door of the system. And these courts try to get them the treatment they need to stay out of court and out of jail. We have a family drug court, we have a mental health court, we have the regular drug court, the diversion court, DUI court, a veteran's court—the problem is they can't even keep track of all of these special courts. And no one has a total of how many kids and parents go through the system and whether they complete treatment and get reunified. No one anywhere in the county keeps that total—each project runs its own data system. And each project is small and worries about its own clients, and competes with the other ones to get resources from the rest of the system."

She laughed. "Expedia can get me a flight from hundreds of airlines to thousands of airports. But we can't track one mom and her kids from one door to another in this revolving door circus we call a system."

She went on. "So she gets referred to the family drug court. They see she's enrolled in our treatment program, and that's fine until somebody points out that she crossed county lines and that would be under the jurisdiction of our county, not their county. They finally work that out, then she says she wants to talk to her 4 year-old. Good therapy for her, good for her kid. So they try to set up a phone call. But the foster agency only takes calls up to 6 pm, and we only allow calls *after* 6. We negotiate that, bend our rules to allow a call at 5:30, and she finally gets to talk to her daughter. Then we start to work to try to get both kids transferred up here to be with her in our program. We have two beds for kids all ready, but the Riverside child welfare people aren't sure they can move the kids across county lines, even though we have the space."

She watched their reactions. Sam and Joshua were both shaking their heads. Sam asked, "How do you put up with all this? It must make you crazy."

Brooke nodded. "Sometimes it does. But by now, we know what works. It took our profession twenty years, but we know that when a mom is ready to have her kids with her, she should have them here."

She smiled. "You may have noticed that women are different from men."

They laughed. "We definitely noticed," said Joshua. And Sam added "*Vive la difference.*"

Brooke went on. "One of the differences is that women recover in relationships. It isn't the medication, it isn't the therapy—as good as we think our therapy is. It's relationships, learning to trust people, learning to cut yourself off from people who are pulling you down. Learning to respect yourself and to trust your ability to be a decent parent, even if you didn't have decent parents yourself. Dealing with the abuse and violence and sexual predators in your own life—more than half of these women were beat up or sexually molested when *they* were kids. And so we bring the kids here whenever we can, and work with moms—we have a small program for dads, too, but mostly moms. We show them parenting skills and work on nutrition and discipline and talk about how different kids have different temperaments. We bring in moms who have been through the program and got their kids back and have stayed clean. And our moms learn they can do this, and it's a huge boost for their own treatment.

"See, we used to say to women 'you go get your own head straight, take care of yourself first.' And for some women, that's the right message. But that doesn't work so good for babies. It's hard to walk up to a crib of a two-month old and tell her that her mom is getting her act together and maybe she'll drop by in six months— or she won't. 'Hang loose, kid.' Babies don't work that way—they attach to adults that they need, or they don't. And if they don't, they deal with that hole in their emotions for the rest of their life.

"We know that because at the same time we've been learning a lot about women in treatment, we've also been getting a lot smarter about infants and toddlers. We've got new neurodevelopmental research that tells us much more than we ever knew about those first two or three years and how crucial they are." She stopped and reached for a card on her desk. "You guys talked to Irena Chervoussian, right?"

Sam nodded.

"She's the best. She trains our staff who work with the little ones." She closed the file. "Now do you want to talk to some of these women?"

"Yes," Joshua quickly answered.

They went into a small conference room where three women were sitting in well-padded armchairs. There was a small coffee table in the middle of the room, which had live flowers and art on the walls which Sam quickly recognized as Latin American. Two of the women were Latinas and the third was African-American. A counselor from the agency joined Brooke and the two men.

Brooke said, "Mr. Leonard and Mr. Bronson are looking at county agencies, and they've been doing some interviews for a law firm on how well agencies serve women with children in the system. They will not use your names or attribute any statements to any of you. They just want to get a feel for how the agencies and the courts treat you."

There was a short silence and then one of the Latinas spoke up. "Mostly they treat us like criminals, since we broke the law. Until I got here, I felt like a criminal, too. I was worried I was never going to see my kids again, and I hated having to deal with all the lawyers and three different caseworkers. I never knew what was happening, all these people in court talking about CPS this and IFSP that and Part C and IVE—they have their own crazy language and none of it made sense. Then my worker from here—the woman who came to court to talk with us and try to get us to sign up for the program—was finally able to explain what all that was and how it would affect me. And I could see right away that I needed to be here and that getting here was the last chance I had to get my son back." She started to tear up. "And they tell me that he can come out here to stay with me in another week."

Joshua asked her, "How old is your son?"

She wiped her eyes and said "He's five. He's been with my sister, but she has three kids of her own and she doesn't really know what he likes." She clutched her hands in her lap and rocked back and forth, smiling through her tears. "I can't wait to see him. I—I kept his teddy bear—he used to like it, but I don't know if he still will."

As they talked to the other two women, Sam and Joshua heard sad variations on the same story. One woman said she was enrolled in what the county called "concurrent planning." But the way the program worked, as she saw it, much more emphasis was given to getting her son's possible adoptive parents used to the idea of parenting a drug-exposed child than getting her through treatment with a strong relationship with her baby. "It's not about me," she said fiercely through her tears. "It's making sure that nice middle-class family knows what they're getting into when they try to raise my kid."

The final conversation was with the African-American woman, who had said little in the session. She began slowly, saying. "When I first got here, they kept telling me 'You've got to do your part. Only you can turn it around.' OK, I get that. But I tried to get into three other programs before I got here. And I tried to get my daughter tested, and they said there was a five-month waiting list. And then I tried to get some dentures, because I had messed up my teeth doing meth. And when I went out on job interviews, they took one look at my mouth and turned me down. I want to work, I *need* to work to support my kid,"

She paused and glared at them. "I've got to do my part. Right. But only me? Yeah? So what about you guys with all these programs and all the money that goes into these programs? When is it that you have to do *your* part? The judge wants to hold me responsible—fine. I'm responsible. But aren't any of you responsible, too?"

As they walked out to the parking lot, Brooke said. "You guys *were* good listeners. Thanks for coming. I hope it helped."

"It really did. We're very grateful. You have a great program here."

"One final thing to remember—for every women here there are dozens of others who need to be. We do good work, and so do some other programs. But there aren't enough of them—and there aren't enough good ones. I don't mean to run down any other agencies, but most of them don't have the same mix of programs we have, and most of them can't afford to have the kids with the moms. And as you saw, making that happen is often despite the agencies' efforts."

"In the best interests of the system," Joshua said.

Brooke nodded. "Yes. That's how it works, all too often."

They drove back into the city, thinking about what they had heard. Then Joshua, seemingly randomly, asked Sam, "Sam, why aren't you married?"

"Tried it, kid. Liked it a lot. It's the natural state of human existence, my Franciscan sojourn to the contrary."

"So?"

"So I failed the course. Then I lost my confidence."

"What do you mean?"

Sam sighed, and said, "I think you have to deserve a great woman—or mate, if that's your choice—to ask her to sign on to living with you while you turn all wrinkled and smelly and forgetful. You have to have done a lot to earn that. I lost confidence that I could deserve that."

Joshua was quiet for a while. Then he said, "Maybe it's grace— maybe you don't deserve it, but you get it anyway."

Sam looked at him. "Did you study journalism at SC—or theology?"

Joshua smiled. "Actually, I took some courses at Hebrew Union College."

Sam asked, "And now you're going to tell me that my ancient Catholic texts about grace being a New Testament idea are mistaken."

"Not mistaken. *Hesed*—mercy is one translation—is undeserved kindness in Judaism. Maimonides wrote about it. Like that bumper sticker: 'Commit random acts of kindness.'"

Sam was silent, thinking. Then he said, "I'm going to ponder that one, kid."

Joshua smiled and said "OK." He added, "Don't wait too long."

CHAPTER 26

Law office

Nicole had asked Sam and Joshua to check in with her as they got close to their mid-point in the interviews. They scheduled a time and met with her in her office.

She listened to their briefing, and then said "No surprises, right?"

Sam said, "No—but a depressing refrain of 'not my job.' After a while all the interviews begin to blur into each other. Except for Dr. Chervoussian, so far they're all more or less saying 'it's not our responsibility.' They just can't accept that part of the job is working with people they don't control. They all want to stay inside their own little boxes."

"Any good suggestions for change? Any positives to balance the bad news?"

Joshua spoke up. "Some of them just make excuses, but a few really want to make a difference, and their frustration is not having the resources or the backing from their bosses to do the job differently."

"Different how?" asked Nicole.

"To work closer with other agencies." He told the story about the case of the woman who was caught between two counties and the timetables of two different agencies. "And so the caseworkers had to work it out informally, because the formal rules were the barrier."

"Work it out, then ask forgiveness instead of permission."

"Exactly."

Nicole was watching Joshua closely, realizing that he was much more than just Sam's assistant. Something about Joshua rubbed Nicole the wrong way, but she couldn't put her finger on it. He rarely treated her with the awe that her own interns and other early

20-somethings usually showed as they worked with her. Maybe, she thought, it was his self-assurance, going far beyond what she felt a recent graduate was entitled to display. But whatever it was, it bothered her.

Nicole then said, "I really liked the sections you included on the front-line workers and the kids you interviewed. That added a lot. It made it real, and got beyond all the interviews with the officials you guys talked with."

"That was Joshua's idea. He did most of those interviews."

"He did? Nice work," she forced herself to say, beginning to realize that Joshua was rather extraordinary. She wondered if she had misjudged him at first.

As they were getting up, Sam said, "We're going to see Supervisor Calver next week, as you suggested. Should be interesting."

Nicole said, "I'm not going to tell you to handle him carefully, because you'll handle him however you want. But he's a key player—he's taken the lead on several of the children's initiatives in the county."

"We know."

Later, Joshua and Sam were driving back to Sam's house to finish their notes on the last sessions. Joshua was quiet, and then asked Sam, seemingly out of nowhere, "Sam, what do you think of Nicole?"

Sam got the sub-text, he thought, and answered carefully. "She's very strong," he paused, "and less self-sufficient than she lets on."

Joshua looked puzzled. "That seems contradictory."

Sam laughed, "She's a woman, Josh. Of course she's contradictory. It's in the design specs." He went on. "She's very wrapped up in the work she does—and that's good. But she's still normal enough—non-workaholic enough—to want something more, I suspect."

He waited, and when Joshua was silent, he asked, "You thinking about applying for the job?"

Josh looked embarrassed for a moment, and then smiled, with what Sam had come to think of as his *I'm growing up faster than you think* look. "Maybe."

Sam was quiet for a while, and then said, "You could handle it. She could too, probably."

Sam and Joshua had made arrangements to go to a dropin center in Pasadena for older foster kids, some of whom had 'aged out' of the foster care caseload but were still in touch with the other kids they had gotten to know through the training programs the agency ran for foster kids.

As they drove, Sam looked out the window at a supermarket parking lot. A uniformed boy was slowly gathering the carts that had been left all over the lot. "Josh, you know there are two kinds of people, right?"

Playing the straight man he knew he was supposed to be, Joshua asked, "Two kinds of people?"

"That's right. There are people who take their shopping carts back to where they belong and people who just leave them in a parking spot. Tells you a lot about someone—whether they think about other people or just have their head up their own ass."

"Makes sense to me, Sam," Josh said as he marveled at Sam's philosophy of life, with its hard ethical core.

For his part, Sam enjoyed listening to Joshua when he added his ideas to the interviews. Sam had come to believe that every older professional, say, over 60, should be assigned a younger worker whose job would include monitoring the senior. A scale could be developed, Sam thought, in which the younger worker would score the senior for excessively self-referential comments, off-topic wanderings, and recurring blathering about how things used to be done or what was tried years ago and didn't work. Once a certain score was reached, the younger worker would gracefully signal to the senior that his contribution to the meeting had maxed out, and the senior would not be allowed to speak any longer.

Elderbabble, Sam thought, was both an occupational and a gerontological hazard—and he dreaded it.

Foster youth home

When they arrived at the center, a rehabilitated two-story home in one of Pasadena's older neighborhoods, they were shown into a small conference room where they saw four youth who looked between 16 and 20, sitting in chairs.

Sam explained what they were doing and thanked them for their time. Before he could begin asking questions, one of the youth, a scraggly-bearded, lanky white kid, asked "I thought you guys were looking into that baby who got kidnapped. What's that got to do with us?"

Josh, whom Sam had agreed should lead the discussion, answered, "We're trying to understand the whole child welfare system, from prenatal to aging out at 18 or 21. You guys are at the far end of that chain, so we wanted to get your outlook on how the system has treated you. How would you summarize it?"

The young man looked at Joshua as if he had said *we're trying to see if any of you have two heads.* Finally he answered, "We're at the far end, all right. We're at the forgotten end, mostly. You know what independent living is?"

Joshua responded, "I think so. It's the services you're supposed to receive if you're getting ready to age out of the system. It's supposed to prepare you for making decisions about work, college, and spending money and taking care of yourself. So how well does that work?"

The kid began to answer, as the body language of the other three youth showed how much they also wanted to chime in, leaning forward, and looking at each other with smiles. "We don't think much of it, really. A staff person from one of the county contractors comes out and talks to us in the foster home or group home we're living in, lecturing us on how to do all that stuff and giving us some kind of test that scores our ability to do all that."

By now the other male, a Latino with a close-shaved head, was anxious to get into the conversation. "Yeah, and when you ask them where you can get a job or how you can get scholarship information about colleges, they give you a bunch of phone numbers. I can get phone numbers off the internet, man—I don't need some counselor to give me phone numbers."

One of the two girls, an African-American with a pretty face and close-cropped hair, said "You need to understand, man, we're the losers. We're the kids no one wanted to adopt, and none of our relatives wanted to take us in. So we're at the bottom of the barrel."

Josh asked her, "So what could they be doing better?"

The second girl was also African-American, short and petite. She spoke up and said, "If you guys are supposed to be looking into what happened to that baby, you should pay attention to where some of those babies come from." She laughed. "Some of us are real breeding farms, dude. I know at least four girls who were in my independent living classes who got knocked up and dropped out of the program because they were pregnant. No money, no job, about to age out—not much else to do but sex, and so some of us do a whole lot of bim-bam. Sometimes that hatches a baby."

Joshua smiled and asked her, "Do they give you birth control?"

She smiled back and said, "Yes, if you ask for it. But most of them don't. Me—I love that shot you get every three months. Works fine for me." And then she gave Josh a kind of leer that Sam delightedly watched Josh try to ignore, resulting in his being at a loss for words for the first time since the investigation began.

Sam asked, "They've changed the foster youth program so that they can give you services after you're 18. How's that working out?"

The Latino answered, "That's how we get to live here. And that part of the program is pretty good. Having a place to live that isn't some dump in a lousy neighborhood helps a lot. I'm trying to get into LA State, and being here gives me a lot better chance than if I'm couch-surfing with some other guys."

He frowned and looked at Sam. "You know the question you aren't asking, man?" Without waiting for Sam to answer, he went on. "You're not asking us what works—what we like. What I like is when some dude like us—some guy or chick—woman—I mean," he quickly added, glancing at the girls, "when somebody comes here who has been through all this bullshit and who is just a few years older than us. Peer counseling, they call it. That works, because it isn't some guy with a bunch of college degrees who talks down to us. It's somebody who's been through it."

Sam smiled and said. "Makes sense. Got it."

They continued the conversation for an hour or so longer, and both Sam and Joshua ended up more impressed with the kids than the services they were getting.

Family Drug Court

Sam and Joshua met next with the court coordinator for the small family drug court that the county had set up. They met in the county courthouse, in a tiny cubicle where the coordinator had her office. The coordinator, Geneva Robinson, was a forty-something African-American woman who seemed unsure of why Sam and Joshua were meeting with her.

"Let me understand," she began as Sam and Joshua sat down in two chairs squeezed into the small office. The chairs had been brought in from an adjacent conference room, and clearly the cubicle was not designed for three people. "You're here to talk with me about the drug court, but this case was never under our jurisdiction. So I'm not sure why you're here."

"We're trying to get an overview of all the agencies involved in cases like this one. We've reviewed your annual report, and it said that about one-third of your caseload includes cases with children under three."

"I see." She was not comfortable with their questioning, and seemed disturbed that they had read the report.

"How many cases does your court see each year?"

"We do intakes on about a hundred, give or take."

"And how many fit your eligibility?"

"Well, that's very hard to say. Obviously a lot of parents with abuse or neglect cases could benefit from our services. But we only have enough funding to serve the hundred. I suppose there are three or four thousand a year who fit our profile."

"How successful is the court with the parents you serve? How many of them graduate from the program, and how many are reunified with their children?" Sam could tell that she was bothered by their questions, and he was trying to ask them as gently as possible. But it wasn't working.

She frowned. "Well, you need to understand that we're not funded to do evaluations. Our information system mostly tracks people who enter and exit the court's treatment programs. You'd have to ask child welfare how many of them are reunified—we don't have that data. That's not our responsibility."

They were driving along Sunset on their way to their next appointment which was scheduled on the West Side. Sam idly looked out the window and saw two lithe young beauties strolling along one of the winding streets coming down from the foothills.

"*Young girls are coming to the canyons . . .*" he sang, softly, only slightly off-key.

"What?"

"It's an old lyric. From the Mamas and the Papas."

"Who?" But Sam could tell he was teasing him this time. "No, wait—my dad used to listen to them. Folk singers, right?" He nearly snickered, and Sam was wounded.

"You disrespectful young punk. All you've learned from tagging along with me, and you still won't pay attention to the music I've tried to drill into your thick skull."

"Yes, sir. That's right, sir—I should pay more attention." He was trying to keep from laughing. "That historical music is really very interesting to me, Mr. Leonard. Truly it is. It's amazing to hear what people in those days listened to, it is just amazing."

Sam pretended disdain, but he really loved that the kid had gotten to a point where he gave back as much as he got. For Sam, the back and forth verbal fencing with a smart, young man or woman was golden, for it acknowledged that he was worth fencing with—not a desiccated remnant of an irrelevant time.

So he relished his time with Joshua and wondered what he would do for fun after the project was over.

CHAPTER 27

Nicole had suggested that Sam and Josh interview Dorothy Easton, the executive director of a national women's organization based in LA that represented women in legal cases where a baby had been drug—or alcohol-exposed. As Sam reviewed the organization's materials prior to the interview, he saw that the organization, National Advocates for Women's Reproductive Rights, had taken a rigid position against universal screening for prenatal exposure. The organization's website said that "prenatal exposure to any specific drug or alcohol is not evidence that the baby was harmed by the exposure." The organization had assembled studies showing that cocaine, heroin, alcohol, and marijuana did not always lead to disabilities, and used those studies to imply that prenatal exposure should not be a policy issue. Sam expected that the meeting would be tense, given the focus of the investigation on a drug-exposed baby.

NAWRR offices

Sam and Joshua arrived at the offices of NAWRR, which were in a nondescript three-story building in Culver City. As they walked into Easton's office, they were greeted by a short woman with curly grey hair and a brighter smile than Sam would have predicted.

"We've been expecting you," Easton began.

"Why?" Sam asked.

"Because this Baby Isabel case is the kind of media hysteria that leads to more prosecution of pregnant women. It happens over and over, and our job is to keep it from leading to more legislation and prosecution by loony judges who would make it worse."

"Media hysteria?" Sam said. "A baby was kidnapped."

Easton said, "Yes, and that's a very serious crime. But I'm sure you're familiar with state legislation that has criminalized the private behavior of pregnant women in ways that has deterred thousands of women from seeking help from treatment agencies."

She gestured at a map on the wall. "The states marked in red are those with laws or current legislative proposals that would criminalize prenatal exposure."

Sam said, "Yes, we're aware of such laws. We're not proposing anything like that, and no one we've talked with has, either. But do you agree that the critical issue is to get pregnant women who are abusing drugs and alcohol into treatment as early as possible? And getting help for their babies to screen them for the effects of drugs and fetal alcohol exposure?" Sam decided to press the point. "And isn't prenatal drug use already illegal, regardless of the effects on the fetus?"

"Yes, treatment is the goal. But the assumption that all these babies are damaged is unwarranted."

She kept her eyes moving back and forth between Sam and Joshua, intently watching their reactions to her words. "Mr. Leonard, I doubt that you want or need a detailed legal review of the issues involved in prenatal exposure or the dozens of cases our organization is involved with. We could go on all day and barely scratch the surface of the cases we're working on right now, in states all over the country. But here's the bottom line, so far as your report goes. First, the county does a lousy job of getting pregnant women with drug problems into treatment. You'll find that once you interview the agencies that run those programs. Pregnant women aren't even 2% of the total admissions to treatment. Some priority."

Sam nodded.

She went on. "Second, if your report includes the conventional recommendation for universal screening, we're going to oppose it and so will many women's groups. Not because treatment isn't sometimes needed, but because the track record in this county is for agencies to go punitive instead of preventive—to take babies away from these women without offering them a chance to get into treatment if they really need it."

Sam asked, "So you're not saying screening is a bad thing in itself? Isn't screening the only way to identify those women and their babies as early as possible?"

"We're against screening that leads to removal and that is used in a biased way against women of color and poor women. There are women among our groups who are . . ." she paused and looked for a softer word, "a bit more intense about these issues. They tend to frame the issues as racial, even though there's ample evidence in California and elsewhere that it's middle class, educated white women who use the most drugs and alcohol during pregnancy."

She continued, "If women who seek help get punishment instead—they won't seek help. It's really as simple as that. These laws do nothing to increase access to treatment. They spend more money removing babies and locking women up than they would spend for good treatment that included mothers and their infants in the same program."

"Family treatment," Sam said.

"Yes, family treatment. That's the answer, not punitive responses that break up families and criminalize women."

"So your organization supports family treatment but not screening to identify the women who need it?"

"Screening and testing should be done only with fully informed consent of the pregnant woman."

Joshua had been silent, making sure he understood Easton's position. He had carefully read the materials on their website and the several YouTube presentations Easton had made. Now he leaned forward and asked Sam's question a different way. "But if women aren't routinely screened for drugs and alcohol as part of prenatal care—how will anyone know they need help? They're routinely asked in a prenatal exam about their weight, nutrition, exercise, their health history. So why not ask a few questions about drugs and alcohol? I'm sure you know there are validated tools that have been used as part of prenatal screening across the country. Why not endorse that as a way of getting more women identified who need treatment?"

"You're asking a good question, Mr. Bronson. The answer is that every woman should have the right of privacy to decide what she wants to discuss in a prenatal visit with her doctor. And we simply don't trust the agencies that would have access to this data not to use it in a punitive way."

"But your website includes statements by many medical organizations opposing punitive action against pregnant women; it says nothing opposing screening."

Easton was beginning to get irritated, seeing that both Sam and Joshua were asking the same question over and over. "I'm not sure I'm being clear. We simply don't believe that screening can be done in a non-punitive way."

It was a stalemate, Sam realized. There was ample history to support Easton's concerns—especially in the more conservative states that had the worst legislation. Thinking about Luisa Contreras, Sam knew she wouldn't emerge as a heroine if the full details of her pregnancy were revealed. The media would over-simplify: babies are innocent, mothers who use are guilty—case closed.

Yet Easton's position was one of the most important barriers to universal screening, and it would cause progressive legislators to think twice about endorsing what would be painted as an anti-mother approach.

Sam and Joshua thanked Easton, who asked for a copy of their report as soon as it was completed. As they left, Sam said to Joshua, "Lots of history there—and a lot of it isn't good. She's got a good point—but it's a better point in South Carolina than it is in Southern California."

Just then Sam's phone rang. He picked it up and said "Leonard here." As he listened, his eyebrows went up and after a pause, he said "Supervisor Marvin, I'm with my colleague who is working with me on the project. Do you mind if I put you on speaker?"

Hearing a soft yes, Sam clicked on the speaker, and said to Joshua, "Josh, this is Supervisor Marvin. He would like to meet with us."

Marcus Marvin was the dean of African-American politicians in Los Angeles, and had occupied that role for two decades. He had emerged from South Central Los Angeles with a great voice that had been recognized by a first-rate music teacher, and had gone on to a career as an opera singer who also made several popular albums that went platinum. He had invested his earnings in housing and shopping centers in Los Angeles, and then moved into politics. He was in his third term on the Board and had never been challenged after winning his first election.

Sam went on, "Supervisor Marvin, what would be convenient for you?"

Marvin answered "How about next Tuesday at nine?"

Sam said, "Next Tuesday at nine would be perfect, sir. We'll see you in your office then. Thank you."

Supervisor Marvin's office

They met with Marvin in his office in the Board chambers. Pictures of him with five Presidents—Reagan, both Bushes, Clinton, and Obama—hung on one wall, with African and Latin American art on the other walls. A poster featuring a much younger Marvin as the lead singer in Othello was the only other wall decoration.

Marvin was soft-spoken, with a gentle smile that Sam knew concealed one of the finest minds ever to grace local government in California. He began by asking Sam and Joshua "Well, how goes your exploration, gentlemen?"

Sam said, "Supervisor, we have found that all the agencies blame all the other agencies, and none is responsible for what happened to that little girl."

Marvin smiled again, and said "As they said in that strange opera Mr. Gershwin wrote, 'it ain't necessarily so,' Mr. Leonard." Then he got a much more serious look on his face. "I hear you're looking into more taxes to pay for some of what needs to happen in DCW."

"Yes sir. Do you think you could consider supporting an increase in the alcohol tax?"

Marvin looked at them sternly, all geniality gone. Then he said, "Well, let me tell you a story. You may remember that about the time of the '92 disturbances, we lost several dozen liquor stores that went up in flames. Now, we had a fine young woman who's now in Congress who went around door to door after the disturbances and asked people if they wanted the burned-out liquor stores to come back or some grocery stores instead. Turned out we didn't need ten times as many liquor stores in South Central as in the rest of the city." He turned and looked at the map of his district, running across the downtown area and the central part of the larger city.

Then he wheeled back and leaned forward. "I'll be your first vote on that, gentlemen. Do you have any idea where you'll get the other two?" He paused, and then added, "Would you like a bit of advice?"

"Yes, sir," Sam said.

"Don't count on Calver. And don't count Berenson out."

Surprised, Sam said, "All right. We'll tuck that away."

Marvin was silent for a few moments, and then said, "Years ago I was singing in New York, and some producer decided we needed to do some 'early music.' So they found this 13th century opera, 'Herod and the Slaughter of the Innocents.' They cast me as Joseph, against a gorgeous blonde soprano. Forgot her name, but she was good." He fell silent again. Then he said, "*The innocents*. Guess you can't get more innocent than the babies you're talking about. Someone told me you were using the number of 20,000 babies born every year."

Marveling at his sources and realizing that someone had briefed him on their questions, Sam said, "A little more than that, Supervisor."

Shaking his head, Marvin said "The innocents. Well let's see what we can do to help them. Should have gotten to that long ago"

He stood up and walked them to the door, saying, "You fellows keep punching, and let me know what I can do to help."

They thanked him, and as they walked down the corridor out to the lobby of the building, Joshua said "I feel like I finally met a good politician."

Sam chuckled. "They exist, Josh. Whatever color they are, they're golden. And sometimes they make a real difference."

CHAPTER 28

Law office

Nicole had asked Sam and Joshua to meet her in her office. When they arrived, Nicole was looking glum.

"What's happening?" Sam asked.

"I'm just trying to figure out how we're going to deal with Wilma Holmes."

"Who's Wilma Holmes?" said Joshua.

Nicole sighed. "She's a classmate of mine from law school. Know-it-all type, only the problem was she really did know it all. Or most of it. Very, very smart, and very, very unscrupulous. We tangled several times in law school—and since. She went to work for the legal rights office for the Children's Law Foundation and we went up against each other in court three times while I was with the DA." She frowned. "I'm 0 for 3, and she'll never let me forget it."

"So how does she get into this case?" Sam asked.

"She called yesterday and said she was coming in to talk about Baby Isabel. Said something about a class action case that would take on all the county agencies that are doing—in her words—'a totally shitty job' on cases like this."

She got up from her desk and poured herself a cup of coffee from the dispenser on the bookshelf behind her desk, motioning with her cup to ask if either of them wanted some. They shook their heads no, and she continued. "She could really screw things up. If she gets into it, the agencies are going to stop talking to you for fear they'll say something that could get them sued or make them look bad." She looked at her watch. "She'll be here in a few minutes."

When Wilma Holmes walked in, Sam could immediately see the contrast with Nicole. Wilma was blond, though somewhat improbably, with dark eyebrows. She wore her hair long, well below her shoulders. She was thin, with a figure shown off by her low-cut blouse worn with a tightly fitting suit. Sam's trained eye noted in rapid succession that she'd had augmentation and that it had been remarkably successful. Her face was angular, with fine cheekbones and lips that were a 9.0 on the Julia Roberts-Angelina Jolie scale.

"Hello, guys," Wilma said, as she swept into the chair nearest to Joshua. "I hear you're the new super-sleuths Nicky has hired to dig up the dirt so she can bury it."

Nicole quickly said, "Unless you want to be Willy for the rest of this meeting, drop the Nicky stuff, Wilma."

"My, aren't we sensitive today?" Wilma said, as she looked over Sam and Joshua with a frank stare. "So what are you guys turning up?"

Nicole quickly said, "You'll be able to read the report when it's out, Wilma. Tell me what you want."

As Wilma turned back to Nicole, Sam watched Nicole watching Joshua's reaction to Wilma. He filed it away for his next counseling session with Joshua.

Wilma turned quickly to business after her fencing with Nicole. "Nicole, you've got a real problem this time. The county agencies have done a terrible job on these drug babies, and we've decided it's time to turn on the spotlights. The Baby Isabel case will be the one that finally gets people off the dime."

Nicole, speaking as though she were talking to a slightly retarded person, said "We agree, Wilma, and that's why we're looking at all the agencies. I'm sure you see why that makes sense."

Wilma laughed and said, "Makes no sense the way you're doing it. These *journalists*," saying the word as though she meant *clowns*, "will write their story, but you and I both know it's going to take legal action to make a difference."

"So what kind of legal action did you have in mind?"

"We're going to wait for your report, Nicole. But we think all the agencies should be sued under CAPTA—none of them are doing CAPTA reports the way the law specifies. And we're also considering a new interpretation of reasonable efforts. What the county is doing for the moms in these cases is giving them a referral and then washing its hands. That's nowhere near what reasonable efforts should mean."

Nicole frowned. "Good luck with that one. The case law is pretty clear that the county just needs to send them to treatment and parent ed and then see what they do."

Wilma gave Nicole a scornful look. "And that's all you're going to do—give them a referral slip and pretend that will make a difference?" She wagged her finger at Nicole, and added, as she rose to leave, "You're not going to be the heroine on this one, Nicky. See you around."

As she left, Nicole gave her back a full Italian salute, right arm extended above her left hand as it slapped onto her inner elbow.

Sam laughed and said "Good thing she doesn't get to you."

Nicole smiled, and said, "Not a bit. Never has, never will." Then she laughed. "Is it that obvious?"

Sam said, "I just hoped you weren't going to swing on her."

Nicole said, seeming embarrassed, "They had to pull me off her once. We had just finished finals in a third year class on civil rights legislation. She walked out early and when I finally finished, she was standing outside smoking with some of her groupies, and she said, 'Hey, Nicole, was it too tough for you?' I just lost it. I was interviewing for a clerkship and it hadn't gone well. The test and Wilma's mouth were the last straws." She shook her head. "Wilma was smart, but she was also smart about who she got close to. There were stories about how friendly she had gotten with some of her professors and older students who were in a position to help her." She got a mischievous look and added, "For a while we were calling her Willya instead of Wilma. Willya Dume."

She went on. "She's 100% right about reasonable efforts, though. I've had one of our interns doing some work, and we may have a surprise for her on that one."

Joshua asked "What's CAPTA?"

Nicole said, "The Child Abuse Prevention and Treatment Act. It's not a lot of money, but to get it the state has to promise they will do two things—which they and the counties aren't doing worth a damn. Wilma's right about that. The county is supposed to report all drug or alcohol-exposed births from hospitals to child protective services. And all kids under 3 in child welfare cases are supposed to get developmental screenings by the Part C agency—that's the county's developmental disabilities agency. Neither one happens for 90% of the kids that need it."

"Now I remember, that came up when we talked to the public health people. Sounds like the County is pretty vulnerable," Sam said.

"Maybe. Feel free to mention it in the report. But there's no followup from the feds at all. Congress passed the law and got it right—but the feds pretty much ignore it. No enforcement effort at all. It's one of those things the feds "encourage" but don't even monitor. And Congress ignores it even after they stick it in the law. So whether a legal battle would produce anything is not clear. But Wilma doesn't care. She gets a headline and her funders see her kicking ass. So she may well go after it."

CHAPTER 29

The Desert

After the biker attack, Joe decided to take a risk and see what was happening back in the Valley. So he called his cousin Charlie.

When he came to the phone, Joe could tell that Charlie was nervous, He was almost whispering. "Hey man, where are you? Been reading about you in the paper, guy. You're in trouble with the cops—and you're in a lot of trouble with the crew."

"What do you mean, with the crew?"

"They're looking for you too, man, and you'd better hope the cops find you first."

"For getting shot at by the Vatos? You *told* me to sell over there, Charlie!"

"That's got nothing to do with it, man. Right after you went into the hospital, they arrested about twenty guys, almost all from our crew. They all think you snitched, Joe, and they're really gunning for you."

"I had nothing to do with that. The cops who asked me about selling got nothing from me, Charlie."

"Maybe I believe you, Joe—but the top guys don't. El Jefe wants you brought in for discipline, and he may put a contract on you. I know some guys who are already looking for you. Some of them went to Aunt Josie and hassled her. Stay low, Joe." And he hung up.

Joe knew it was time—it was past time. The cops were still looking for him, and the gang might be soon. The dust-up with the bikers might get back to the cops if they contacted the Marine base. Eventually one or the other would figure out where he was, however well Dolores had hidden her trail. Farmer might get pressured to tell the cops, or the gang might send out more enforcers to pressure Aunt Josie or Luisa. Joe had to worry now about how to get Isabel back without getting himself shot up again. And he had to worry about keeping Dolores out of it.

Joe walked back inside the mobile after his call from Charlie. He told Dolores about the call.

"So this guy—this *Jefe* guy—has threatened you?"

"Charlie thinks so. Says there may be a contract out on me."

Dolores was furious. "What an asshole. First, you didn't rat anybody out—you're getting blamed for what some stupid gangbanger did when he got pulled in by the cops. Second, you got shot because you did what they told you to do, trying to make a sale across the line in somebody else's territory." Then she fell silent and looked out the window at the Whipple peaks.

Joe started to get worried. "Look, it'll blow over. There's nothing we can do about it. No way are they going to find us out here." He paused, watching her start to pace around. "Dee, I'm starting to think I need to go back, get Isabel into a good place, and take my chances with the law."

Dolores didn't respond. Watching her, he knew she was thinking about something crazy. In her world, the bad guys attacked and you attacked back, only smarter and harder. But that wouldn't work with the gangs—Middle East rules weren't Valley rules.

"What are you thinking about?"

"About how much I hate all those gang-banging, drug-hustling bastards. They're just like the fucking Taliban—they terrorize people to a point where everyone gives up and lets them make all the rules." She went back to the window, frowning.

"Maybe. But you had 150,000 troops behind you over there. Here, it's only a few cops, and some of them are corrupt."

Then he made a mistake, and knew it the minute the words came out of his mouth. "Give it up, Dee. You're not ready to go up against anybody right now."

She wheeled around from the window and said "You think so, little brother? You think I'm not ready?"

"No, no, I didn't mean that." Desperate now, he added, "I need you here—Isabel needs you here."

"Back off, Joe. I'm going to think about this some more. But I'm not sitting in any fucking rocking chair waiting for those assholes to come after you and the baby. That's not going to happen."

Joe watched her grab her cellphone and walk out into the front porch to make a call. *Who the hell was she calling now?* he wondered.

During the next few days, the threat from the gang wasn't brought up, and Joe hoped that Dolores had forgotten it or decided to let it pass for the time being. So he was totally surprised when he woke up one morning to find her packing a canvas camo bag with what looked like two automatics and several clips of ammunition.

She grabbed her keys off a hook in the kitchen and said, "Take care of Isabel. I should be back before dark. I'm taking my car—I switched the plates out again."

"Where are you going? You can't just drive off—and why are you taking your arsenal along?"

Dolores smiled and patted his shoulder gently as she headed for the door. "Don't worry, Joe—I have some backup."

And all Joe could think as he watched her drive out across the desert was *I never should have told her.*

Dolores had made two calls. First to Farmer to ask him to get in touch with his contacts in the LAPD Valley division and find out where the head of the Valley Muerte gang lived. Then she had a long talk with Lassiter.

Both calls were productive. Then she made another one.

After a three-hour drive, Dolores arrived at the near-mansion owned by Carlos Anaya, *El Jefe* of the Valley Muerte organization. It was a two-story stucco building on two acres in Woodland Hills, with a long curving driveway in front and an unobtrusive guard house built into the wall at the front gate. They waved her through, and she drove up to the front of the house.

A head-shaved, muscle-bound flunky came out and took her inside. A young woman was waiting and gave her a thorough pat-down. She had left her guns in the car, concealed behind a compartment. She knew they would find them, and she wanted them to—as a sign that she was serious.

She was shown into a large room where Carlos Anaya was sitting in a large armchair. He was a heavy set man of about forty, with a Pancho Villa mustache. He was wearing a guyabara shirt and what looked to Dolores to be snakeskin boots.

He waved her into a chair. "I heard you wanted to talk to me. Always happy to meet with the neighbors. Though I guess you don't live around here any more."

"Yeah."

"Charlie tells me you're Joe's sister. Joe the snitch."

"Look, Mr. Anaya, Joe didn't tell the cops anything. Whatever they found out about you, they got from somebody they pulled in. Look for whoever got arrested and released in the last few weeks. Joe got shot and then disappeared, so he was easy to blame. But he didn't do it."

Carlos got a distant look on his face, and Dolores could tell he was weighing her claim against his own mental lists of guys who had been hauled in.

"Here's the deal, Mr. Anaya. I have some friends—some brothers, actually. Some of them are watching this house, and the rest are on standby where they can be here any time you mess with Joe."

"Brothers? Black guys?"

She smiled at his mistake. "No. In the Corps everyone is brothers and sisters, and these guys are part of my family. I took care of them over there, and they watch out for me over here. You people talk about *La Familia* all the time, but this is a real family. We've gone through shit you never dreamed of. So if you come after Joe, we come after you. And we will take you out, and then the Vatos will take over your organization in a few days. It's that simple."

Carlos narrowed his eyes and glared at her. "I kill and bury people who say things like that to me." Then he relaxed, and smiled. "But you have a lot of balls coming in here and talking to me like that."

Dolores replied, "You and your little entourage here may have killed some people. But you would shit yourself and start whimpering in the first sixty seconds of a real firefight."

"You sound like a very tough woman, Miss Brenner. I hear you have some kind of medal for killing a bunch of ragheads over there. See, I have a kid in the back room who spends all day googling for me. You're famous, *chica*.

"Use my name. I've given you the respect of using yours."

"How do I know you aren't bluffing? What if there aren't any people out there?"

"I knew you'd say that. Listen very carefully."

At first there was nothing. Then three distinct *plink, plink, plink* sounds came.

"That was three of your upstairs windows. There are definitely people out there. They have silencers, and they are well hidden."

Carlos stood up, shouting, "You come in here and start shooting up my house. *My house?* I cannot allow that, *puta*. I don't care if the whole fucking Marine Corps is out there."

She stared him down, saying softly, "We could arrange that if you'd like." Then she backed off. "Mr. Anaya, we respect you and we're not here to take your business away from you—as disgusting as it is that you prey on other people's diseases. We're here for one reason—to make sure you back off any threats to Joe. That's all."

He was still furious. She could hear the underlings scurrying around upstairs, and she could imagine them setting up defense positions.

Then she watched him calm down, sitting back down in his chair, thinking hard. He asked, suspicious, "How did they know to shoot when you said to? You're wired. But we shook you down when you came in."

"No, sir, I'm not wired. *This whole house is wired.* War gives people the chance to invent all kinds of stuff. Don't make us use it."

He was getting angry again, more now out of frustration than at her. "You can't just come in here, threatening me and shooting this place up. You're not the law."

"Some of my brothers work in the dark, Mr. Anaya. No one would ever find them." Then she laughed and added, "What can you do? You're going to go to the LAPD for protection? *Buena suerte*, Carlos. And if you call anybody in the Corps, you'll find that people go on leave all the time. What they do off-duty is their own business. Face it, Carlos, you're not a very sympathetic figure if you start whining about being targeted."

She leaned forward. "Like I said, it's simple. Back off of Joe. He didn't do anything to threaten you or your business. Then forget about it—and about us."

She rose and waited for his response. He glared at her, but only said, waving his hand "Be gone—get out of my house. I'll check to see if you're right about Joe. Don't ask for anything more."

As she drove away, Dolores thought two things at once: *That's all I wanted* and *I really need a drink.* She held her right hand out from the steering wheel and watched it for a moment. *Look, no shakes. Good.*

When she got back to the mobile, Joe was furious. "Where did you go this time? And who did you see?"

"I went *out there*, Joe. It's going to be fine." And as she explained what had happened, Joe went through the stages from disbelief to relief and then back again to wondering what the hell she had really done.

CHAPTER 30

Department of Child Welfare

Sam and Joshua had scheduled their final agency interview with a deputy administrator in the child welfare agency whom Nicole had insisted they interview. She said that she had worked with him on several cases and he was, in her words, "the most competent, knowledgeable person I ever encountered" in the agency.

They arrived in Nate Rubin's office, where the balding, slightly overweight official greeted them courteously. They explained what they were doing, and he responded, "Yes, I've heard about what you're doing. It's created a bit of a stir."

Sam said, "Really? How so?"

Rubin answered, "You're asking good questions, questions about how we all connect with each other. And I gather you're not accepting the usual blame game."

Sam said, "Well, we're not trying to point fingers at anyone. But there does seem to be a lot of finger-pointing going around—usually at the other guys."

Rubin laughed. "That's par for the course, I guess. It's 'their fault.' It's always the child welfare agency they come after. We're the easy target. But the hospital never even reported this baby, even though there's a federal law that says they're supposed to tell us."

Sam said, "They say they did."

Rubin frowned. "Maybe. But what that usually means is that the hospital social worker called our hotline, and left a message. There's a countywide protocol for formally reporting drug-exposed births in writing on a form we developed, but very few of the hospitals use it. I'll check to see what really came in."

He looked at them, trying to gauge their interest in what he was beginning to say. "You see, what you're looking at, the drug babies, is a problem we've had that goes all the way back to the mid-80's. We've tried everything, but never in an organized way. The problem doesn't belong to any one agency, which is why you're getting all this blame the other guy stuff. The hospitals are involved, we're involved, the health clinics are involved, and lots of other agencies are involved—or should be. But nobody is in charge. I saw an estimate a few years ago that for every baby we find that is drug—or alcohol-exposed, we miss twenty other ones. Most of them just go home. This little girl made it into the headlines because somebody snatched her. But almost all the other ones just go home. And then they show up in our caseload a few years later when someone sees that she isn't being taken care of. Or when she gets to be in third or fourth grade, and she's acting up enough to disrupt a classroom. Then it gets to be the schools' problem, and they shunt her off into special ed. She gets a little older, and mental health takes her, and they want to send her out of state to some lock-up program."

He frowned. "See, all we really do to try to get out in front of this is to set up little programs, little token-scale programs. Then somebody asks 'what are you doing about this, why don't you have a program?' And we give them a full-scale WADI—'we're already doing it.'" He laughed. "Word actually means dry river bed in Arabic. *Wadi*—good word for a lot of what we do. Dry river beds."

He had talked for a long time, and Sam and Joshua could see why Nicole wanted them to talk with him. He had an overview that was rare, able to see more than his own agency's defensive tactics.

Sam asked, "What about the feds? They make a lot of rules you guys have to operate under. What role do they play in all this?"

Rubin sighed. "I don't understand the feds any more. I just don't get them. I started out working for the federal government, long ago. I was in the old Budget Bureau in 1965, right in the middle of the early days of the skirmish on poverty. And I worked with Cabinet Secretaries and assistant secretaries and deputies for this and that. Worked with a lot of civil servants and interns. They had a great intern program in those days, bright young kids who were just starting out, had been inspired by Kennedy and actually wanted to work for federal agencies on the domestic side."

He shook his head, looking sad. "But now—I don't know. They are so bloody timid now—everything is a caution sign with them. They're yellow light people."

"Yellow light people?"

"Yeah. Caution, watch out, don't take risks, don't upset anyone. Don't stick your neck out, don't get involved with new programs until they become the conventional wisdom, and then only fund little programs. PPD I call it: pilot project disorder. Everything is a pilot project, almost nothing gets continued after the three-year pilot project funding runs out. And so everyone at the local level runs around and tries to get funded from the next federal pilot project, whether it's what they really want to do or just a diversion. And the feds don't seem to care. They just keep spinning out these new programs, little programs that try something new. Only now they call it 'evidence-based practice.' Means they've tested the new programs in a completely unrealistic environment and found that they worked, compared to some group of poor kids who didn't get the new program."

He went on. "They pretend that a project is a program, and then they pretend that a program is a policy. But it's not. It's just a cover story to show people when they ask us what we're doing about some problem. We show them the project and usually they go away without ever asking us how many kids *aren't* being helped by the project. What is it with these people—did they skip arithmetic in school? Can't any of them *count*?"

He said, "Look, there are some good feds. I don't mean to condemn them all, any more than all the people here in the county agencies are no good. There are some policy people who have come into the government from outside, and they know a lot about how the programs do and don't work. And there are some civil servants who are both civil and see themselves as servants—and they're worth their weight in gold. You get to work with one of them, someone who knows the ins and outs of programs and knows how to move resources and has a solid sense of what's going on around the country even if they have no travel funds—they can be great. I love working with the good ones." He sighed. "But the time-servers and the yellow-light people out-number the good ones by far, from what I've seen lately."

Then he paused, and looked at them. "I know I'm sounding cynical, and I don't mean to. It's just that I've seen a lot in 47 years of doing this work with kids. One thing I've learned after all these years: When agencies behave like children, kids get hurt."

He went on. "I've been too negative, probably. That's what people tend to call you these days when you're realistic. There *are* people who can put it together—who get the idea of working across agencies, and know that if you go it alone, one agency by itself— you'll get what you asked for. And then you end up left all alone without the resources you need. Some people in some of these agencies, including this one, totally get that. They work out on the bridges, on the edges, and some of the people back in the agency put them down because of it. Kind of like the Foreign Service— they talk about diplomats going native and seeing things from the vantage point of the country they're assigned to, instead of ours. But the agency people here who understand the moms and the kids best are *themselves* the best practices. Turns out best practices usually come from the best practitioners. And we've got some of them. I don't mean to make it sound like there aren't any."

He stopped and looked over at his wall, which had a demographic map of the county. "But there aren't nearly enough of them. We've got ten million people out here in this country that's pretending to be a county. And there's maybe a few hundred people in the agencies who really understand how to work across the bridges. There just aren't enough of them."

He leaned forward and continued. "Here's the other part of it. The bureau chiefs in county government have become their own little fiefdoms, because the leadership at the top in some of the agencies is so weak. These little sultans run their own projects, keep their own budgets under tight control, and don't have to work with anyone else. In some ways, it's the worst possible time to get these guys—and gals—to work together, because the little sultans are now in charge in so many of the agencies. And the same thing happens a lot of the time in state or federal agencies. Without a great agency head, the little chieftains run their bureaus without much guidance—and they love it.

He looked at them, and then added, "If you guys can put together a report that captures some of this—that cuts across the agencies and the programs instead of just blaming one of them— you could make a difference. Nicole is a fierce fighter, and when she asked me to talk with you, I was glad to. Give it your best shot."

Sam said. "We will. We are." He thought they were done, but it turned out Joshua wasn't.

Joshua asked," What kind of turnover do you have in the agency now?"

Rubin said, "A lot. You know, a lot of these workers will be retiring soon. The boomers are getting old, and many of them have enough saved—if the state doesn't take their pensions away—to quit and take things easy."

Joshua leaned forward and said, "About how many will that be? What percentage, roughly?" The interest in his voice broke through, and Rubin looked at Sam with a questioning look.

Sam shrugged, and said "Kid sees things from the other end of the telescope, I guess."

Rubin laughed and said, "It could be as many as a quarter of the workforce—many more in the top ranks, I would think."

Joshua, unembarrassed by Sam's remark, said "So a whole new generation of supervisors could be coming into place. What will they be like? Will they be different?"

Rubin said, "Well, I've actually done some reading on that. And I've talked to the new people we've hired in the last year or so. One school of thought says they are much less driven than we were— much more likely to be 9 to 5 types who live for their non-work lives—families and leisure. But another school says these kids, especially the ones who come to work in an agency like this one, are likely to have a deeper commitment to the work and much less tolerance of hierarchy and rules. Open to new ideas, not stuck doing it the old way because we always did it that way. Familiar with horizontal networks, because they grew up on the Internet and use Wikipedia and social networks. So maybe they won't get stuck in vertical chains of command." He smiled. "They may know how to connect things, having grown up with everything connected to their damn smartphones. Could be interesting."

Then he held up his hand. "I know you guys are wrapping up your interviews. But I want you to talk to one more guy—a guy in our numbers shop named Will Coburn. He's the best, and he can help you understand what's really going on with some of the agency reports they've given you."

Sam quickly agreed and made the appointment while they were still in Rubin's office.

As they walked down the corridor toward the elevator, Joshua said to Sam, "What a resource. He knows so much, and had an acronym or a phrase for everything. Yellow light people, PPD, WADI. Guy needs a glossary."

Sam nodded, and then asked, "Josh, why did you ask the question about turnover?"

"I keep reading about the generational switch, and it just makes me wonder if it means things could be different. If this interagency stuff is about to shift, in ways people aren't really ready for. You know, Sam, we're going to have a lot of bad news in this report. It would be good if we can point to some things that are getting better." He corrected himself. "That *might* be getting better."

Sam said, "Good point, kid," and again realized how lucky he was that Ernie Scott had sent Joshua to him. "You know, you're right that there are thousands of guys like that who are retiring or about to retire. The boomers are going off to their lakeside cottages and their doublewides—the unlucky ones will go to their singlewides. And young sprouts like you will replace them—and no one knows quite what will happen. But it could make a big difference."

CHAPTER 31

They arrived at Coburn's office later that afternoon. Coburn was the complete opposite of what they had been expecting when Rubin described him; he looked more like a blond surfer than a numbers guy.

Coburn greeted them and sat them down across from his desk. Behind him were four oversized monitors and a row of bookshelves full of multi-colored binders with numbers on their spines.

Sam thanked him and began by asking, "How would you summarize the county's performance in working with kids in the child welfare system, given all the data you have access to?"

"That's simple, Mr. Leonard, Mr. Bronson. We're succeeding." He stopped and watched the surprised reaction he had expected, smiling in a weird way, seeming to say *threw you a curve on that one, huh?*

"Succeeding?" Sam asked, trying to keep a tone of incredulity out of his voice.

"Yes. The most expensive thing we do in this agency is to stick kids in foster care and other institutions. Depending on what kind of care it is and how old they are, that can cost anywhere from two thousand a month up to five thousand a month—or more. And so success means that we've cut foster care entries by 25% from where they were ten years ago, even with a lot more kids in the county today."

He leaned back and smiled. "That's success—at least as the budget guys and the politicians define it. We spend less money—we must be doing something right."

Joshua waited a moment, and then asked quietly, "Is that how you'd define it?"

Unsmiling now, Coburn said "We're off the record here, right?"

Sam nodded. "Yes. No direct quotes."

"Then the answer is *hell, no*. Unless you believe that a miracle has happened, a miracle that somehow cured abusive families of their disorder and addiction, then taking fewer kids into care is nothing but a huge gamble. We're hoping—betting is a better word—that those kids we leave home with those parents will be OK. Some will be, some won't."

He frowned sadly. "Seventy deaths in three years? That's the tip of the iceberg. We numbers people talk about 'metrics.' Seventy dead kids is one hell of a troubling metric, in my opinion."

He went on. "Look, the reality is that a lot of the parents we deal with aren't going to get their act together. They're going to be offered voluntary services, and they're going to turn them down or drop out. A third or more don't even show up at the first detention hearing. We tell them they're going to lose their kids, and they don't even show up to contest it. So that's a third, roughly, who aren't even going to try. And on the other hand, there's a third or so who are going to make it—they got into the system because they messed up, but they have enough going for them in basic decency and intelligence or terrific support from someone who cares about them—and they're going to make it. That leaves us with the middle third, and that's who we're really struggling with. There's no magic or accuracy to these numbers, by the way. That middle group may be as big as a half, and in some places it may be much smaller than a third.

"So we're working with parents who give a damn—or who might. But the fiscal Titanic that we've all been floating around on for the past few years is slowly sinking. And the simple fact is that you can just move the bar on the kinds of abuse and neglect we tolerate up to a point where you take in fewer kids and fewer parents. And then we save a ton of money."

He looked at them with his goofy smile. "So, you see—we're succeeding. As long as you measure it by what we're spending. Or not spending."

Sam didn't want to over-react to what Coburn had said, but he needed to get past the cynicism or whatever it was that was making him explain the system in such simplistic terms. "So how *should* we be measuring it?"

It was as if Coburn had been waiting for the question, because he pounced on it. "If we cared about the kids, we'd be watching two things very carefully. First, how many of them re-enter the system after they go back home, or after we make a judgment to leave them home when we think something might have happened. Second, we should be watching who is coming *into* the system, and how they're different from who was coming into the system five or ten years ago. My bet is that we would see that much harder cases are coming in now, because we've screened out all but the hard cases. And that means those families need a lot more services—just at the time when we've been cutting the services they need."

Joshua asked, "So what is that re-entry rate now?"

Before he answered, Coburn looked through some papers he had brought with him. "Here it is. I wanted to make sure I gave you the right number. It's a little over twelve percent. So—success again—nearly nine out of ten of those kids we send home stay home."

Joshua asked the obvious follow-up. "How many kids is twelve percent?"

"You're catching on, Mr. Bronson. Because that is exactly the right question. It's 828 kids—828 kids that re-entered foster care within twelve months of our sending them back home to live with their parents. If you go back three years, the number is more like 30%. And that, of course, doesn't include kids who were sent home and were re-abused but no one made a report." He fell silent, watching both of them.

Sam finally spoke up. "So what's the answer? Nobody bats 1.000, but obviously eight hundred kids who got sent home and then got abused again is a problem."

Coburn was again quick with an answer. "For openers, we need to get the right numbers. Now, it's like each team gets to keep its own batting averages, instead of the official scorer." He looked at some notes he had beside him on a lined pad, and Sam realized he had prepared for their interview with some care. "We play some other numbers games, too, gentlemen. One of the ways we make the numbers look good is by sending kids to live with their relatives. Nearly forty percent of the kids we have in foster care are with relatives of some kind."

"That's better than putting them in a home or institution with strangers, isn't it?"

"Sometimes. A better word is usually, I guess. But here's the thing. Many of the parents who abuse or neglect their kids seriously enough for us to remove the kids to foster care are really in bad shape. They abuse drugs or alcohol, they have mental illness of some kind, they're barely holding down jobs or may have their own learning disabilities. Three-fourths of them are women, and most of those women were themselves abused as kids."

He paused, and the sad look came over his face again. "And many of these addiction and aggression disorders are *family* disorders—they run in families. You can catch them from your parents, or other relatives who are abusive. And so good old Uncle Earl or Aunt Sally who may be willing to take the kids in may have lots of their own problems. But they didn't get caught, so we call them a placement and the kids go off with them. Mental illness and addiction sometimes just happens to people—but a lot of the time, you catch it from your kin. So celebrating kinship placements seems a little too easy to me, after twenty years of watching kids go home to some pretty rough places."

"How do you solve that one?"

"You screen the hell out of those families and kinfolk who step up and say they will take these kids, and you try as hard as you can to tell the difference between the real saints and the ones who are not so saintly. Look, some of these people should get instant halos—grandparents and aunts and uncles who thought they were going to retire and take it easy and then they suddenly end up with a six-year old, and they're starting elementary school parent-teacher meetings all over again. And sure, they get financial help. But the financial help doesn't do much for a seventy-year old who stays up all night waiting for a teenager to come home or an aunt who has been teaching school for thirty years and wants to go part-time and then finds out what summer camp costs, along with babysitters and the shoes and the Iphones that all the other kids have."

"So those are the good guys?"

"Those are the super-good guys. But not all of them. Kin placements fail, and sometimes they don't fail, but the kids end up not doing much better than when they were home with their birth parents. All I'm saying is that we should screen them just as carefully as we do strangers or institutions, and do more follow up than we usually do with kin placements."

Then he added, "And the final numbers game is called 'differential response.' That's where we get a report, and we think there is a real problem, but we don't open a case. We just make a referral to a 'community agency' that is supposed to work with the family—on a voluntary basis, of course—and keep that family out of the system. That helps keep the numbers down, and if we do that for the less serious cases, we can shift the numbers into that category for as much as ten to twenty per cent of all cases."

Joshua asked, "If they're less serious cases, why's that a problem?"

"If they're less serious cases, but we're pretty sure abuse or neglect happened, the families still need help. But the very agencies we are referring them to are the ones that are getting their budgets cut—some so badly they're shutting down, others by one-third or one-half of their total operations. So the idea that these families are going to get some help is a stretch, because we don't track them at all, by the way—we just count the ones we refer out, not what happens to them. If it were a football game, we'd be making a handoff to the injured reserve—and then we'd turn around and not even watch to see if they make yardage or get thrown for a loss."

Joshua asked, "One final question. Are there any big pieces of the solution that we haven't asked about?"

Coburn smiled and said, "Only one. How do you pay for it?"

Joshua said, "And how *do* you pay for it?"

"We make polluters pay for the mess their pollution causes. Why this county doesn't tax alcohol enough to pay for the mess caused by people who misuse the product is a mystery to me. A study done at Columbia a few years ago documented that on average, 11% of a state's budget is cleaning up after alcohol and drugs—much more alcohol than drugs, except for the prisons part. Highway patrol, DUI court cases, hospitals with terminal cirrhosis of the liver cases, mental retardation, special education, and so on. Eleven percent—that's a ton of money in this state."

Sam and Joshua thanked Coburn and walked out, marveling at his grasp of the big picture and seeing why Rubin had wanted them to talk with him.

The next morning, at their breakfast warm-up meeting, Joshua proposed to Sam that he spend a few days meeting with line workers in sessions to be arranged through the unions and workers' organizations in the agencies. Sam could read the message that Joshua wanted his own part of the project, and he agreed that Joshua could go ahead, not without some anxiety that the kid would be dealing with some fairly senior union reps in doing so.

Joshua spent four days interviewing workers as Sam worked on the report. The workers he talked with were delighted, pointing out that they were rarely consulted in this kind of investigation.

Back at Sam's house, Joshua debriefed Sam on the main points of the interviews he'd done. "Sam, they were all over the place. Some really wanted to have a more constructive role, and totally understood why agencies needed to work together more closely. They had some really good ideas for dealing with the fragmentation. And others were full of excuses or dismissed the whole idea of working across agency lines as impractical."

He looked at his notes. "One of them, the guy from the supervisors union, went on for nearly an hour telling me why the confidentiality barriers to working together prevented them from ever sharing data about kids. But Sam, another supervisor told me that there are at least five different ways to handle confidentiality."

He glanced at his notes. "A judge gives a court order, the data is de-identified with all names and other personal data stripped out, the information relates to child abuse, aggregate numbers only, research provisions—all ways you can deal with the barriers without getting into trouble. And the guy said that in his experience, whenever a worker in another agency cited confidentiality as a barrier to cooperating, it was nearly always a measure of distrust more than a genuine legal problem. They didn't *trust* the agency or the worker who wanted the data—so they hid behind confidentiality."

Joshua frowned. "Sam, we need to make sure we don't just scapegoat these workers. Some of them said pretty much what we heard from the higher-level people—they want to do a better job, they know they need more tools to do it, and they care about the kids,. Some of them are going into homes that you or I wouldn't go into without an armed platoon. And some of the younger ones I talked to are trying to pay off more than $50,000 in grad student loans that they had to take out to get their MSW degree."

"Point taken, Josh. I'm really glad you did the interviews. Great work, kid."

CHAPTER 32

Chief Administrative Officer

Nicole had called Sam and asked him to join her in a meeting with the County Chief Administrative Officer, Dr. Franklin Hamilton. Hamilton had gotten wind of the report Sam and Joshua were preparing and had called Nicole complaining that his agencies were being "badgered" and threatening to end the county's cooperation with the investigation.

Nicole explained to Sam as they drove over—Joshua having been delegated to continue his meetings with line agency staff—that Hamilton was a long-time county official, an African-American who had started as an intern forty years ago and had risen to the top of the county government.

As they entered Hamilton's office, Sam's first judgment was *an older Samuel Jackson*. As Hamilton began talking, he revised it to add *with James Earl Jones' voice*.

Hamilton began by leaning forward and saying to them, with an angry look on his face, "You are trying to make my agencies look bad."

Sam had been pushed around by some of the toughest elected and appointed officials in the country, and he was not feeling in the mood to be all that subservient. Speaking deliberately, slower than usual, he said, "With respect, sir, some of them already look pretty bad without any help from us."

Nicole saw quickly that she was going to have to play peacemaker. "Dr. Hamilton, we aren't gunning for any agencies. We're trying to document how well they work together. One of the mistakes we've all made in the past has been to assume that we could focus on one agency at a time. Sir, the point here is that what happened to that baby gave us a chance to look hard at a lot of agencies—and make sure that no one of them gets the blame alone."

Hamilton was quiet for a long time, looking at both of them. Then he said, "And that's supposed to make me feel better?"

Sam was getting angry despite himself. "Again, sir, with respect, your feelings seem less important than the lives of the 20,000 or so babies born with the same problems Isabel Contreras has." Then he smiled—or tried to. "Speaking only for myself, of course."

Nicole scowled at Sam, realizing that Hamilton had set him off in a way she hadn't seen before. "Let's calm down, gentlemen. What my firm hopes is that we can come out of this with a set of steps that we all agree could connect these agencies better. And we agree that there have to be some new resources on the table to make that real and not just another token add-on project or two."

Hamilton said, "And where are these magical new resources supposed to come from, Miss Larwin?" By now Hamilton was refusing to look at Sam at all.

Nicole said, "As you know, the state has given counties taxing authority for alcohol and tobacco supplementary taxes. A nickel a drink on all types of alcohol yields about 200 million dollars for prenatal screening and an interagency agenda to deal with the effects of prenatal exposure."

Hamilton laughed. "A nickel a drink? That's been tried twice in the last twenty years and it failed miserably. And how do you think you're going to get that through a Board that's 40% owned by the alcohol lobby and 60% pledged to never increase taxes?"

Nicole answered, "We've had some preliminary discussions that seem to suggest the votes might be there."

"Well, more power to you. If someone wants to take on the alcohol lobby, they're welcome to charge up that hill. And we'll see which of the emperors want to ride along with him."

Then he leaned forward and glared at both of them. "What I will not tolerate, however, is any more badgering of my agencies. They have suffered cut after cut from that bunch of . . ." He caught himself, and started again. "From the Board, which is fond of attacking my agency heads and then cutting their budgets. I'm close enough to retirement myself to tell you that I am not going to take that bullshit any more. I'm sick of the posturing. These agency heads have been trying to make things happen with budgets that we have been forced to cut *beneath* the bone, and I will not pretend any longer that this kind of posturing is acceptable."

Nicole said, "We understand, Dr. Hamilton, and that is why we've put the language in the report about needing more resources."

Sam decided he had pushed hard enough, and said, "Dr. Hamilton, if there is someone in your office that you'd like us to talk with to get an overview of how the agencies work together, we'd be glad to do that. Just let us know who you would like us to talk to."

Still glaring, Hamilton said, "Talk to whoever you want. My budget people understand what's been happening to these agencies, in some ways better than any of the agencies themselves." Then he calmed down, visibly working to control himself. "You should call Deborah Lowry and tell her I suggested you talk with her about agency budgets."

As they walked out to Nicole's car, Sam shook his head and said, "Pretty defensive—too bad he's mostly right."

Nicole said, "Yes, but you can tell he's had it with the attacks from the Board. Be sure to call Lowry. She's very good and she knows every line item in the budget forward and backward."

CHAPTER 33

The Desert

Joe gradually saw that Dolores was different somehow since she had come back from LA. She didn't tell him everything that had happened, but he knew she had gone to see El Jefe and had come away with some kind of assurance that he was no longer a target. He marveled at her guts and her connections with the Marines.

As he thought about what she had done, Joe envied Dolores having something he had never had: a family that backed her up without reservation. Since Esther's death, he had never had that kind of backup. For Dolores, he knew that it gave her a strength that he hoped she would be able to hang on to as she continued her own recovery.

But what was happening with Dolores was more than how she had handled the confrontation with Anaya. It was her ease and competence in dealing with Isabel, an ease that helped him understand how much he lacked the ability to provide the baby with anything like the care Dolores had given her.

He couldn't ask any more of Dolores than she had already given him. And he couldn't raise Isabel by himself. That left two options, Joe thought: *Drop her at a fire station—or bet on Luisa getting it together.*

He couldn't drop her off and walk away, knowing what he had learned about what might happen to her. And he also had to worry about her safety when he took her back—and his own. The bikers had been taken care of, and it looked like Dolores' trip to see Anaya had quieted things down. But there was still the police.

He had been reading the *Times* every day online, and had read about the search for Baby Isabel. The story also mentioned an investigation by a legal team headed by Nicole Larwin, who used to work for the DA. Larwin was looking into the role of all the agencies that were involved in the Baby Isabel situation. Someone named Sam Leonard had been hired to work with Nicole Larwin's firm on the investigation.

Joe started thinking about what that could mean to him—and to Isabel.

It was June and the desert was heating up. Dolores had bought a good thermometer and had logged the heat day by day on her calendar. It had already hit 100 for fifteen days in a row, but the August 110-plus days were still ahead. She had a supply of gasoline for her backup generator, but the solar panels were working well so far, and the AC was effective.

When Joe went outside for his morning walks, he was careful to take water in two canteens and a liter in his backpack. By 9 am the horizon had already begun to shimmer, which was his signal to head back to the mobile.

He never took Isabel out of sight of the mobile, and only in the earliest part of the morning, when it was still relatively cool. She seemed to like being outside, and when he picked her up in the morning for their porch-sitting sunrise, she would get excited and start kicking her legs. Joe noticed after a few weeks that her kicking was no longer random, but usually accompanied her being excited or dissatisfied about something.

They dressed her in lightweight outfits and sometimes just carried her around in a diaper and no shirt. Her hair was quite curly, and had begun to frame her face. Dolores had some photographic equipment she had bought in the PX, and took some beautiful shots of Isabel and Joe, Isabel and Sancho, and, with Joe's help, Isabel and Dolores.

Then Isabel became a talker, or at least a pre-talker. The startled cries that she'd make when she first got to Dolores' had given way to softer babbling, which grew more frequent when Joe or Dolores talked to her. She would begin making small popping sounds with her lips, which gradually turned into *buh, buh, buh* sounds. It was funny, and they ended up laughing when she would make the sounds and then stop, waiting for them to respond. When they did, she'd start up again, waving her tiny arms and looking at them and making the *buh, buh* sounds.

Dolores had brought a scale with her when she moved in. She told Joe that she worried about just sitting around gaining weight so she checked it regularly. It was accurate to a tenth of a pound, so they could keep an eye on Isabel's weight gain by weighing themselves and then picking her up. Isabel was up to twelve pounds, two ounces, which Dolores said was good, given where she had started out.

And Joe knew that they had done all they could for Isabel's health. He also knew that every day he stayed he was risking Dolores' health now.

CHAPTER 34

Supervisor Calver had been one of the "five emperors"—a label used by the media for the Board of Supervisors—for longer than any of the others. He had first been elected in the 1970s as a young reformer out of the Valley, an active Democrat. But over the years, his politics had centered and his contributions had multiplied. Now he was so well-funded that only relative unknowns cropped up every four years to give him token opposition. Sam and Joshua drove out to his district office in San Fernando to meet with Calver.

Calver's office was in a new building, and occupied an entire floor. Remarkably good-looking young assistants scurried around, and a receptionist took Sam and Joshua into an inner office. The door said Calver, A.S. in large ornate script. Calver's full name was Allan Stanley Calver.

Calver was a heavy-set man of average height, wearing his hair fashionably long. After the introductions, Calver asked, "So what have you been looking at?"

Sam said, "We've interviewed lots of agency people, some front-line staff, and some clients. We've been trying to get a handle on how the agencies work together, because the Baby Isabel case seems to be partly about how whether those connections work. We've also looked at the statements the Board has made over the years as various crises and problems have come up in the area of children's programs."

As Sam launched his questions, Joshua began handing him the relevant documents, not unlike a nurse handing a surgeon the right scalpel before the surgeon asks for it.

Calver frowned as Sam mentioned reviewing the Board's statements. "And what have you found?"

Sam paused, wondering how frontal he should be. He decided to go for the middle ground between soft and hard. "Year after year, some crisis comes into view—a kid is killed, an agency that works with kids gets caught misusing funds. And you guys consistently make statements about how things should be improved." He paused, watching Calver. "And the interesting thing is, when Joshua reviewed the agency budgets each of those years, there didn't seem to be much correlation between what your colleagues said and what the budget said."

Calver laughed, humorlessly. "You've been comparing the speeches with the spending."

"Exactly."

"Well, maybe my colleagues and I are guilty of rhetorical excess from time to time. But politics is partly about rhetoric, and we can't always back up our speeches with cash. You may have noticed there's been a depression going on in most state and local governments recently."

"We know. And agency people talked to us about the cuts that the Board has had to make. But no one has told us about any programs or interagency efforts that were given enough priority to exempt them from the cuts. The cuts were nearly all across the board—as if all the programs were equally important and worked equally well."

Calver said, "I would agree we should make smarter cuts. But you go around exempting one group from cuts and pretty soon everyone wants to be exempt."

Sam asked, "Isn't that what priority-setting is about? Isn't that the function of the Board?"

Glaring now, Calver snapped, "Well, I always appreciate folks coming in and telling me what the function of the Board is, Sam. And we do set priorities." Realizing that he was sounding angrier than he intended, Calver toned it down. "But tell me what you had in mind."

Sam went on. "A few years ago, one of the dozens of interagency advisory groups started looking at prenatal drug exposure. They pulled several agencies together, looked at federal laws and regulations, then took it to their policy group."

"What happened?" Calver asked.

"Absolutely nothing."

"Why?"

"No one would say on the record. But we were told some of the policy people said it was too messy, the hospitals wouldn't cooperate, women's groups didn't like the idea of expanded prenatal screening because it violated privacy. But the thing that struck us most was that no one in the discussion ever suggested taking it to the Board—to any of you."

"We get a lot of reports, Sam. But not everything comes to us."

"Of course not. But this was the hardest look at prenatal exposure that we any group had ever taken before—and it never came to the Board."

"Well, maybe it should have, and maybe it shouldn't. There's no way of knowing what we'd do about something like that until we see it. Too bad we didn't."

He paused, and then went on. "Sam, I know you know this. You've been a reporter, you've been around government. Each agency has its own constituency, its own workers, its own clients. Sure—they ought to work together more often. And there are some things we could do—some we've already done—to try to bridge those gaps better. But, Sam—and I know you won't quote me—the reality is that *no one gives a royal red rat's ass about coordination.*" His voice had become very intense, and his eyes were locked on Sam's. He went on, jabbing his finger down onto the table. "There aren't a hundred voters in this whole county who care about that stuff, and all the advisory commissions and everyone else who has been calling for better coordination over the years wouldn't know how to work an election to save their souls."

Sam was marveling at the depth of Calver's cynicism—and realism—when he realized that Joshua was asking a question.

"Then how do you make the system work better when it harms kids by its fragmentation?"

"Good question. Mr. Bronson. My question back to you is how do you pay for the staff it would take to make non-trivial changes in those systems?"

Sam decided to come back into the conversation. "A few times in our interviews the question of a county-based alcohol tax increase came up. You raised the tobacco tax by a buck and a half—why not raise alcohol a nickel a drink?"

Calver looked at him, silent. Then he spoke, slowly. "That idea would go nowhere."

Joshua glanced at a piece of paper. "You won last time by 20 points, Mr. Calver. Doesn't that give you some political capital to spend?"

Looking only at Sam, Calver smiled. "You're training a tough journalist here, Sam." Then he looked back at Joshua. "Maybe I do have room to make that proposal, Mr. Bronson. And maybe I could get another vote on the Board. But my chances of getting three votes are next to zero. There's a lot of beer and wine sold in this county."

Joshua wasn't backing off yet. "So are you saying you would consider supporting it?"

Calver said. "I might." And then he stopped talking, obviously hoping that he could finish the session.

Sam decided to try another tack. "In some of our interviews, agency staff told us that they get monitored for what they do separately—never for what they do together. Could the Board reinforce working across agencies by making that change?"

Calver said, "We've done some of that, I think. I know we set up a coordination unit in the CAO's office a while ago, and they have a fancy dashboard of information items that cut across agencies, and our staff look at that on a regular basis."

"But are there any measures of what the agencies do *together* that you monitor? And does anyone running an agency ever get graded on results they get by working with the other agencies?"

Calver said, "I'm not sure. Let me ask my staff about that and I'll get back to you."

They wrapped up then, as an aide came in and tapped her watch so that Sam and Joshua could see Calver nodding to her. Calver's final words were "Let me know if I can help you, gentlemen. Just let me know."

Walking out to the parking lot, Sam told Joshua, "That may have been the best political science course you ever took, kid."

Joshua said. "Yeah. But why do I feel like I need a bath?"

Sam laughed. "You probably didn't notice the staff. Quite a healthy-looking crew. And well-scrubbed."

Joshua smiled and said "Is healthy-looking your euphemism for incredibly well-endowed women and guys who look like they're all models?"

"Something like that. Politicians do tend to seek out and attract those kinds of people."

County Budget Office

Deborah Lowry, the CAO's budget chief, agreed to meet with Sam and Joshua in her office in the County Administration Building. Lowry was in her late forties, with short, curly hair and attractive features. Standing nearly six feet tall, she motioned them to chairs set around a small table in her office.

Sam explained that the CAO had urged them to meet with her and discuss their report. He assured her that all their interviews were off the record and that no one would be quoted. Sam added, "The CAO felt we might be somewhat unfair to the agencies."

She nodded. "Yes, he called me and told me about your meeting. Look, I'm not going to bore you with the numbers. I'll give you the latest budget," she gestured to a thick document on the table, "but the bottom line is that the county budget outlook sucks. So if Dr. Hamilton felt you were going after the agencies because they aren't doing something they should be, of course he's going to point out that most of them have had cuts of up to 25% in their core lines of business for the past three years. You can bang on them because they haven't gotten some of their main mission done, but you can't do it without pointing out what they've had to work with."

She pointed to a chart of the county organizational structure on her wall. "In some of those agencies we've got some first-rate managers, and we've got some duds, too. You can't reduce leadership to some easy formula, but if you could, I'd be willing to bet that one-third of those agency heads would be gone after the results came in."

Sam said, "We understand that. We've met with some outstanding staff, and some others who aren't that inspiring. What we're looking at is how well they connect with each other—whether they can put the pieces together for kids like that baby that was kidnapped."

Lowry said, "County government is a pretty fast track here, Mr. Leonard. But you still get some show horses and some agency heads who got their jobs by waiting everyone else out. And the budget stuff crushes all of them. They get rolling with some solid efforts to change things, and the ground gets cut out from under them. And something like this Baby Isabel thing comes along and everyone wonders whether this is just a few days' headlines or whether it is going to be a spotlight that won't go out for quite a while."

She was quiet for a moment, then said, "How well do they work together? Much of the time, they don't. Agencies usually see that as an extra—if the feds pay for it, or they can get a private grant, they'll do it. But it's not what they get scored on, so it's at the margins."

She smiled. "I get very few budget requests from one agency head for increases in another agency's budget."

Joshua asked, "What about new revenues?"

Lowry looked mildly surprised, and then asked, "You watch much TV? Not much call for more taxes these days."

Joshua persisted. "Some of the agency people talked about alcohol taxes, with the state letting the counties raise their own rates if they want to. Does that make any sense, given the effects of alcohol use on your budget?"

She looked at him carefully. Then she said "Interesting. Where do you get the votes for it? When that actor led the crusade for higher tobacco taxes in the 90's, he totally chickened out on going for alcohol taxes."

Sam responded. "Our interviews suggest there might be three votes for it. We're going to do some more probing. But does it make sense? The projections say a nickel a drink could produce as much as two hundred million for treatment and prevention."

Lowry kept looking at them with new interest. "Two hundred million. That would do some good. Of course, we'd try to plug budget holes with it. So you'd need some kind of maintenance of effort language. But it could help, if the votes were really there."

Sam marveled at her ability to see the flaws in the argument while agreeing with it at the same time. They talked further and she agreed to look at their report with an eye toward its budget implications.

As they were reviewing their notes at Sam's house in Orange, Sam received a call from Nate Rubin.

Rubin came straight to the point. "There's one more thing I needed to pass on to you guys." He hesitated, then continued. "I wasn't sure I would tell you, but I've been thinking about it, and it fills in some of the pieces."

Sam was quiet, well aware that whatever it was, it was bothering Rubin and he would tell it in his own way when he was ready. Then he asked, softly, "Do you want to tell us what it is? You're on speaker with Josh and me."

"I *have* to tell you. But first I have to ask you to protect the source. I heard this from a person who is easily identified, since there were only four people in the room when it happened."

Ever the journalist, Sam easily said, "Sure. We can figure out a way to conceal it—or get it from another source who confirms what you tell us." Then he shut up, waiting for Rubin to cross whatever line was bothering him.

Rubin sighed and said, "It goes to what we were talking about with the Board's hypocrisy. After one of the child killings last year, there was a big furor in the *Times* calling for action. So the Board voted for more money for DCW, to make sure they could monitor kids who were sent back home from foster care. Calver was the leader on it, and got most of the publicity. There was an editorial commending him for his leadership."

He went on, and Sam could hear the anger in his voice. "And when it came time to actually move the money, two weeks later, after the furor had blown over, Calver put a hold on it. He did it in a closed budget subcommittee meeting, and he did it in a way that made it look like they'd given DCW new funds, but then they took the same amount away in the personnel line—so they really got nothing."

Joshua couldn't help himself. "What a phony."

Rubin said "Yeah. Look, the way to handle this is to go to the budget staff and ask them if the increase was offset anywhere else in the budget. I guess you could tell them that you noticed it as you were going through the budget. See, the person I'm trying to protect is a staff guy who was so disgusted at what Calver had done that he passed the story on to me, hoping I could do something about it. But I didn't—until now."

When Sam called Deborah Lowry in the budget office to confirm the story, she was quick to admit it—and Sam even got the impression that she was glad to get the real story out.

CHAPTER 35

For their final interview, Sam and Joshua had decided to try to get some historic perspective on the problems they had been wrestling with in their interviews. A professor at Cal State Fullerton, Alex McMorris, had been mentioned by a few of the interviewees as someone who had written about interagency coordination throughout his career. They set up an appointment and drove down to Fullerton to meet with him.

California State University, Fullerton Department of Public Administration

McMorris was in his late 60's, tall, with a full head of white hair, glasses that he wore low on his nose, and Dodgers pennants all over his walls.

Sam chuckled and gestured at the pennants. "Thought this was Angels territory, Professor."

"Never, Mr. Leonard. Been a Dodgers fan since the days when I was at Occidental and we could get in free after the 7th inning. Made a great study break, only ten minutes away. Today they'd probably run us off. Great team, great history, but these days it's all about the bottom line."

"Yes, sir. Go Blue." Sam opened the interview by saying, "As you know, we've been looking into the ways that agencies in the county work together on problems like the Baby Isabel case. And we understand you've been studying coordination issues for a long time. We thought you might give us some deeper context for these connections and the problems they bring."

McMorris sighed and said, "Well, the first thing is to nail down some of the language. We used to call it "coordination" in the mid-60s, when the federal government first realized that having several hundred programs all trying to make cities better and end poverty might not be the most efficient way to go about it. Then

173

in the 70's they called it "services integration." "Collaboration" had a long ride, and recently some are calling it "interoperability." But whatever you call it, it's damned hard—and damned important."

He went on, watching them to gauge their interest in his history lesson. "The armed services have been trying to accomplish their own kind of services integration since 1947—and they admit they still have a long ways to go. You see, gentlemen, we are in the middle of a war between two great trends—the trend to specialize and the trend to synthesize. We are great at deconstructing things—atoms, literature, our politics—those things, we divide and subdivide like crazy. But at the same time, we are great re-assemblers and integrators: biophysics, neurochemistry, psychohistory. These are fields that used to have their books and disciplines all to themselves, and now they get smashed together. So now, it's how well they fit together that determines whether we can make sense of them, not how well we can fragment them.

"So getting agencies to work together is riding the tide in one way, and going uphill in another—to mix my metaphors a bit. Now, I've read a bit about your Baby Isabel, and it seems to me that this problem of prenatal drug exposure is a near-classic example of a problem that doesn't belong to any one agency. So it has to belong to lots of agencies who aren't very good at sharing problems."

Joshua spoke up. "That's sure what we've been hearing, Professor. They're great at pointing fingers, not so good at sharing responsibility."

"Agreed." He leaned back, watching them to make sure he didn't veer off into a dry lecture. "Gentlemen, here are the few lessons I would hope you consider in your report. I've spent lots of years trying to make sense of this. First, coordination isn't real unless it's driven by the customers—by what kids and families need. It isn't about what the agencies want to coordinate, it's what the kids and families need so *they* can make sense out of it. Second, don't waste any time on symbolic coordination crap that is just bloody meetings for the sake of meetings. Years ago, I learned a great State Department acronym: BOGSAT. Bunch of guys sitting around a table. Useless! Coordination isn't meetings—it's results, and if you can't measure whether you get better results by working across agency lines—stop wasting time in dumb meetings where everyone just talks about what they did last month and no one mentions whether the customers are better off."

He jabbed the table, full of intensity. "It's not what the agencies are doing—it's whether kids and families are doing *better.*"

"Third, if the budget guys don't believe in it, it will all become token and symbolic, and it will quickly lose credibility with the front-line people. Figure out if coordinated services work better— and get agencies to agree that they'll measure what happens to those customers that they hand off to each other, instead of washing their hands once they make a referral." He paused. "Know what a referral is, gentlemen?"

Joshua knew a rhetorical question when he heard it, and asked, "No, Professor. What's a referral?"

"A referral is bloody *malpractice,* Mr. Bronson. If all you're doing for your customers is giving them a phone number to call someone else, you are engaged in malpractice, not collaboration. And it is profoundly unethical to do that to people who need help from you—to people you are being paid to help."

He visibly calmed down, and they could see that the referral game was one of his real hot buttons. "Fourth, the people who really run the government have to believe in coordination, or it won't happen." He paused, waiting to see if they would ask the obvious question.

So Sam asked, "And those people are . . . ?"

"Purchasing—the contracts office. Government buys a lot more these days than it does itself, and so the contracts you write have to reinforce coordination, or everyone will just work down the same old vertical silos. And then the contracts will merely reinforce fragmentation."

Joshua had been writing furiously, even though McMorris had given them permission to tape him.

"Fifth: Someone said that information and water will be the most important commodities in the 21st century, and so far it's looking like that's right. What private companies can find out about us these days is enormous, and unprecedented. The Amazon and Barnes and Noble online stores know every book I've bought for the last decade. The public sector has got to catch up. These agencies could have known about Baby Isabel before she was born. Now I know there are civil liberties folks who worry a lot about privacy, and every one of these agencies has someone who is poised to yell 'confidentiality!' as soon as they try to share data on their clients. But we could save a lot more of these kids if we just put what we already know about them in one place. You've read the horror stories about the county agencies whose workers had PDAs with client data but didn't have the wireless connections to access any of it. There's no excuse for that."

McMorris gestured to a whiteboard on the wall with a set of flow diagrams. "Here's the deal on information systems. The private sector and the defense intelligence people, actually, have developed software that will let almost anything talk to anything else. Data matching used to be tricky, but when you're combing through billions of phone calls looking for keywords in a hundred languages and codes—you have to know how to search and put pieces together. So the tools are there, whether you agree with their use or not.

"But our agencies might as well be in the 19th century when it comes to using cross-systems data. They have some of this software, but they've rarely using it at its maximum capability. The health people in the private sector are much further along, because it costs money when you order too many tests of the same person or prescribe medicines that are incompatible. Eventually somebody gets a lawyer—no insult intended to your sponsors—and the lawyer sues the hell out of you. So they are getting much better at finding people across different systems. "Interoperability" is the new phrase, and it's something the human services need a lot more of, for all the privacy issues it raises. But most counties are doing it mostly for billing—not to find these little kids as they wander across different systems."

He paused, and smiled. "Lecture almost over. Sorry, I go on a bit sometimes, but this matters, as you know.

"Finally, there has to be some leadership somewhere. Collaboration is not just equals sitting around looking at each other. Someone has to care about it enough to put their name on it and to have good staff reporting to them on what is happening— and what isn't. Often, gentlemen, it's what collaboratives don't do that's more important than what they do. A lot of them don't measure their results, don't talk about the underlying values that they disagree about, and don't pool their resources beyond token out-stationing of a few workers in a few pilot projects. If collaboration is what we do only when the feds pay for it—it isn't very important. Leadership means going after the real money, and that means redirecting the funding already here, not new federal grants."

Sam asked "You've looked at the county over the years. What are the chances that they can get their act together and work across agencies more effectively?"

"I'd give it a one in three chance. Maybe better, if you guys write a tougher-than-usual report and the leadership of the county feels like it has to respond with something more than a one-day press release."

Sam smiled. "Those aren't very good odds."

"Mr. Leonard, I know your work and I admire the hell out of what you did in Mexico. If you write a kick-ass report, with the help of your young sidekick here, those odds might get better. Might make a nice bookend with the work that got you that Pulitzer."

"Thanks—I think."

Then Joshua surprised Sam by challenging McMorris. "Professor, when we met with Supervisor Calver, he seemed awfully skeptical about what you've been talking about. He said, if I remember right, that 'no one gives a royal red rat's ass about coordination.' How would you answer him?"

McMorris laughed. 'That's the kind of pungent language politicians can use and that's forbidden to academics." Then he was silent for several moments, thinking how best to respond. "He's right that you'll never win an election, or get many votes, based on a stirring call to coordination. Mario Cuomo said it all when he said 'we campaign in poetry, but we govern in prose.' The coordination work is prose at its most painful: protocols and memos of understanding, unique identifiers and negotiated interagency outcomes. The data people make it real, when they mash together what two agencies do for the same families. But they can rarely make it interesting. But let me go back to my first point—it makes a big difference for a kid or a family when you realize that they don't walk in the front door of the agency with a single problem painted on their forehead. What you two have been doing is about drugs, in part, and the treatment people have this awful term that means a lot: co-occurring disorders. They did a study in Illinois a while back and found that 92% of the clients with substance abuse problems were also coping with mental illness, domestic violence, and crappy housing. Fix one of those, and you've done next to nothing. Try to fix all of them—and you're wading deep in the swamps of coordination."

He paused again, making sure they were following him. "The school reform people have had a lot of trouble understanding this, most of them. From birth to high school graduation, kids are actually in school about 9% of their lives. And for at least a third of the kids, something powerful has to happen out there in the other 91% of the time to make a real difference in the classroom. So you can't just blame the schools—or the teachers."

He smiled and then said, "So what I would say to Supervisor Calver is voters may not care about coordination, but anybody who cares about kids had better pay attention, or they're just doing symbolic work that misuses scarce money. And they're wasting it at a time when we can no longer afford it."

As they stood up to leave, Joshua noticed two quotes McMorris had placed on his wall amidst the Dodger paraphernalia. He read them and then asked McMorris if he could have a copy. McMorris handed him a book and said, "They're in there." He added, "Thanks for what you're doing. You're asking the right questions, and that's more than half the battle, I've found."

The quotes were

I found that the entrepreneurial spirit producing innovation is associated with a particular way of approaching problems that I call "integrative": the willingness to move beyond received wisdom, to combine ideas from unconnected sources, to embrace change as an opportunity to test limits. To see problems integratively is to see them as wholes, related to larger wholes, and thus challenging established practices—rather than walling off a piece of experience and preventing it from being touched or affected by any new experiences.

Rosabeth Moss Kanter, *The Change Masters*

"I never could stomach these nationalists," Merlin exclaimed. "The destiny of Man is to unite, not divide. If you keep on dividing, you end up as a collection of monkeys throwing nuts at each other out of separate trees."
T.H. White, *The Once and Future King*

Sam drove back, and as they came onto the 57, Joshua said, "That was incredible. What a resource."

"Old guys rule, kid."

"Yeah. Sometimes." He was quiet for a while, and then asked, "So are we going to write a kickass report, Sam?"

"Josh, writing is the all-night party. Editing is the morning after. Now it's time for the morning after."

Over the next four days, fueled by an excess of both caffeine and cigars, Sam drafted a first cut at the full report from their notes and his earlier drafts. Joshua added a section on the interviews he had done with county line staff and the interviews with former foster youth. Then Sam drove off up Highway 395 to his favorite writing spot, a friend's home looking out over the Sierra at June Lake. He edited, sent drafts to Josh, edited some more, napped, watched the sun drop down behind Carson Peak a few times, and then drove back to Orange, tired and deeply gratified at the work he had been given to do.

They finished the draft and emailed it to Nicole. Then they decided to celebrate with a dinner at the Orange Hill Restaurant, high on a small hill overlooking Orange and much of central Orange County.

CHAPTER 36

Law office

Sam and Joshua walked into Nicole's office, late in the afternoon. She had asked them to stop by after her appointments so they could go over the report.

"Sit down, guys." Nicole tapped the report on her desk. "Pretty powerful stuff."

"You said you wanted the real deal."

"Yes, I did. And I got it." Then she laughed. "Tell me why you put in the section about elected double-talk."

"We thought you might want to talk about that."

"Oh, yes. Look, I'm going to go to bat for this report, and I think we'll get some good media coverage. But I need a solid defense against the pushback from the politicians."

Sam began to answer her. "You know who we talked to—you saw the list. All the people you suggested, and a lot of others as well. And most of them told us about their agency, and about the resources they had, or didn't have. But very few of them ever talked about the elected officials in the county. It's as though they exist on a different plane, so far removed from the agency world that it doesn't even occur to most of them to pressure the Board for action. And all the advisory groups and advocacy groups buzz around and issue reports. But none of them ever holds the Supervisors responsible when things go wrong. It's always 'bang on the agency' time. The Supervisors are mostly exempt from any of that pressure."

"The five emperors," Nicole said.

Sam went on to give her the outlines of the story Rubin had given them about Calver intervening to cut the budget in secret. When she asked if that would be in the report, Sam said "Not yet. We may need to use it as a bargaining chip."

Nicole's eyebrows went up, but she could see from Sam's face that she shouldn't yet ask any questions on that point.

Joshua joined in. "We spent some time looking at budget hearings and what the agencies asked for and what the Board finally gave them. We also reviewed four of the recent media storms after a kid died." He grimaced. "It's pretty disheartening. The Board members posture, issue press releases, talk about the agency failures and how important kids are—and then they cut the budget and ignore the data that the agency and the CAO keep sending to them."

"All right. Let's leave the double-talk reference in. Let me talk about the content." She picked up her copy of the draft report, which Sam could see had dozens of comments written in the margin. "The conclusions have got to be more than 'things are fragmented.' 'We need more coordination,' or 'we need a strategic plan.' All true—but all same old, same old."

Sam responded, "We've got three main themes, Nicole. We talk about accountability, legal changes, and taking prenatal drug exposure seriously. The end of the executive summary tries to nail each of these down so that what's new jumps out, instead of being buried in a long list of 'gotta do's.' If we don't do that, the agencies will just come back with a long list of 'gonnas'—what they're *going* to do."

He handed her a one-page summary. Then he added, "There was no villain, Nicole. You knew there wouldn't be. There were just lots of people, some very sharp, some not so sharp, who rarely saw their job as going outside their boxes." He paused, frowning. "It would all be very boring and bureaucratic—except it's really about babies, and not just the boxes that agencies hide in."

She took the summary, read it quickly, and nodded. "Let me be a cynic for a minute—or a member of the Board. But I repeat myself." She waited for their half-laugh, and went on. "This is just another plan, some more projects, better oversight. I give it one chance out of three. Maybe four."

Sam laughed. "We got those same odds from the professor at Cal State Fullerton whom we talked to." He leaned back in his chair, gathering his arguments. "Well, maybe—you seem a little pessimistic to me. But even given those odds—what are the odds of the status quo making things better?" He kept his tone reasonable, knowing that she was giving them good feedback in the midst of her tough questions.

"None—and I agree with you on that. We'll take the shot, Sam. But I'm trying to figure out what will improve the odds. Somehow we've got to make this more than one more report. You guys have done a great job, but I need to figure out how to get a real push behind this. Let me think about it and catch up with you later in the week."

After they left, Nicole spent some time laying out her options on a legal pad. She could go to the DA and try to convince him to bring formal charges against the agencies. She knew that would be a tough sell, because picking on the agencies didn't make any friends, and what they had done in the Baby Isabel case was less important that what they hadn't done. She could go for hearings at the Board of Supervisors, but as Sam had pointed out, that was likely to lead to more grandstanding and little action.

Then she began to think about the grand jury. In California, the grand jury has a role that goes beyond reviewing indictments for criminal behavior. Each county grand jury had the option of picking a topic of governmental performance and doing a year-long report. Some of the reports turned a bright spotlight on problems, and a few actually resulted in getting something done. One of the adjacent California counties had done an excellent report on prenatal substance abuse several years ago that Sam had referenced in his report. And a report by the local grand jury on the probation department had eventually led to a federal civil rights investigation that had shaken things up a lot.

The grand juries tended to be made up of retired professionals who had the time and interest to spend hour after hour during a twelve-month period going over reports and testimony. The more Nicole thought about it, the more she thought the grand jury might be the best way to get some action. So she started drafting her recommendations.

Nicole had put together what she called her "A team"—Sam, Joshua, and Millie Parkinson, a colleague from her law firm who handled media relations for the firm. Millie and Nicole had become close friends after a minor blow-up in the firm over how female partners were being treated. During the conflict, they had both taken some risks and won a change in promotion policies for women. Millie was a few years older than Nicole, a short, elective blonde, with a face that was usually smiling, even when she came out with the raunchy language she had learned working in a US Senator's office for ten years.

Millie sat reading Sam's summary. She looked up at Nicole, frowning, and said, "So they're all to blame. That's no headline. And it's not much of a case in court." She softened her words by smiling at Sam and Joshua, and said "There's some great stuff in there, guys. I'm just looking out for the PR side."

Sam nodded, but before he could respond, Nicole shot back, "It isn't about headlines, it's about kids."

Millie said, "Thank you, Crusader Rabbit. But after your slogans, what have you got, Nicole? And how are we going to get something done that makes a difference? This baby comes back sooner or later, the kid goes to jail, things get back to normal. So how can we use this to get something done?"

"We need to release this report and turn on every spotlight we can find. And we need to make clear that the Board of Supervisors is where the buck stops."

She knew she was playing a hand with some missing cards. But she got up, went over to the window in the conference room where they were meeting, and looked down at the street below. She saw a woman pushing a baby stroller slowly up the street toward a discount store. And she wheeled around and said "Millie, we aren't going to do it the usual way. I've fought to do this right for three months, and I have to tell you just issuing a press release is not the way to do it."

"So how are you going to do it, hotshot?"

Sam, watching the interplay between the two women, knew that he should stay quiet.

Nicole closed her eyes, put her hands together in front of her face, as if to pray, and then stared at all of them with as strong a look as she could muster. "We have uncovered a pattern of negligence that is harming thousands of kids. And it goes all the way up to the politicians, and so we need to have the guts to say it. They promised to do something about all this, and then they cut the budget when no one was looking and ignored what they knew was going wrong until the next kid died.

"I've read the Board's oversight hearings for the last five years. They're a *joke*. If I lost this job and had to go teach somewhere, I'd like to teach politicians how to use budget hearings to do their jobs better. It's simple. You ask a question one year, they write it down and ignore you. You ask it the next year, they see you're serious, then you ask it the third year—and finally you get some action. And none of them have ever done that. They jump around and pontificate when the cameras are on and then they go off to the next fundraiser and kiss some more butt."

Millie was still frowning, but listening. "So what do you want? We release this thing and go after the Supes, and there's going to be a firestorm." She knew that Nicole would not be pressing this hard if she didn't think she had a very strong follow-up.

"That's right. And that firestorm is going to make it very hard for politics as usual to win the day. Millie," she said, gesturing to Sam and Joshua who sat mute, "these guys are very good. I went with them because I wanted the toughest report I could get. Sam has a Pulitzer, for God's sake. And they've uncovered more in a few weeks of digging than we've ever had on the table before. We've been going one by one with these agencies—when it's all of them. And that's what this report says."

"Tell me what you think should happen, Nicole." She looked at Sam and Joshua. "You guys can join in, you know."

Sam quickly said, "We intend to. For now," he said with a smile, "we're just basking in Nicole's praise."

The half-joke lightened things up a bit. Nicole took a deep breath. She had thought a long time about the answer to this question. "I want five things. First, we need a special committee of the Board to react to this report. If they just send it off to the CAO, they'll produce reams of paper and it'll all be forgotten."

Millie and Sam nodded; Joshua stayed unmoving. Nicole went on. "Second, I want to go to Judge Nakai and ask him to demand an annual report from all of these agencies, with specific benchmarks on all the data our report says is missing—drug-exposed births, referrals for developmental assessments, whether parents actually get into treatment and how long they stay there. A real dashboard focused on these babies, like the report suggests, something we can use as a scorecard every year on whether programs are doing their job.

"And third, we need to set out a new legal standard for child welfare cases. We've been using this vague 'reasonable efforts' standard for years, which basically means give the parents a shot at getting their kids back, but with no requirements for what the agencies have to do to make it real. We need to show the judge how to go from reasonable efforts to a standard of reasonable *effectiveness*—to make sure these programs work for parents who are trying to get their act together. We've got to break this pattern of just starting up new, tiny programs every time there's a new crisis. We've got to get out of what the report calls the 'pilot project syndrome.' "

Millie said, "Let's get some of the legal research team from the firm to take a look at that. Nicole quickly responded. "I've already had the interns do it—we think we can make it fly."

Millie, shaking her head, said "I have no doubts about your guys, but I want to make sure the firm will back you. Let's run it by a couple of the partners who deal with the County."

"OK, if you want." Nicole went on, looking down at her list. "Fourth, I think we should take the report to the grand jury and try to get them to pick this as one of the topics they're going to work on for the next year. We issue this, and we have a two or three day media splash."

Millie interrupted, "At best. Maybe one day."

"Right. And then it's over. But if the grand jury spends time on this, their report will keep it alive, and let the agencies and the Board know this is not going to go away.

"And fifth, I want to propose legislation for a new county alcohol tax to pay for all this. The state has authorized county add-ons to alcohol taxes, because they figured they were never going to get a statewide increase. We tax alcohol lower than almost any state, because the wine and alcohol lobbies are so powerful. So let's go for it in the county."

Millie sighed. "That's a broader agenda, for sure. I just don't know if we can sex it up enough to make it seem like a campaign instead of a dry government document." Then she wagged her finger at Nicole. "But listen, Nicole. Every political instinct I have tells me you need to line up some support or this is going to be one or two days worth of headlines, and then it'll sink like a rock."

Josh finally spoke up. "And what about the workers? And what about the moms and the kids?"

Nicole, irritated that he had added something not on her list but grudgingly wondering if he had a good point, asked, "What are you proposing?"

"The report says that the front-line workers have caseloads far beyond their ability to keep a close eyes on the kids left at home—and on kinship placements. What if some of the new money went to lower caseloads? And what if some of it was set aside for college scholarships for older kids aging out of foster care—kids who go to college at much lower rates than other high school graduates?"

Sam added, "It humanizes your action list, Nicole, adds something for people instead of all the other stuff. As important as a dashboard and the legal changes are, they sound like bureaucratic mumbo-jumbo. Josh is right, this puts the people most affected back into the short list."

Nicole quickly answered, "Which is now a longer list. But you're right. Thanks, that's a good add."

Josh smiled at her, with an expression that seemed to say *You really ought to take me more seriously, you know.* And Nicole filed her reaction away for future reference.

CHAPTER 37

Judge Nakai was old-school, and he was tough. Nicole had brought cases before him several times, and had won more than she lost, but she had needed to go out to the edge of assertiveness, and he was very sensitive to his judicial prerogatives. She had called and asked for a chance to brief him on the report before it was released.

Nicole was shown into the Judge's chambers when she arrived. It was noon, and he was eating a salad. His office was modestly furnished, with a Western landscape on one wall and two prints that Nicole assumed were Japanese on the other wall. There were no pictures other than a small framed photo of the Judge with what looked like three generations of Nakais.

The Judge showed her to a table and offered her some salad. She politely declined, and began.

"Judge, I wanted this meeting to explain why we aren't bringing a formal case and why we're taking the approach we will be recommending in our report."

Nakai raised a hand and carefully said, "Be careful of our boundaries on *ex parte*, Miss Larwin. If you anticipate that any actions from this report may reach my court, we should not be having this conversation."

"Your Honor, I'm hoping this conversation will be primarily concerning your role as the presiding judge rather than your role in any one case. We are proposing a somewhat novel approach to reasonable efforts, and I wanted you to know before the report is issued what we are doing and why. Two of the recommendations, Your Honor, bear upon how child welfare cases in general are pursued and how the outcomes of those cases are assessed by the court system."

"Very well. Proceed."

She filled him in on the background of the Baby Isabel child welfare case, including the involvement of the several agencies that were involved or could have been. She explained that she had decided not to bring any formal action against any county agencies. Then she went on to describe what the report would say.

"The first change we are proposing is a shift from reasonable efforts to reasonable *effectiveness.*"

His quizzical look made her hasten to get to the second issue. "The second is to measure that effectiveness differently than we now do, by providing an annual report by your Court that summarizes the outcomes of treatment for all parents in the child welfare system or with positive tox screens at birth who were referred to treatment programs. The two concepts are linked by the need to determine a reasonable effectiveness standard as it would apply in any one case based on much better information about how well agencies do on *all* of their cases."

She watched his reaction, but he was not revealing anything yet.

She continued, "At this point, Your Honor, there is no valid answer to the question of how many child welfare clients have substance abuse problems. Everyone says "70-80%," but there is absolutely no set of numbers collected in this county that can document that. In fact, the state has actually reported to the feds for years that only 4% of all removals to foster care are based on parental substance abuse. That's the lowest figure in the country— Oregon reported 66%."

Nakai scoffed. "4%—that's ridiculous."

"Yes, sir, it is, But it's also a diagnostic of how bad our data is. And just as bad as not knowing that overall number is that we don't have an answer to the second question: how well do treatment agencies in the county do in serving child welfare parents?"

Nakai responded, "Well, yes, that would be good to know. But what does that have to do with this idea of reasonable effectiveness?"

"Judge, bear with me. I apologize for going through some ancient history, but we have to go back to *Brown v Board of Education* to understand these issues."

"What on earth does this have to do with segregation, Miss Larwin?"

"Your Honor, that case was decided on the law, but the plaintiffs rested a major part of their arguments on social science. Many studies had proven that segregated education had harmful effects on black children. Ken and Mamie Clark showed how segregation affected those children's mental status—the pictures of themselves that they carried around in their heads. We've all read about the doll tests that were used, with black kids choosing white dolls because they were 'better.' The social science affected the law, by showing that harm was being done by segregated schools."

She went on, seeing Nakai nod. "We all learned about footnote 11 in law school, the summary of the social science that led to the overturning of *Plessy*. Footnote 11—where the Court had to pay attention to social science."

"All true, all good legal history, Miss Larwin, but where are you trying to take me?"

"Right up to *today's* social science, Your Honor. We have twenty years of evidence—the term of art is evidence-based practice—that uses scientific methods to determine which social programs are effective and which are merely well-intentioned. When a judge tells a parent that a life-altering decision—terminating her parental rights forever—will result if she doesn't get into drug treatment and stop using drugs, we are assuming that the critical factors are her access to treatment and her willingness to stay in treatment until she completes it. But, Judge, we now have reams of studies that show that not all treatment is equal. Some treatment programs use evidence-based practices, and some definitely don't. And so when we accept the federal law's requirement that the state make reasonable efforts to keep that parent with that child, it will be our position that we are required to do all we can to make those efforts *effective*. We cannot simply hand a parent a referral slip and say go get sober unless we know we are sending her to a program that will give her a reasonable chance of success."

She paused, and added, "I know you're familiar with the recent state action against several treatment programs that were over-billing for cases they took."

Nakai asked, "So you are trying to take us beyond reasonable efforts—which is the law. But where do you want us to go? And how can we go there if the law stops at reasonable efforts?"

"With respect, Your Honor, the law stopped at *Plessy* before the *Brown* decision. But if we are making these fundamental decisions about parents' rights, and we know that some of the programs where we send parents just aren't effective—we need a new standard. A standard of reasonable *effectiveness*."

"But what does that mean?"

"It means that we need to have a reasonable expectation that the programs we send people to will be successful with parents who do their part—who enroll, stay in the program, and comply with the program. There is no absolute guarantee, Judge. Even great programs can't make up for some parents' lack of motivation. We've learned a lot about parents' motivations, and their readiness for treatment—whether they really want to stop using and get their act together. They have a disease, but like diabetics and people with hypertension, they need to take the medicine that reduces the effects of the disease. That's what we can expect and demand of them. But what we can expect of ourselves and the programs we fund and refer parents to is that those agencies should be just as responsible for compliance with proven methods as parents are compliant with staying in treatment. Otherwise we are asking them to take medicine that won't work."

Nakai sat still in his chair, hands folded on his desk, never taking his eyes off of her, listening intently. Nicole tried to keep the flow going.

"Let me read you a quote from one of the clients that Sam Leonard and his assistant interviewed. She really nailed it." She reached over to one of the piles of papers she had spread out on her side of the table and began reading. '*I've got to do my part. Right.*

But only me? Yeah? So what about you guys with all these programs and all the money that goes into these programs? When is it that you have to do your part? The judge wants to hold me responsible—fine. I'm responsible. But aren't any of you responsible, too?"

She went on. "Finally, on this point, we have some indications that advocacy groups are likely to raise this issue in the near future. They read the statistics also, and they know that referrals are being made to the kinds of agencies that have been getting much closer looks from auditors lately. Sooner or later the mis-billing and the ineffectiveness problems may bump into each other, and advocates are likely to use that to press for more oversight and more emphasis on resources for the best agencies, instead of demanding that all the agencies be funded regardless of their track records."

Nicole stopped reading and looked at Nakai. She had talked a lot, and she had pushed him. She had carefully studied his decisions on significant cases and she knew he had a lower reversal rate than any judge in the County. Asking him to advance the interpretation of reasonable efforts as far as she was doing meant she was asking him to take a sizable risk.

But she also knew that Nakai was 69, and had spoken with other judges about retirement. And her gamble was that he would consider the possibility that he could mark the end of his career with a major step forward, a capstone that would be remembered long past his many routine cases.

Five years before, Nakai had given the annual address to the county bar association. In it, Nicole had read, he had spoken at length about judicial responsibility to take note of what was happening in the larger society "beyond the legal box," as he put it. The speech was not only a thoughtful response to the "originalists" who attacked judges for making new law. It was also a plea for a wider lens, a longer view past isolated cases to the social currents that ran beneath the law.

Now Nakai leaned forward and said, "I'm going to think about what you've said, Miss Larwin, which is what you wanted me to do when you walked in here. I will see how your report makes your case for this 'reasonable effectiveness' doctrine. Perhaps you're right. Perhaps we have relied too long on a narrow interpretation of reasonable efforts. And maybe the social science you cite has something to tell us. I will listen. Now tell me about the second part—this annual report you are recommending."

"Thank you, Your Honor." She took a deep breath and went on. "You and the other judges and DCW send parents to these agencies to get parent education, drug treatment, mental health treatment—and then you decide whether they get their kid back or you terminate their parental rights to that kid. I know you know this, Your Honor—but that's a life-changing decision. You are permanently changing that kid's life, either way."

Nakai sat with his hands folded, unmoving. Nicole kept building the case, only occasionally glancing at her notes. "But no one adds it all up. No one counts which agencies helped parents, which had dropouts, which ones did a better job than other agencies with the same kinds of families in their caseloads. Some agencies do it on the cheap so they can get county business when the purchasing office funds contracts based on the lowest unit cost. Others get funding from dozens of different sources, so they can supplement the county funding and provide a much richer program with much deeper dosage of services for the parents and their kids. But there's no measuring stick, no baselines against which those agencies are compared each year. That's what the report recommends, that the presiding judge ask for an annual report on all the cases where kids were removed, assessing how the agencies performed in serving the parents referred to them."

Nakai said, still frowning, "These are very difficult parents to serve, Miss Larwin. The success rates in some of these programs are not very high. It's not just about the agencies. As you've noted, it's also about these parents' addiction, and the violence and trauma in their own lives. You can't just blame the agencies."

Nicole said, "That's right, Your Honor, and the report says that. For some of these programs, a 15% success rate is great, because the families they are trying to help don't want it or can't accept it—or just don't show up. A third or more of the parents don't even show up at the first detention hearing. But that's why it's so important to get accurate performance data out there. An agency that makes 30% when the baseline is 15% is doing a great job. But when some agencies claim a 80% success rate because they don't start counting until the client finishes the program—it's smoke and mirrors data. That's what an annual report would do. It would cut through all the agencies' hype to force them to measure what they do against a common benchmark. And the judges would have a better handle on how well these agencies are doing their part of the job."

Nakai frowned and then said, "As I said, I'll look at the recommendations in the report. I can see some value in asking for an annual review of what they're doing in more depth than what we do now. That makes sense to me. But I'm making no commitments beyond that."

Then he leaned forward and asked, "Are you talking to the Board about any of this? They spout off about the lousy job the agencies are doing and then they turn around and cut their budget and fire the agency head every time there's a crisis. Is the Board part of this?"

"Yes, Your Honor. We've talked to Calver and Marvin, and we're going to talk with Berenson. The report will be very blunt about their pattern of big talk and little follow-through with funding. We agree that the Board's role is critical."

"Very well. Keep me posted on what you're doing. And I appreciate your bringing this to me in advance of the report." Nakai stood up and for the first time in the meeting, smiled at Nicole.

As she walked out to her car, Nicole felt she had done well enough to be able to tell the team and Millie that Nakai was briefed and potentially supportive. That was all she could hope for at this point.

CHAPTER 38

County Grand Jury conference room

The next day, Nicole finished the preparations for her presentation to the grand jury, which had been sworn in for its year of duty only three weeks before. She had reduced Sam and Joshua's report to a five-page summary and a Powerpoint with highlights. The challenge was convincing a sub-committee of seven members that the Baby Isabel case was a window into much larger issues.

As she walked into the grand jury room, she saw a group of four men and three women, ethnically diverse and all appearing to be in their sixties and seventies. The foreman, a Latina, introduced herself as Marina Ortegon, and invited Nicole to begin.

She took about twenty minutes to make her presentation, and concluded by asking for questions. The first was from the foreman.

"I think you've convinced us that this is an important issue, Miss Larwin. But it also sounds like a very big issue that could end up taking all of our time for most of our year. Do you think we can get staff to help us with this?"

Nicole said, "I would advise you to ask the agencies for some of their best people to work with you. We can give you a list of the staff who were most helpful during our interviews. I'm sure that some outside experts such as Dr. Chervoussian should also be glad to make themselves available."

The next question was from a white-haired man who had been frowning during most of the presentation. "From what you've said, I gather these agencies have had a difficult time getting their act together. What do you think we can do that would make a difference?"

Nicole answered, "As you know, grand jury reports are taken seriously and covered by the media. So I think . . ."

The man interrupted her. "So our report gets one day of headlines. Then what?"

Nicole calmly resumed, "Then, I would hope, the Board of Supervisors would review your recommendations and . . ."

He interrupted again. "But they already have the recommendations of the report you've given us in summary form here today. What more can we say that isn't already in the report?"

The foreman, with some irritation, said, "Mr. Boggs, perhaps you could let Miss Larwin finish what she is trying to say."

Nicole smiled and said "Thank you. I'm confident that if an impartial group with an overview of the entire county government were to agree or disagree with the recommendations of the report prepared by Mr. Leonard and his assistant, the Board would take that very seriously and move to adopt some or all of the recommendations." She paused and decided to go back to a point she had tried to make in her presentation.

"The most valuable part of your role could be your ability to look beyond individual agencies to the pattern of fragmentation that Mr. Leonard described as the problem. As the report makes clear, there were more than a dozen agencies that had some impact on Isabel Contreras' life—or should have. This is not a report about one agency that isn't doing well—it's about an entire pattern of agencies that aren't working together as well as they should. It affects more than 20,000 babies born each year in this county. Your reactions to those conclusions could affect thousands of children and their families."

Boggs was not yet convinced, sitting with his arms crossed and leaning back in his chair. But Nicole could see nods around the table.

Then an African-American woman spoke up. "I was a nurse at USC Hospital for thirty years. I saw so many of those sad little creatures I started to believe it was normal." Her voice got strained and she had a very sad look on her face. "But it *isn't* normal, and if something we do in this committee could make any difference at all, I'm for it."

Nicole decided to wrap up and let them debate it among themselves. "Thanks for listening, and I want to assure you that my staff and I are available if you have any further questions as you review the report. I hope you'll consider taking this on. It could be very important if you weigh in on this, and we would welcome your help."

Two days later Nicole got the call she was waiting for from Marina Ortegon, telling her they had voted to take the issue of interagency efforts aimed at prenatal exposure as their top priority for the year ahead. Nicole thanked her and made an appointment to meet with the subcommittee.

CHAPTER 39

Law office

Next Nicole called Sam and asked him and Joshua to come back and see her.

When they arrived, she got right to it. "I want you to go see Supervisor Berenson. You interviewed Calver, but you need to see her, too. Talk to her about the alcohol tax."

Sam looked amazed. "Marvin mentioned her, but Berenson? She's a rightwinger. Why talk to her?"

Nicole laughed. "Sam, I'm surprised at you, stereotyping people like that. Yes, she votes against most social programs. But it's because she keeps asking the right questions. She sits there and asks, over and over "does it work?" And the agencies come back with head counts instead of answering her question. I've seen her vote to double the budget for programs that have proved they work. She did it for early childhood education two years ago when the child care people stopped arguing for higher salaries as the solution and began showing how the kids in the best programs were doing better reading in first grade. She's a listener, Sam, as well as a conservative. Go talk to her." Then she laughed. "I think you'll enjoy her, despite your stereotyping, Sam."

Supervisor Berenson's office

So they did. Supervisor Berenson was in her early sixties, with shoulder length grey hair and what Sam, with very little sense of women's clothes, imagined to be a designer suit and pearls. She represented the West Side of the county, and had acted in movies of the 60's, though never in lead roles. She and her husband were major donors to several charities, and she had gotten into politics from her active role in the county's arts community.

Her office was a definite contrast with Calver's, with art work that Sam assumed was on loan from various museums. The furniture probably exceeded Sam's house in value, and he sat down gingerly, hoping nothing broke.

Berenson began with a faint smile. "Welcome, Mr. Leonard, Mr. Bronson. I gather you have put together a report on this tragic case of the baby being kidnapped out in the Valley. I'm looking forward to reading it. How can I help you?"

"We've developed some recommendations based on what we heard from the several county officials we have talked with, Supervisor Berenson. Nicole Larwin thought it would be useful to get your reaction to some of them."

The Supervisor's eyes twinkled with amusement. "That usually means someone is afraid I'll oppose what they've come up with, and they're trying to feel me out in advance. Well, I've spent time in Hollywood, and I've never been averse to a little feeling out. Or up, as the case may be."

Sam was able to keep a poker face, but Joshua gasped, giving the Supervisor the reaction she seemed to want. "I'm sorry, young man, have I upset you?"

"No, Ma'am. Sorry I reacted."

"That's all right. I find it important to clarify the difference between conservatives in politics and conservatives in manners. I never wanted to be called a stiff-necked old broad."

"No danger of that, ma'am."

"All right. But if you call me ma'am again, I will have you escorted out and I will conclude my business with this distinguished looking Pulitzer-holder." And she beamed at Sam.

Sam decided he had better get to the point before Josh found himself evicted and he ended up accosted. "Supervisor Berenson, one of our recommendations is for a small increase in alcohol taxes in the county. As you know, the state has now given the county the authority to raise alcohol taxes in each county. A nickel a drink— beer, wine, and hard stuff—gets you 200 million bucks in LA County alone." He paused and waited for her reaction.

"$200 million? How do you know that?"

"Alcohol Justice—an organization that works on alcohol issues. They have this calculator on their website. Figures it out for every county or state."

"You don't say."

"That's right. If that amount were applied to prenatal screening and interventions that have been proven effective for children who were prenatally exposed, it could make a huge difference."

She frowned. "Mr. Leonard, I hate programs that don't work. I hate spending money on them, and I hate the pretense that they are helping people. It is government at its worst: symbolic allocations to non-existent results. Now, you let me move funds from the worst programs to the best ones every year, and give me budget staff to figure out the difference—and I'll give you an add-on to the alcohol tax. A nickel a drink, when we've already got 3 bucks on a pack of cigarettes? A nickel a drink doesn't seem too bad if it really helps kids. But the deal has to include getting rid of programs that aren't worth a damn."

Sam said, with some amazement, "There really is such a thing as a true fiscal conservative."

The Supervisor laughed and said, "You say that like you found out there really is a Santa Claus."

"Yeah. But I thought Santa Claus was a lot more likely to exist."

She smiled. "You know, my great-grandmother marched with Carrie Nation. My mother had a hatchet Grandma Bessie swore she used to chop holes in beer barrels." Laughing, she added, "I always wondered why the church people rolled over so easily for the alcohol lobby."

Then she looked at Sam with a mock-stern expression. "It's not just fiscal conservatives you don't understand, Mr. Leonard. It's moral conservatives, too."

And to Joshua's great amusement, Sam, the ex-Franciscan who quoted the New Testament from time to time, was totally silent and clearly uncomfortable.

As they left, walking down the corridor in the County Hall of Administration, Joshua said to Sam, "Nicole was right. She's remarkable."

"That she is. I'm just glad we got out of there with our clothes on. What a character. But she came through, and it really calls the question with Calver. Which is what Nicole wanted."

CHAPTER 40

The Desert

Joe and Dolores had begun one of their marathon talks about when he should take Isabel back, and Dolores was summing up.

"Joe. I want you out of here—you know that. But little brother, they're going to lock you up if you just drive into LA and turn her over. I wish you'd think about the fire station deal. They'll take care of her and you can get away. You could even take her over to Lee's station and they would come get her from there."

Joe shook his head. "That just doesn't make any sense, Dee. First, I'd spend years looking over my shoulder waiting for somebody to throw handcuffs on me. Second, I really did break the law—for a good reason, but it was wrong to take her. And I guess all that old atonement stuff they used to teach us at St Anthony's hasn't worn away."

He went on, trying to make her see it. "I took the baby and I sold Luisa the drugs. If I drop her at a firehouse and drive away, I'm pretending I have nothing to do with her. And then taking her has no meaning. I took her to make her life better, and I have to be responsible for breaking the law when I did it—whatever my reasons."

"But you don't have to go to jail. What good does that do Isabel?"

"It's not for Isabel. It's for me, it's wiping the board clean, the way Sister Maria used to do at St Anthony's. Remember, she'd clean those boards every afternoon—except when she kept one of us after school to do it—so she could have a clean start the next day. That's what I think atonement means. A clean start. So I have to take the punishment."

Then he went over to Isabel's crib, watching her sleep. "And there's no way of knowing what would happen to Isabel. She could

202

end up in some real bad places if Luisa never gets her act together. All our work this last few weeks—somebody could undo that by just not caring about her and turning her into just another case."

He walked over to the window and looked out at the desert. "Being out here has made me think a lot about what I could do instead of hustle. I really could go back to school—I could give community college a shot, and see if the music thing goes anywhere." He smiled, with some sadness. "I hear you can do college classes in prison now."

While he had been in high school, a teacher had tried to get Joe to apply to college. The teacher, Steve Buchholtz, had Joe in one of his music classes, and had heard him play the guitar. For a class assignment, Joe had written a song and had played it as part of his final exam. Buchholtz had given him an A, and told Joe after class that he had a true talent at song-writing. He explained that Joe could get a scholarship and would be able to transfer from community college to a four-year college that had good music training.

Joe thought about it for a while, but it was the first time anyone had ever said anything to him about his music. No one he knew went to college, and it sounded like a world with people and ideas hopelessly distant from what he knew.

But Buchholtz was persistent, and finally he persuaded Joe to go on a tour of Cal State Northridge and talk with the admissions staff. Joe caught the bus to CSUN and found his way to the admissions office. When he introduced himself to the receptionist, he was handed off to a recent CSUN graduate who was interning in the admissions office. The graduate asked him what he wanted to major in. Joe wondered what the right answer was, and then said "Maybe music." The student gave him a look that said *what do you know about music*, and then after talking in a bored manner about his own experience at the University, gave Joe a brochure about the college and an application kit.

After a very brief session with an admission counselor who urged them all to apply and discussed financial aid for about five minutes, using a lot of abbreviations that Joe had never heard before, Joe ended up with a group of ten other high school students who were visiting the campus on an orientation tour. They were all from Valley high schools, and, Joe quickly realized, they were all first-time college prospects. They wore high school clothes, t-shirts and jeans, except for two of the girls who were dressed in too-tight skirts and blouses.

And the key moment of the tour for Joe was when they walked by two students with CSUN sweatshirts sitting on a bench outside the student bookstore, and he overhead one of the students say to the other, "Look, man, more *mojados*." And then they laughed.

The Spanish word for wetback is at least as demeaning as the English, and Joe quickly saw how much the label upset the students in his tour group. The disdain from the college students was almost physical, a rejection and a stereotype that dismissed all of them. It didn't help at all that both of the students who had laughed at them were Latino.

And Joe thought to himself *this just isn't for me—this isn't who I am*. It wasn't right then, and he guessed it never would be.

And so he lifted his head up, looked around the campus and the buildings, and carefully put the brochures and the application packet he had been given into the nearest trash can on the concrete walkway between the buildings. Then he walked to the bus stop, sat down, and waited for his bus home.

Joe put the memory away and went back to Isabel's crib. He sat down with the guitar and began to play, and as he played, he wondered what it would be like to learn about how to write music from a real composer.

CHAPTER 41

Sam and Joshua were at Sam's home, working on some final edits to the report. A call came into Sam's cell, just after he had received a text message from Nicole that read *My office just got a call from a guy who says he has Isabel. We couldn't trace the call—looks like it's a one-time cellphone. He said he will only talk with you. We gave him your cell number. Talk to him and then call me immediately.*

Sam answered the phone saying, "Sam Leonard here."

"Mr. Leonard, my name is Joe Brenner. I know you're working for Nicole Larwin on the Baby Isabel case." There was a pause. "I have her with me, she is fine, and I want to talk with you about bringing her back."

"Joe—can I call you Joe?"

"Sure."

"Joe, if you know we are working on the case, you know there are a lot of people concerned about her. You also probably know we get hundreds of crank calls. Can you give me some proof that you have her and that she is OK?"

"She's fine. She has a tiny birthmark on the back of her neck that looks like two dots, one on top of the other." He paused, then went on. "We are with my sister, who was a combat medic with the Marines. We would like to bring her into the 29 Palms base and have an escort into the city. Some people I used to." he paused, "used to work with may be trying to get at me, and I don't want Isabel harmed. Somebody already came out here and tried to shoot our place up. The Marines helped us, because my sister was a medic." He added, "And I want immunity for my sister—she didn't do anything wrong. She got a Silver Star in Iraq."

"How can I reach you?"

"You can't. Talk with Larwin and the cops and I'll call you at 5 pm today to work out the details." And then he hung up.

Sam had put his phone on speaker so Joshua could hear it.

Joshua said, "Wow. Sounded authentic to me."

"Me, too." Sam was dialing Nicole on her personal cell, and she picked up after the first ring.

"Nicole, he sounds legitimate. He knew about the birthmark. He wants to bring her into 29 Palms—looks like his sister has some connection with the Marines there. He's scared someone is going to try to take him out."

"How is the baby?"

"He said she's fine. No way of knowing, but the kid sounded like he had his act together, even though he's scared. No one has been able to locate his sister?"

"The detectives on the case found a guy out in Havasu who knows her, but they hit a stone wall with him. He's an old boy friend who's protecting her. She has pretty bad PTSD from what the detectives were able to find out from the Marines and the VA." She was silent for a moment, then added, "So she's out there somewhere between Havasu and the base at 29 Palms. I guess we let him bring her in, but if he wants to talk to you first, we're probably going to ask you to do that. We'll be tracking you, but from a ways back." She paused. "Sam, you don't have to do this."

"I know. Look, Nicole, there are no indications that this kid is violent, and everything we've heard about him says he really cares about the baby. I think it'll be fine." Josh was nodding and pointing to himself. "Josh and I both want to do it."

Abruptly, Nicole said, "All right. I'm going to have to clear this with a bunch of people, so give me an hour or so and I'll try to get back to you. Might be a good idea to get in your car and head toward 29 Palms."

"We're on our way."

So Joshua and Sam started driving. They knew they would eventually be tracked, but could see neither aircraft nor cars that seemed to be following them. They could see dark clouds off to the south and east, and heard on the radio that an early monsoon had moved up from Mexico and was expected to bring heavy rains out over the desert.

They drove out the 10 and got to the emptier, more desolate areas near the 29 Palms turnoff. Joshua asked Sam, "You ever get tired of looking at all that?"

"No. You?"

"Sometimes. Then I start to think about how all this was underwater for so long and how wet it was then and how dry it is now." He looked off to the storm clouds. "Most of the year, that is. So the history makes it a little more interesting."

"Good, kid. Think about how it was, and not just how it is. Out there where history backs into geology—that's the way to really understand California. If anyone could ever understand California."

Sam went on to talk about his love of his bizarre native state, and Joshua listened, fascinated at how much Sam knew about the state, and how deeply he felt about its history and its potential. He knew that Sam had been at the center of some extraordinary events in the state's recent history, working as a journalist and as the middle man negotiating between the Governor and the leader of a human rights movement based in Mexico.

"You ever read Frank Norris, Josh?"

Joshua shook his head, looking thoughtful. "Wait. Frank Norris, wrote *The Octopus*? California railroads? The Trust?"

"That's right. Glad to see USC still gets some of it right. Frank Norris called *The Octopus* 'A Story of California.' He nailed it, way back there in 1904. Norris and old Upton Sinclair. Wrote these great novels called muckrakers, novels about bad guys screwing the little people. They called Norris and Sinclair 'social realists.' Thick novels, not always easy to read. Lots of preaching. But more of California in them than a lot of the current stuff, the so-called 'noir' stuff about LA. Norris died young, at 34. Could have written five or six more California books—would have been great to have them." Sam looked over at Joshua. "History lesson over."

Joshua said, "Thanks, Professor."

They stopped at a gas station and called Nicole. She sounded harried, and asked them where they were. It was about 4 pm. And Sam reminded her that they were supposed to talk to Brenner at 5.

"I know, I know. Look, this is just as messed up as I expected it would be. There's a faction that wants to tail you guys and let the meeting happen, and a faction that wants to talk to the Marines, and another group that wants to go in with a full SWAT team and try to rescue her."

Sam said, "Nicole, he's determined to bring her in by himself. You can swoop down with a SWAT team and all that paramilitary crap and take your chances. But I'd trust a decorated vet and the Marines to get this one right—and going in trying to snatch her could be very dangerous." Then he added, "Who's going to make the final call?"

"She was taken in LAPD territory, so the Chief and the DA and DCW will all be involved. I'd say it's the Chief's call, ultimately."

"We'd be glad to talk to him if that would help."

"I'll tell them."

Half an hour later Nicole called back, and said the agencies had finally agreed. When Joe called Sam back at 5, he made arrangements to meet him at the front gate of the 29 Palms Base at 8 am the next day.

As Sam and Joshua drove up to the gate at the Base to figure out where they were going to spend the night, they saw the clouds building up.

CHAPTER 42

Joe had finally decided that he was going to take Isabel back and trust that Nicole Larwin would make the right decision about Isabel—and about him.

He and Dolores packed up the items they had accumulated for Isabel, moving slowly and quietly. As he looked out the window, he noticed that the late afternoon sky had darkened considerably, looking like thunderstorms. The weather the night before had predicted the first of the monsoon rains that usually began in July and run on through August or early September.

Dolores saw him watching the sky and said "It's the monsoon, coming early. We're on high ground here, but you have to cross three or four washes to get back to the 62 and head on into 29 Palms. Be very careful—some of those overpass bridges can get shaky if you hit them just when the first flood of water comes down the wash."

Joe took his cellphone, but he knew it wouldn't work well for much of the trip back. He and Dolores made a plan which she insisted on, harking back to her patrol days, in which Joe had to call in every half hour. Joe thought she was over-controlling, and said so.

Dolores was furious. "Listen, little brother. You may be a big-time drug dealer and all that. But I have been through stinking weather and incoming fire beyond your worst nightmares. You check in every half hour—you have Isabel, dummy, and we aren't taking any chances. I'd come with you, but I'm . . ." she paused, and Joe saw that she was struggling to say the words. "I'm just not ready yet."

"Not a problem. We need you here in case anything happens."

Dolores walked away, and Joe could tell that part of her anger was about the risks of their trip and part was about the loss of Isabel. She came back with a small, multi-colored blanket that Joe was surprised to recognize as one that had been in their home. Dolores, frowning, said "You probably remember this, Mom said she had gotten it from one of the grandmothers in Mexico, I don't remember which one. She used it for me and then for you. I always kept it, thought I might . . ." But she couldn't finish the sentence.

And as Joe watched his tough, war hero sister weeping quietly over Isabel's crib, folding and re-folding the little blanket, and then thrusting it into the large backpack Joe would be taking, he knew that neither of them would ever be the same. And as he watched Sancho put his head down on the floor, watching them carefully, but making no move toward the crib, he knew that the dog was also going to miss Isabel.

Joe walked over and gently rubbed Dolores' shoulder. "You're going to get better, Dee. I know you are. You helped Isabel get better. You helped her so much. And now you're going to get better."

"Maybe." She tried to smile, and couldn't quite make it. She put her arms around him, quietly crying. "I'm going to miss you guys. You write me and tell me what happens. And I'll . . . I'll try to come and visit you. Maybe with Lassiter."

"That would be great."

Joe set off early the next morning along a dirt road that led southwest. Their plan was for him to stay on dirt roads that would end him up on the 62, rather than doubling back to the 95. It was riskier because of the weather, but it was much more secluded than the 95, which was cruised frequently by the Highway Patrol. Dolores had explained that in her explorations of the area, she had found a decent road that Joe's Escape should be able to travel. The problem would be the rains, because there were two bridges over usually dry river beds on the way to the 62.

The rain from the monsoon was falling hard as Joe moved out. He had wedged Isabel's carrier in the back seat between layers of blankets, close enough that he could reach her with the bottle he had in a portable cooler that was plugged into the AC outlet on the console.

The first ten miles went by quickly, but Joe could see sheets of water coming in from the south, and the road was getting wetter and more slippery with every mile. Then he came to the first bridge. The water rushing under it was moving faster than anything Joe had ever seen before. He stopped the Escape on the approach to the bridge, studying the water roaring down the wash, and then called Dolores.

He raised Dolores on his second try with the cellphone, but he could barely hear her and wasn't sure she could hear him at all. "Dee, I'm at the first bridge, about fifteen miles from your place. Bridge is still there, but water is up almost to the top of the road. I'm going across—will check in once I get to the next bridge."

He hung up, and slowly crossed the bridge. The wheels spun and the Escape slid sideways in two places, but they got across.

Five miles further, with the rain coming down as hard as it had since he left Dolores' place, he stopped as he saw the second bridge. By now, the water was coming over the top of the bridge, and he could see the supports of the bridge, which were old railroad ties, moving visibly under the onslaught of the flood coming down the wash. As he watched, the bridge lifted up and then settled back down.

It was obvious that the bridge was about to break loose from the supports. Joe tried to look upstream and downstream to see if there was any other option, but the rain made it impossible to see more than thirty feet away from the car. Isabel was whimpering, and as he turned and tried to give her a bottle, he felt the Escape moving with the water that was spilling over the edge of bridge onto the road. For a moment, he regained control of the car and tried to accelerate, but then he felt a lurch, and something struck the back of the car. There was debris all over the wash, some of it large sections of sagebrush, and he could see that some of the debris was up on the road, pushed by the flow of the water coming off of the bridge. His wheels spun, and he felt the car drop down into the hole he was digging.

They were stuck, and the rains were coming just as hard. He pulled out his cellphone and called Dolores.

Hands shaking, Dolores called the number Lassiter had given her. "Sergeant Lassiter, please. It's an emergency."

He came on the phone right away. "Lassiter, you asked me to call if we needed help. My brother is stranded between our place and the 62. He's at the second bridge. He's going to need a tow. And Sarge, when you get there, don't be surprised—he has a baby with him."

"A baby?" Lassiter was quiet for a few seconds, and then his voice came back, more guarded. "Have anything to do with that little girl that is missing?"

She paused. "I won't lie to you—he's got her. But he's taking her back now. She's been out here because she was sick, and her mother can't take care of her."

Lassiter briskly said, "Once a medic, always a medic, Dee. I'll have some of my guys head out there. Can you tell me where you think he is?"

"He's been checking in every half hour. He last called from Old Woman Road, and he said he was twenty-two miles from here. That should help you nail him down."

"I can't get any choppers up in the rain, but we'll got 4-wheels all over the place. They're on their way. I'll call you if we hear anything."

Joe tried to remain cool. If he had been alone, he would have left the car and tried to fight his way to higher ground, but carrying Isabel, he was afraid he would drop the carrier in the water and lose her. He thought he had gotten through to Dolores, but he wasn't sure he had connected. He tried to remember what he had read about the monsoon—the question was how quickly the heaviest of the rains would head north and east and how soon after that the water would subside.

Fifteen minutes went by, and then he thought he saw a lighter trace of clouds off to the south. The water in the wash was no less than it had been, but as he watched, the rains definitely lessened.

Isabel had taken the bottle he had given her and went back to sleep, with occasional twitches of her legs against the carrier. Then, looking back through the windshield at the far side of the wash, Joe saw three high four-wheel vehicles painted with camouflage pull up to the edge of the wash. Then, for the second time, he heard Lassiter's voice from a loudspeaker. "Joe, it's Lassiter. Stay there. We'll send someone across for you and the baby."

Twenty minutes later, they were across the wash. The Marines had quickly unloaded a basket unit which they hooked up to some kind of propellant and a rope, which they then shot across the wash. Joe secured the rope to the trailer hitch on the Escape. A Marine came across on a pulley lift to anchor the rope, and went back to get the basket. He crossed again, placed Isabel in a chest carrier, and took her across. Then he came back and took Joe across, followed by a basket full of supplies from the Escape. The unit had obviously practiced the maneuver many times, and Joe marveled at how quickly and easily they ferried Isabel, himself, and the supplies across the roaring waters. As he looked back at the bridge he saw that it was still standing, but with only one support left under it. And then, as he watched, that last support gave way and the entire bridge fell into the wash.

Joe walked over to Lassiter and said, "Thanks—again, Sergeant. You guys come in handy."

"Wish they were all that easy." He glanced back at the bridge. "That is one hell of a *wadi*—that's Arabic for dry river. Glad we could help you—and Dee." He looked at Joe, frowning a bit. "How are you going to get that little girl back where she belongs?"

"I may need a lift. I'm connecting in 29 Palms with some people who can help me get the baby back where she belongs." He realized that Dolores had told Lassiter that he was taking Isabel back. "I just hope I don't get arrested before I can get her back to the county." He paused, thinking of the threats Luisa had passed on, and added, "Or something worse." He explained the threat from the gang, and as Lassiter listened, the sergeant got a grim smile on his face.

"Well, maybe we can help with that, too. I have to make a run into LA sometime this week. If you come back to the base and let me get squared away, we can give you a decent escort. The brother of a Silver Star Devil Doc gets top treatment, no matter what he may have done in a good cause. I don't think you'll have to worry about some asshole thugs coming after you." He smiled. "Actually, we'd welcome the practice."

CHAPTER 43

When Sam and Joshua arrived at the front gate at the 29 Palms base, they were escorted to the base commander's office. When they walked into the training room that had been set aside for what the Marines were already calling "Operation Isabel," they could see right away that the Marines had taken over. In the training room, what amounted to a full-dress nursery had been set up, with Isabel happily babbling in a regulation green crib, two nurses and a doctor standing by in their operating gear. Joe was looking semi-comfortable in an armchair with Sgt. Lassiter seated on his right.

Colonel Herman, the base commander, introduced himself and got right to the point. "Here's our view, Mr. Leonard. This young lady," he motioned to Isabel, "was brought onto our base by Mr. Brenner. We know he has broken the law, he knows it, and he's ready to accept the legal consequences. He's doing the right thing now to bring this baby into proper care. What's more, he has been threatened. We have assured ourselves that the threat is real. And since he is related to an outstanding corpsman who took fabulous care of our Marines in a hard place, and he and his charge are now on our base—we are going to protect him and this baby with all the authority and firepower we have at our disposal. Now we will cooperate with civil authorities, and I have already been in touch with the Chief and the DA. But we will not relinquish care of this little girl or Mr. Brenner until they are both safely in appropriate custody in Los Angeles."

"Sounds good to me," Sam said amiably. "He has asked to speak with us. May we talk to him?"

"You may. I've set up a private area over in the S3 conference room next door, and I've asked Sgt. Lassiter, who has good rapport with Mr. Brenner and his sister, to stay with him while you talk."

"Very good, sir. Thank you."

And so, after Joe walked over to the crib and made sure Isabel was content, Joe, Sam, Joshua, and Lassiter moved into the small audio-visual area where a table and chairs had been set up in the midst of TV cameras and projectors and screens.

As they sat down, Sam smiled at Joe and said "Guess this is a little more elaborate than the private conversation you thought we were going to have, eh, Joe?"

"Yes. But we're very grateful to the Marines, who have saved our butts twice so far, and I'm very glad that Isabel and I got here safely." He paused, and Sam could tell he was getting to the hard part. "What I want to talk with you about, and through you to Miss Larwin, is what happens to Isabel. I know I won't have much say about all that, and that the agencies will do whatever they're going to do. But from what I read about the investigation that you and Mr. Bronson are doing, you may be one of the best chances Isabel has to be where she needs to be while Luisa tries to clean up her act and get custody back."

Sam replied, "We'll do what we can, but it's up to Luisa more than anyone."

"I know. But when we were taking care of Isabel, I read about programs called family treatment, where the baby could stay with the mother. Can she get into that kind of programs if Luisa enrolls—and can Luisa get past a waiting list?"

Sam thought back to their session with Dr. Chervoussian, and her emphasis on attachment disorder and the value of family treatment that kept mother and baby together. With the help of a little research on his own, Joe had instinctively gotten to a critical issue about Isabel's future: where she would spend the next few months, assuming Luisa got into treatment.

Joe was right—he had little bargaining power. The media spotlight on Isabel's return was going to paint Joe and Luisa as the bad guys who put Isabel in danger, and getting Luisa into a good program was not going to be easy.

Sam told Joe they would do all they could to get Luisa into a program where she could spend time with Isabel. Remembering their earlier phone conversation he added, "Nicole Larwin is going to try to make sure that there will be no charges against your sister."

Then he paused and fell silent, looking at Joe with a strange expression on his face.

"Joe," Sam said softly. "Joseph. You took the baby to what you thought was safety. Out across the desert, you protected her so she could become what she's supposed to be." He chuckled and shook his head as he looked out the window at the desert landscape. "Looks a lot like Egypt to me. And I suppose we could find a Herod or two back there in the city."

Joe had no idea what the old guy was babbling about.

But Joshua knew. Ernie Scott had told Joshua once when he asked about Sam that the Franciscan part of Sam had never left him, and Joshua had seen the proof. Sam's lens on the world sometimes boiled down to pure New Testament basics, and Joshua was glad to have been able to see that side of the occasionally gruff old man.

By the time they were ready to leave the base, four hours later, Baby Isabel had been adopted by Lassiter's unit. Colonel Herman, after being assured that they were headed back to the city, had given his full approval for escort vehicles and a detachment of Marines to accompany Lassiter and Joe in a staff car with Isabel.

They were loaded up and ready to leave. Sgt. Lassiter had been placed in command of the detachment, and the two Humvees of armed Marines were placed in front of Sam's Highlander. Lassiter had spoken to Dolores to make sure she was safe, and promised her he would swing by to check on her once the detachment returned.

He had also assured her that some of what he called "our toys" would be up over her mobile from time to time, keeping watch. Dolores had heard about the miniaturized drones—some as small as a hummingbird—that were being used for surveillance. She reminded herself not to swat any large insects that seemed to be hovering around.

As they pulled out of the base, Joe looked around at the convoy—for that is what it had become. He knew it was to honor Dolores' bravery, but it had also become a steel umbrella over Isabel.

Joe had read somewhere that nearly three million Afghan girls were now in school because of the protection now provided to them by their own woeful government, backed by American firepower. That firepower, at huge cost in lives and money, was arrayed against the Taliban which had barred all girls from attending school when they governed Afghanistan. And as he watched some of the warriors who had helped erect that umbrella over those girls, he was proud of his country, for all its failings. They had protected the three million, and now they were protecting Isabel. And he hoped that all those who would now take over her care would prove worthy of the shield she was being given on this drive into the city.

He had done what he could for Isabel, with Dolores' help. He had given her an oasis of time in the desert—an oasis where she was cared for so she could begin her long journey toward a better life than her odds at birth had promised.

Joe may not have atoned for what he had done to Isabel. But he had tried. He knew he could have walked out of the hospital without looking back—he could have forgotten about Isabel Contreras. But he had not fled from what he had done; he sought to atone as best he could. It was wrong to take Isabel, but Joe knew with a certainty that it would have been wrong to leave her in the hospital, trusting that "the system" would have done the right things to give her life better odds of success than she had when she was born

Joe was smart, but he had lived in a small world, a world walled in by Mike's anger, Esther's love, and the brown stucco and frame neighborhoods of the Valley. His world was about to shrink even more, down to the size of a prison cell. But he had finally come to believe that it would then expand, far beyond the narrow ruts he had worn in his life with drug dealing and isolated music-making.

Caring for Isabel and risking what he had for her had moved the boundaries of Joe's world. And now he knew that doing something for someone else had done something remarkable for himself: it had widened his horizons far outside their original territory, giving him a glimpse of the larger world he was going to live in for the rest of his life.

Which one do you take after? Joe finally knew the answer.

They were about an hour out of 29 Palms on the 10. Joe had been very quiet. Then he turned and looked at Sam in the back seat. "Mr. Leonard, can I ask you a question?"

"Sure, son. What do you want to know?"

"You talked to all those agencies, you did that investigation. Do you think they would have taken good care of Isabel?

"You mean, did you do the right thing?" Sam asked, knowing what Joe was really saying.

"Yeah, I guess that's what I'm asking."

Sam looked at Joshua, and nodded. "We did talk to a lot of people, Joe. And a lot of them said it wasn't really their responsibility. Seems to me somewhere along the line you decided it *was* your responsibility. You may not have done it the right way. But you tried to give that little girl a better shot than she would have had in the system." He looked over at Joshua, wanting him to weigh in.

And Joshua said "You did a brave thing, Joe. You broke the law, but you did a brave thing. You've got a chance now to turn your life around. Up to you."

"I know." He looked down, thinking about the days ahead, living behind bars. Then he looked back at Sam and Josh and said "Thanks."

Joshua leaned forward and turned on the CD player in Sam's car. And Joe heard the opening bars of the Ronstadt collection of lullabies, *Dedicated to You.*

"Dolores put this in your backpack and told us it was there when we called her. She said Isabel should have it with her wherever she goes next." He paused. "She said maybe Luisa would play it for her if she gets into a program where Isabel can be with her."

And as Isabel smiled and began babbling with the music, a tear slid down Joe's face.

And so Joe and Isabel arrived three hours later at the headquarters offices of the county child welfare agency, where a special infant care unit was waiting. Isabel was lifted out of her carrier and placed in a well-equipped baby carriage. The Marines gathered around, each waving their own goodbyes to the baby they had guarded.

And Joe was promptly arrested, given his Miranda warnings, and taken to the county jail.

CHAPTER 44

Law office

Sam and Joshua came into Nicole's office for a debriefing. Sam looked very concerned. "Nicole, you've got Joe in jail for the time being, and you'll have to figure out what's going to happen to him. But you know that there's a threat against his life, and jails aren't the safest place in the world to hide out from gangs. One cellphone call to the wrong guy and he gets shanked. How are you handling that?"

Nicole nodded and said "We talked about that. He's in isolation and the DA personally made a call to the warden to tell him to watch out for Joe. He did the right thing—finally—and we're going to try to keep him safe."

"Can we give Joe assurances that Dolores will not be prosecuted?"

Nicole laughed. "That's not a problem. Sure, she harbored a criminal. But nobody's going to prosecute a Silver Star war hero who has been taking care of a sick baby. We'll probably work out some community service deal with the base at 29 Palms."

Changing subjects, she said, "We may have a problem with the tax increase, guys. Calver is refusing to go along. Looks like the alcohol lobby may have gotten to him."

Sam smiled and said, "With your permission, I'd like to go talk with him again. We've picked up some intelligence on some of his issues with DCW, and I'd like to see if he's concerned about his image."

A bit nervous, Nicole said, "All right. Be careful. He's a wily bastard."

Before Sam could respond, Joshua laughed, and said "We've got one of those on our team, too, Nicole."

After talking with Nicole, Sam made an appointment to meet with Calver. He told Joshua he wanted to do it alone, since Calver wouldn't want any other witnesses to complicate the discussion.

Supervisor Calver's office

Sam arrived at Calver's office, and after passing through the various barriers of beauty, he was shown into Calver's office.

Calver waved Sam to the chair beside his desk, and said, smiling, "Mr. Leonard. Always a pleasure. What can I do for you?"

"I hope this isn't inappropriate. But we're wrapping up some of the final work on our report, and I wanted to confirm a question that arose when we were going over the budget." He then outlined the secret DCW budget cut made by Calver that Rubin had told him about, and added quietly, looking straight at Calver, "There's really no reason this has to be part of our report."

Then he paused, and continued looked steadily at Calver with his reporter's *don't bullshit me now* look. "What's your thinking on the alcohol tax increase, Supervisor?

Calver looked back at him with barely concealed anger, knowing instantly what the question was about. Then he asked, "Have you ever been in politics, Sam?"

"No. I've seen it at pretty close range, though."

"I guess so. Well, I've been thinking that tax might be a good idea, now that you mention it." He waited, and seeing no reaction from Sam, quickly asked, "Is that all?"

"Yes. Thanks, Supervisor."

"Don't mention it." Calver's tone was dismissive, but Sam knew he'd gotten what he wanted. Like all good political bargains, what hadn't been said was what mattered most. Calver had heard the threat, as Sam intended him to, and Sam was fairly confident the vote would be there.

Board of Supervisors Conference Room

The Board convened for their regular Tuesday morning meeting. They were going to get a presentation from Nicole on the report Sam and Joshua had prepared, and Nicole had asked both of them to be in the audience.

During the Board meeting, Calver spotted Sam and Joshua in the audience. At the break, Calver walked over to them and looked at Sam, unbelieving. "You came back to this? A man like you, with a Pulitzer and all that? You came back after your report was finished? Why?"

Sam smiled and said, "We wanted to see if you were going to follow through. We're journalists, Mr. Calver. We deal in leads. We wanted to see if you would be the lead in the story—or just one of the bit players."

Calver walked off shaking his head.

Joshua said to Sam, "You really don't like him. Why?"

Sam replied, "Because he was once somebody with guts and values. He could have gone all the way—big majorities, all the money he ever needed. He's smart, but he settled for just having the local power. He never wanted to risk it on the state game."

He sighed, and then said, "I care too much about this state, Josh. I've dealt with three governors and watched four or five others try to do the job. There was a shot, once—" he stopped and shook his head. "There's a guy named Leon Panetta, you've read about him. Worked for Tom Kuchel back when there were still liberal Republicans in the Senate, then he was a Congressman from the Monterey area. Ran Clinton's White House after the Monica thing. Then ran the CIA and the Defense Department. He was going to run for Governor once, but he could never get the $25 million it took in those days to run statewide. Now it takes maybe $100 million. He would have been the best Governor since Pat Brown."

He paused, still musing about what might have been and what it could have meant to the state he loved so much. "Josh, I measure them all against those guys. On his best day, Calver could maybe shine their shoes."

CHAPTER 45

Department of Child Welfare

Luisa had begun her effort to get into treatment. It was to prove a journey as difficult as Joe's time with Isabel in the desert—only Joe knew where he was going, and Luisa was truly lost.

Her first try was as uphill as any route she could have chosen. A well-meaning counselor assigned to her from the county child welfare agency told her about a program in the Valley which allowed women in treatment to enroll in a program that permitted clients to live with their children, enrolling the children in child care while the parents were in addiction recovery counseling. The program included parenting education and therapy, which encouraged the women to explore the underlying causes of their addiction in their own family history.

As Luisa heard the program described, she thought it sounded too good to be true. It turned out to be exactly that. The first hurdle was being accepted in a program that had few vacancies and a long waiting list. Luisa had been told that women with younger children like Isabel were given priority for admission, but that turned out to be words written on a piece of paper negotiated among agency heads. The document had little impact on the daily realities of what treatment agencies actually do. She was finally told that the program did in fact have a vacancy but that since she had been diagnosed with bipolar disorder, she wasn't eligible because the program did not treat women with both mental illness and substance use disorders.

By that time, four weeks had gone by and Luisa had a hearing with the judge who was handling her case of child neglect. Unfortunately, the judge who was handling her criminal case scheduled a hearing the same day, and when she showed up for the criminal case, she was marked as non-compliant in the child abuse case because she had not kept her appointment in that court.

Her case worker, an overworked twenty-seven year-old who had been with the agency for only six months, was sympathetic with Luisa's dilemma in missing one court date to keep another, but had no idea how to negotiate the tangled jurisdictions of the two cases. Finally her supervisor stepped in and explained how she could get Luisa into the caseload for the small family drug court. The case worker met with the drug court coordinator—a woman whom Sam and Joshua had interviewed—and were told that they had no facilities for infants under the age of one.

The next attempt was to enroll Luisa in a women's treatment program that had a vacancy, but could not take Isabel, who would be referred to a foster care center near the program. The problem this time was that Luisa was living with a cousin in the Valley, and the program with the vacancy was in Long Beach. So after a two-hour bus ride one-way, Luisa would be able to participate in the program, but would get back to the foster care center after their closing hours and could not see Isabel except for an hour on Saturday and Sunday. When Luisa's case worker asked if the treatment program could vary their hours, she was told that a change would mean that Luisa was not putting in the minimum number of hours needed for completion of an intensive out-patient program. When she asked the foster care center if they would vary their hours so Luisa could be with Isabel at the end of the day or for longer on the weekends, she was told that their visiting hours were long-standing agency policy and could not be modified.

Luisa sat with the caseworker trying to sort out the latest disappointment and figure out their next step. The worker was glum.

"There was nothing about this in graduate school or in our orientation. *Nothing.* I feel like I just started work and have no idea what to do."

Luisa refrained from pointing out that the problem was not really about the worker, but about Luisa and Isabel. "Maybe I should just do the bus ride to Long Beach and see Isabel as much as I can. It's only for six months."

Irritated, the worker said, "But we have these new guidelines about infants and attachment disorders, and we are supposed to do everything we can to connect moms and their kids, especially when they're under one." She laughed, unhappily. "Looks like most of the agencies we deal with didn't get the message."

Luisa had worked hard to hold it together during the weeks of trying to get into treatment. She knew that clients who were seen as uncooperative were shuffled to the bottom of the lists, given the enormous discretion that caseworkers had to give priority to some clients and disregard others. So many women didn't even show up for their hearings, or accepted a referral to treatment but dropped out after a few sessions. And Luisa knew that she needed to come across as one of the cooperative ones if she was going to have a shot at getting into treatment. So she kept her mouth closed, even when she wanted to scream with frustration. She knew she was finally doing the right thing, but without much help from a system that saw her as just one more case.

But Luisa had gotten one break in her moves around the different agencies. A woman named Lani Diaz had called her from a local women's program that provided what they called "recovery coaches." These coaches were women, some with college degrees, some with only high school or less, but all of whom had been on drugs and had lost their kids, and then gotten them back. Their job was to explain the rules—written and unwritten—to women who were new to the system, and to try to support them as they moved from losing their kids into treatment and through repeated court review sessions.

When Lani called her the first time and explained that she wanted to try to help Luisa, Luisa wept with gratitude. Lani had said, "I can't give you a guarantee that you'll get Isabel back, but I can promise you that you'll meet dozens of women with worse problems than yours—and all of them are back with their kids now. You can do it, Luisa. And I'm here to try to help you do it. But it's finally all up to you."

And finally, Luisa had come to a bedrock conviction that helped her put up with the revolving doors. Her talk with Joe Brenner had given her some confidence that Isabel was all right and that what he had done was to try to give her one more chance to be with Isabel. If she kept doing what she was supposed to and managed to get through all the hoops the agencies wanted her to negotiate, Luisa would have a good chance to regain custody of Isabel.

Lani had checked back with Sam and Joshua, keeping them posted on Luisa's progress. Joshua had called Nicole, reminding her of the commitment Sam had asked for to try to help Luisa get into treatment. Nicole agreed to call one of the heads of the family treatment programs funded by the county.

The next day, Lani said to Luisa, "You caught a break, Luisa. Joe made the best deal he could for you, and it looks like they're going to try to honor it." She looked sad. "But it makes me feel bad for all the women out there who are trying to do the right thing and don't have anyone who knows their way around the DA's office—or someone else with a little clout working for them."

CHAPTER 46

County Superior Court

Joe's criminal trial took place three months after he had been arrested. He was represented by a defense lawyer that Sam had located who had worked on behalf of parents—both mothers and fathers—who were trying to get their kids back after they had been removed due to their parents' drug use. The lawyer had asked the judge presiding over the criminal case to allow Joe to make an introductory statement, and the judge had agreed. Sam, Joshua, and Nicole were in the courtroom.

Joe stood up in his prison clothes and began speaking in a steady voice, looking at the judge. "My name is Joe Brenner. I took Isabel Contreras from Memorial Hospital on the morning of April 29. She was two weeks old when I took her. I had bought food and clothing and everything else I thought she would need, and I took her to a safe place where my sister, Dolores Brenner, could help me take care of her. I wanted to keep her safe and healthy until Isabel's mother, Luisa Contreras, could get into drug treatment and do what she needed to do to have a chance at getting custody of Isabel.

"I took Isabel because I felt partly responsible for her, and because I didn't see any way that the agencies that could have taken care of her would really end up feeling responsible for her. For them, she was just 'a case.' They tell me there are thousands of cases like Isabel, and I wanted her to get the best care I could possibly provide for her.

"I also took her because I felt responsible for selling her mother some of the drugs that she used while she was pregnant with Isabel. The guilt that I feel for doing something that may affect Isabel for the rest of her life will never leave me. Her mother used the drugs, and would have probably bought them from someone else if I hadn't sold them to her. But that doesn't make me any less responsible, or any less guilty for what I did.

"My sister Dolores was a combat medic in Iraq. She was decorated for her bravery, and she is now dealing with the effects of the post-traumatic stress that came out of the time she was in Iraq. She saw some terrible things, and she is still trying to deal with that. But together we took care of Isabel, and I believe we did as good a job or better than anyone who would have been paid to take care of her. Isabel was feeling the effects of the drugs and alcohol that were in her system when she was born, and we took good care of her while those effects were wearing off.

"I am prepared to accept whatever sentence this court may give me. I only ask that the agencies that are now responsible for Isabel make as good an effort as Dolores and I did to give her the best possible chance for the best possible life she can have."

Nicole had located Luisa in her treatment program, and had asked her to come testify on Joe's behalf. She said she was willing to do so, and appeared in court with her mentor, Lani Diaz.

Standing up before the judge, hesitant, looking over at Joe and then at Nicole, Luisa said, "I am here to ask for leniency for Joe Brenner. He took my baby from the hospital, and he took care of her when I couldn't."

The Judge said to her, sternly. "But he sold you the junk you used, the drugs that endangered your baby."

"I bought it—I would have bought it from anybody at that point. He gave me a chance to be her mother. She'd be gone if he hadn't taken her. I'm doing what I need to do to get her back, and he gave me the chance to do that."

The rest of the trial went by quickly. The basic facts were not in dispute, and Joe's lawyer succeeded in getting into the record a medical statement about the care Isabel had received.

Before he handed down his sentence, the Judge called Nicole up for a conversation off the record. "Miss Larwin, I have read your brief and I have listened to your comments about this offender's crime and what he did that you believe to have been positive. But whatever he did after he took that baby, he committed a very serious offense. So I am going to pay attention to your recommendation, and sentence Mr. Brenner to a year in prison, with adequate protection from anyone who might want to harm him, with ten years of probation after that." He looked at her for a long time. "I hope you're right, Miss Larwin."

"Thank you, Your Honor. I do, too."

CHAPTER 47

A month later: County jail

Joe's cousin Charlie visited him in prison after he had been there several weeks. He was excited as he sat down. "Joe, you're in the clear with Valley Muerte. Two weeks ago, they found out who had ratted them out, and finally figured out that it wasn't you. No one is after you."

He got a strange look on his face. "Did you know they were watching for you when you came into LA with the baby? Someone had told them where you were—some bikers or something—and they were watching the road. Holy shit, Joe, you came into LA with a Marine convoy! The shooters almost crapped themselves when they saw the guns sticking out of the top of the trucks you came in on. They waited a while and then snuck back into the Valley. No one wanted to mess with you after that, and then they found out it wasn't you who ratted out our guys."

Joe laughed. "OK, one less thing to worry about when I get out, I guess."

"Joe, they want to try to make it up to you, since they know now that you were doing what I had asked you to. They want to give you a new area when you get out. You down for that?"

Joe shook his head. "I'm done, Charlie. I'm moving to Santa Ana and trying to get into community college. Going to study music. Maybe try to get a job doing music in some kids' program. No more selling, Charlie."

"Too bad, Joe."

A few days later, Serena Salas, the nurse Joe had talked with in the hospital, walked into the prison's visiting area, slowly, as everyone did for the first time, scared and uncertain how to behave. She saw Joe and walked quickly over to the chair opposite him.

There was no glass separating them, but the table was wide, and there were signs all over the room that read "*No Touching or Other Contact Permitted. Violators will Leave Immediately.*"

She said, quietly, "Hi, Joe."

"Hi, Serena. Thanks for coming." He gave her the best smile he was capable of just then. It wasn't much.

"I knew it was you that took her, Joe. You asked so many questions about that baby. But I never told them anything. I guess they figured it out soon enough." She was silent, then looked at him with a question all over her face: "Was I right not to tell them?" She started to reach towards his hand, and then saw the nearest guard step forward, glaring at her. She pulled her hand back slowly. She repeated, "Was I right?"

"Yeah, I think so. I tried to make things better for the baby—for Isabel. I think she ended up with a better shot at staying with Luisa, with her mother." He wanted her to understand, and had worked it over and over in his own head, trying to see if he could really justify the crime—and the time it was costing him. "After I checked out what was going to happen, I just felt like I had to do something, because all those agencies that were supposed to be helping the baby were just going to treat her like another number. So I did it."

He stopped, wondering if he should reveal so much to her. He watched her, pretty, small, with her eyebrows lifted up to show him she was listening and trying to take it in.

He went on. "And part of it was I remembered stuff my mother used to do, used to tell us about taking care of little kids. I remembered the question you asked me about which of my parents I took after. And I knew I was partly to blame for what was going to happen to Isabel. And I had to try to make up for it somehow. To atone."

"You're a good guy, Joe."

"Yeah. That's why they're putting me up in this neat place."

Serena smiled, and shook her head. "You did a bad thing for a good reason, Joe. A lot of people do bad things for bad reasons, and then they try to make excuses."

Joe saw that she wanted to believe that he was a decent person. She didn't talk about his dealing—she wanted to talk about what he had done that had been right. So they talked mostly about her work, and her friends, and then at the end, she said, quietly, "I want to see you when you get out."

Joe looked at her smiling face and said, "I want to see you too, Serena. That's a date."

The Desert

Lassiter had kept visiting Dolores. Lee Farmer had checked in with Dolores, and had been very happy for her when she told him she was "interested in" Lassiter.

Lassiter had gotten approval from the base commander to "keep an eye on" Dolores—which was interpreted as a secure cellphone, a regular flyover, and an open appointment with the base psychiatrist. She had not yet showed up for the appointment, but had told Lassiter that she would "soon."

Lassiter turned out to be one of the Marines whose marriage had been a casualty of his second deployment to the Middle East. He had told Dolores that his wife had never understood what military life had meant to him, and that he was at peace with the decision.

Seated in Dolores' living room, drinking the St. Pauli Girl N.A. that they had both decided was the only non-alcoholic beer that didn't taste like weasel piss, Lassiter said, "I was talking with Dr. Ashton yesterday, who told me that one-third of her caseload was women now."

"Yeah, I heard that," Dolores said. "Half combat stuff and half friendly fire in the form of hostile fucking. Not a happy statistic."

"No." Hesitantly, he went on. "She said that she could really use some backup from someone who knew what it was all about. You still have that community service requirement you agreed to, Dee."

Dolores knew what he was doing. She had finally gotten to a point where she welcomed it. She was getting better the way she had gotten hurt: by caring about someone else. Needing to help Joe with Isabel had taken her out of herself, and had shown her how much her skills mattered to another person.

She would never lose the fear and uncertainty that had scarred her in Iraq, but she would also never forget how good it felt to see Isabel recovering and thriving. And working on the Base as a civilian—or even re-upping, which she supposed she would be able to do—would do wonders for her finances. And maybe also for her peace of mind.

Dolores said, "I'm about ready to go visit Joe. You want to come with me?"

Lassiter replied, "Sounds like a great idea. We can get some decent food in LA."

They heard a distant booming sound, like shotgun blasts. Dolores looked at Lassiter, puzzled, "What the hell was that?"

"Guys up in the mountains trying to poach some of the mountain bighorns that live up in the reserve over on the Arizona side. They sneak in there—state has almost no rangers so it's easy for them to get in and try to take home a big rack of horns."

Dolores scoffed. "So manly. Shooting at some animal that can't shoot back. I never got that—seemed like a thing for little boys who never grew up."

"Yeah. Wonder what those guys would do if something started shooting back. Guys rich enough to afford that kind of hunting somehow never ended up in the real show." He laughed.

"Maybe we could train some of the bighorns to shoot back. Or drop in some bighorn robots and set them up to start firing away at some of those hotshots."

"Speaking of manly, stud . . ." She grabbed his belt and motioned with her free hand toward the bedroom.

Lassiter smiled, trying to keep it lust-free, but failing, and said "Have I explained our latest recruiting bonuses for re-ups?"

"First let's see if I have any medical skills left," she said. They had moved to second-stage recreational sex that promised to evolve into something considerably more serious, and Dolores was definitely ready for the move.

And Sancho settled down in his corner, mourning for Isabel, but glad to have new visitors.

CHAPTER 48

Law office

Nicole had stayed in the good graces of the firm, with Millie's help, as the pieces of her strategy had mostly worked out well. The partners gave her some additional staff and two more interns from law schools in the county. And she found herself inventing reasons to meet with Joshua to go over the parts of the report that he had worked on.

She saw that in some ways Josh, despite the decade that separated them, was at least as mature as she was, that somehow he had absorbed lessons of caring and empathy from the people around him that were far deeper than what she could do. She cared about kids—but, she realized, more as abstract numbers, information, and causes. For Josh, kids and front-line workers were both real, and both deserved more attention than they usually received.

He had an openness to people and to learning that was almost child-like, but that also had faint echoes of what Nicole had read about sages and wise men and women in other cultures. It was an acceptance of the world combined with a curiosity about how people reacted to that world. She saw it in his interactions with Sam, and in the questions that Joshua had introduced in the report, which Sam had generously credited to Joshua in his introduction to the report. He had explained to Nicole why they had interviewed the front-line workers, and what he learned from them. Nicole realized that his work and ideas had a big impact on the tone of the final report, and had convinced Sam that it should include what was usually missing—the workers' eye view of the systems.

Nicole tried not to let Joshua's being good-looking matter too much—but she failed. He was tall, and lean, and had an athlete's grace in movement. And so at first she had allowed herself to think of taking advantage of him for mostly physical reasons. But as she had gotten to know him through their reports on the investigation and meetings with him and Sam, she had come to realize that it was very unlikely that he would let her age and his youth become either a barrier or an unfair advantage for her. And so she revised her pleasurable plotting to a more cautious waiting, hoping for an opportunity to respond to whatever move the more confident of them would make first.

Nicole had a reasonably active sex life in law school and during her first few years in the D.A.'s office. She had become very skilled—she thought—at neatly wrapping up relationships that were mostly physical before they became anything else. Nicole had an acute married-but-loose detector, and she was quick to avoid any problems in an atmosphere that often viewed such affairs as normal.

A senior partner in a law firm that did a lot of work with the county had wanted to pursue much more, but she parried it with "too busy" responses enough times for him to get the message that it was over. He had bitterly said to her in their last conversation that she was "afraid of commitment," and as much as Nicole enjoyed the gender reversal, she wondered whether he might have had a point.

But Joshua made her begin to wonder if she had risked missing something.

Sam, of course, had seen what was happening, and casually mentioned to Josh that he thought Nicole was taking a major interest in his work. Josh blinked once, and then smiled. "You know, Sam, I wondered about that the other day when I caught her staring at me twice. You think I should do anything about that?

Sam answered, "My considered advice, as a septuagenarian to a vital young stud, is to go for it." And then he stopped smiling. "But only if you really think she's special. She's a lot more than a fling, grasshopper."

"I know, Old One."

And so he did, and they did, and after two dinners that were proper and fun and just a little bit wary, they fell onto Nicole's queen-sized bed on their third date and never had a bite of dinner. And after a while she felt at ease teasing him about his youthful vim and vigor, and he felt just as comfortable teasing her about her worldly ways and wiles.

And Sam listened to Josh tell part of it, and never asked him more than he wanted to tell, while wondering where it might lead, feeling that both of them deserved the best of each other.

CHAPTER 49

A month later: County jail

And then Joe had a second visitor—and the surprise of his life.

As Tina McGowan walked into the visitor's room and sat down, Joe immediately saw her wedding ring. "Hello, Joe," she said.

"Hi, Tina. What—what are you doing here? Thanks for coming, I mean, but what are you doing here?"

"I need to tell you something, Joe." She stopped, and watched his face carefully. "You have a daughter, Joe. I kept our baby."

Joe stared at her, not sure he had heard her correctly, with no idea what to say. Finally, he got out the words, "A daughter?"

"Yes. She's beautiful, Joe." She reached into the pocket of the jeans she was wearing and handed Joe a picture. He took it and stared at it, eyes wide, unable to speak yet.

Tina said, "Joe, I married a great guy, Greg Wilson. He's fine with my telling you. He adopted her, but he agrees she should know who you are—if you want her to, that is."

Still looking at the picture, Joe said, "Yes. Oh, yes." Then he looked up and asked, "What's her name?"

Tina smiled. "I always liked the name Esther, and I liked what you told me about your mom. That's her name."

And for the second time, Joe wept for the sake of a little girl. But this time it was tears of joy and hope.

Tina said, "Joe, I read what you did for that baby you took. And I knew you had turned some kind of corner, that you were trying to do something right for once. You may not have done it the right way, and it got you in here, but I think I know why you did it. I hope it works out all right for her and her mother."

"I think it will."

"Telling Esther about you is my gift to her—and to you, if you want it. Greg will always be her dad, but I want her to know you. I don't want her to live a lie—she knows Greg is her adopted father, but she doesn't know you and I weren't married. I'll tell her that later, but for now I just want her to know you, once you get out. You're part of her life, and she deserves to know that. And so do you."

After she left, Joe called Dolores as soon as he got a call slot, and he heard her laughter. "So she told you. I knew it, but I didn't think it was my place to tell you. I saw her at the market after I got back, and she had a guy and a little girl with her. After one look I could tell it was yours." She sniffled, and then said, "The little girl already looks a little like Mom, Joe. It's amazing."

"Unbelievable. I'm still getting used to it. But it feels pretty good, so far."

Dolores said, "You're her father, Joe, but he's going to always be her parent. It's going to be a tough job."

Joe said, "Dee, it's maybe the most amazing thing that has ever happened to me. You go along for twenty-five years of your life never thinking about kids, and then all of a sudden this child, this little girl, is out there. And she's a part of me, always will be, whatever happens. First I got to thinking I could make a difference to Isabel—maybe somehow what I did would help her, whatever it meant to me. And now there's Esther. And I have to figure out how I could help her, whatever Tina and her husband will let me do, to help her somehow."

Dolores said, "I'm jealous, Joe. You've got something that you may or may not deserve, but it's going to make your life richer forever, knowing she is out there, walking around with your biology, and Mom's. Tina will do a great job with her, and if you're lucky, she'll want you in her life. Maybe not at the center, but in a backup role that could mean a lot to her some day when she's really having a tough time."

"I'm OK with that. I can do it. I want to do it." And then he said, "I'm going to write her a song."

CHAPTER 50

Nicole had asked Sam and Joshua to dinner to brief them on what had happened.

The waiter at the restaurant Nicole had chosen was young and movie-star handsome, with dark, lightly curled hair and a half smile that seemed to say *I know we're all pretending here, but isn't it kind of fun to do?* His name tag simply said Jack. He said, "Can I help you?"

Nicole checked her first instinct, which was to say *Oh yes, you can, my pretty one.* Instead, noting Joshua's amused look, she said, "Yes, please, we'd like the linguine."

"May I recommend a wine with that?"

"Please."

He described two wines that he assured Nicole would enhance the meal, and Nicole chose the second one. As he walked away, Nicole consciously avoided watching him, and turned to Sam and Joshua, saying, "Forgive me for ordering for you, but I come here often and I really think you'll like it."

Sam said, "My steadfast rule is to let whoever is paying the bills choose the food. Sounds great."

And Joshua said, "After four years of Chano's Drivein on Figueroa being the high end, this will be just fine."

Nicole smiled at him and said "We've had a few meals that must have surpassed Chano's, haven't we, Josh?"

And Joshua, carefully calibrating his response to agree with her without seeming to be bragging to Sam, said, "Absolutely—both home-cooked and on the town."

Nicole laughed, and then said, "A lot has been happening, Sam, and I wanted to make sure you both knew what the report has triggered. You were there for the Board vote on the new tax, so you're current on that. Berenson really has the bit in her teeth on this one. She got the others to agree to a ten percent shift each year from the least effective children and family programs to the ones that are working best. And she's written in a bonus for agencies that work with harder-to serve families, so they won't game the system by screening out more difficult cases."

Sam said "Wow. She's as sharp as you thought. Pretty good stuff."

Nicole went on. "Half of the two hundred million is going for prenatal screening, family treatment, and recovery coaches, just as you guys proposed in the report. We're moving the child welfare agency head off to a part-time consulting position, and Nate Rubin has agreed to take it over for at least two years. Child welfare and treatment have agreed to do annual data matching so they can find families in both systems and track their progress. Turns out we used to do that fifteen years ago, and the software tools that are now available make it much easier. The new money will pay for all of that."

Sam said, "So it sounds like we're more than a three-day headline."

"A hell of a lot more. You guys did great." Then she gave Joshua the 100-watt version of her smile. "And you got to meet some new and interesting people."

Joshua smiled back and said, "Oh, yes."

Sam scoffed, "You young people get all the fun."

Nicole said, "So why can't we find a fabulously wealthy widow for you, Sam?"

Sam smiled and said, "Don't hold your breath. I'm taking a long vacation up in the Sierra. Save your matchmaking for when I get back." He added, "And make sure she's smart and likes Brahms and the smell of cigars."

Sam sat in his Springdale trailer looking out over Lake Mamie, possibly his favorite place on the planet. Mamie was what he thought of as the gem of the Mammoth Lakes region, a lake his family had frequented for long decades.

He had been doing a little fishing, a lot of walking, and making a renewed attempt to write a novel. He had been trying to write fiction for decades, but each time he started, one of two things happened: something more interesting came along, or he read the first few chapters and saw how much his characters just stood around and lectured each other.

But he had decided to try again. And so he sat looking out across the lake to Crystal Crag, trying to breathe life into his book, pleased with his own life and challenged by his work.

CHAPTER 51

Five Years Later

Joe Brenner waited at Disneyland's front gate, as the crowds were beginning to move through the turnstiles into the Magic Kingdom. In the distance, from the trams that brought visitors from the far-off parking lots, he saw a woman walking toward him, and then a little girl dropped the woman's hand and began running toward him, shouting "Uncle Joe, Uncle Joe—there you are!"

As he swept Isabel up in his arms, she whispered in his ear, "Is Esther coming? Can I go on the rides with Esther, Uncle Joe?"

He waved to Luisa, who waved back and turned away to meet a man who had been waiting for her. And then, from another tram that had just arrived, Joe saw Tina and Greg Wilson walking toward them, with another little girl who was waving and pointing to him. And then she ran toward him, and it was her turn to get the whirling hug, with Isabel jumping around them, yelling, "Yay, Esther's here! My friend Esther's here!"

And then Esther tipped her head back and looked at Joe with a very serious face, and said "Are we going to meet your friend Serena, Joe?" And Joe nodded, and she smiled and tucked her head back into his shoulder.

And after making plans with Tina and Greg to meet them back in the parking lot at the end of the afternoon, Joe and Isabel and Esther walked toward the gates, holding hands tightly, as he softly sang to the two little girls,

This is dedicated
To the ones I love . . .

AFTERWORD

Isabel Contreras is a fictional child, but there are hundreds of thousands of Isabels in reality. We find too few of them early enough to help them as much as we could if we looked harder, and we help far too few of them as much as we should after we find them.

This book is about a baby, and about coordination. One of those subjects is eternally fascinating, and one can be terminally boring. But when the setting is social policy, the subject of coordination—or broken bridges, its opposite—is invariably about babies, children, and families.

Many people helped me think about and write this book, and I can only acknowledge a few of them. This book obviously overlaps a great deal with my professional life, but I need to emphasize that no individuals or organizations are the direct models for the agencies and persons depicted in this novel. This is fiction; the reality of the lives affected by substance use disorders and the inadequacies of current responses have been described in many of the products we have placed at www.cffutures.org. But the organization I work for, Children and Family Futures, is in no way responsible for the ideas or conclusions in this book.

I have learned a great deal from Dr. Ira Chasnoff, whose work with substance-exposed children has been a bright beacon in the midst of all the broken bridges we encounter. The agencies Prototypes and Shields are two of the finest collections of concerned people who work in this field, and I have learned much from their professionals and the women and children they care for. And I receive continuing inspiration from the lives of Jamie A. and other moms (and dads) who are succeeding in the uphill, rewarding work of parents' recovery.

The doctrine of "reasonable effectiveness" is not a legal standard today—but it should be. Hopefully, judges and those who advocate for children in the legal system will one day agree.

The novel is set in a large Southern California county, and some of the geography is borrowed from Los Angeles. But it should be said that many fine professionals work in Los Angeles County, and their track record includes excellent people doing the best they can with inadequate resources to build much-needed bridges of accountability.

Sam Leonard returns, as he has in a number of my novels. His experiences in Mexico were the subject of my first novel, *Like a Single River*. Joshua reminds me of some remarkable young men and women in my extended family, from whose lives and outlook I have borrowed.

I want to thank the writers' workshop hosted by UC Davis at Tomales Bay in October 2011, especially the group that worked with the fine novelist Ben Percy, whose comments on an early chapter of this novel were very helpful. A gifted artist, Shelley Furgason, produced the wonderful cover. Helen Gardner did another great line edit. Adam Gardner, a superb First Reader, made some excellent suggestions that moved things along in the right directions.

As always, my wife Nancy Young has given me the gifts of time and inspiration. Our children Rick and Ashley have helped us and challenged us to think clearly about some of the issues in this book. My daughter Larisa and her husband James Owen (USMC 1990-1994) have run interference for me in many ways throughout the writing of this book, and I am deeply grateful to them. James kept me from making too many mistakes, as an Army guy might, about his jarheads. John Allen also helped with the Navy-USMC relationships. And my grandson Nicholas and a boy named Ozzie continue to fill me with hope for the future.

A Report submitted to the Grand Jury

Interagency Dysfunction in County Government: The Blame Game

Executive Summary

By Sam Leonard and Joshua Bronson

This report was developed by a team of legal professionals and their consulting team, in response to a kidnapping incident at a local hospital involving an infant who was born drug-exposed. Our review documented that many agencies, in addition to the hospital and the child welfare agency, were involved in the case—or should have been. The search for this child has ended positively, and we hope her future is bright.

But during the course of our investigation, a number of issues stemming from agency dysfunction were raised by county officials and many others with whom we talked. By agency dysfunction we mean *the inability of county agencies with the responsibility for children and their families to work together effectively to solve problems faced by these children and their parents.*

We found a rhetoric of collaboration, but underlying it was a culture of fragmentation, overlapping roles, and failed accountability. Many more agency officials have mastered the slogans of collaboration than are practicing its techniques and strategies. Fragmentation and politics reinforce a narrowed vision of what is possible in working across agency lines for children and their families.

The problem is not that there are no interagency bodies. In fact, our conclusion is that there are too many interagency bodies, many of which undermine interagency working relationships because they take so much time in generally useless talk and "planning," rather than deliberate action.

We found that resources matter to agencies' ability to perform their own functions and to work across agency lines. But it is more than a resources problem—it is also a problem of leadership accountability.

We also found that federal oversight is more active in the processes of agency operations than in their outcomes, and more often applied in vertical, single-agency scrutiny of county functions than in working across agencies, due to the fragmentation of the federal government and congressional committees.

Finally, as we will detail further, we found a recurring pattern of county elected officials becoming active and vocal during agency crises that received media attention, with virtually no ongoing follow-up to determine if the underlying causes of the crises had been addressed.

Interagency missions and values

Repeatedly, officials and staff told us that certain key functions in serving children and their families were "not our job."

This fragmentation of mission is widely evident in the reported outcomes of the agencies, which are organized primarily by single-agency functions rather than those critical outcomes that can only be achieved by agencies working together. The problem that led to our investigation—the birth of a drug-exposed newborn child—is perhaps the most challenging interagency problem faced by county agencies. We found that more than a dozen agencies were potentially involved in the life of this child as she grows up. Yet the syndrome of pointing fingers at other agencies was widely apparent in fragmented attempts to prevent and respond to this issue, which affects as many as 21,000 children in this county each year. That means that a total of nearly four hundred thousand children and youth under 18 in our county are affected by prenatal substance exposure.

Interagency bodies abound in our county. Several years ago a count of these agencies found over two hundred separate interagency groups that worked on the issues affecting children and youth in this county. The typical group involves monthly meetings at which each agency reports on its own activities, rather than progress made by working across agencies to improve the outcomes that measure the well-being and safety of children. Reporting on what each agency does by itself is what the child development professionals call "parallel play"—toddlers who haven't yet developed enough to play with each other, but who sit in the sandbox and spend most of their time by themselves.

Those few interagency collaboratives that are effective are marked by three qualities: their leadership by professionals who are skilled at working "outside the box" of their own agency's focus, a set of shared outcomes that have been agreed upon by all members, and a willingness to share rather than to shield resources from interagency decisions.

Missing information

In many ways, we were told, the data that is not collected by the agencies is more important than the massive volume of information that is. For example, outcomes in the child welfare system are not available for parents and children affected by substance abuse, even though that substantial number of cases is one of the most important challenges to interagency operations. The treatment system cannot separate out the treatment outcomes of these children, and the child welfare system does not track the treatment outcomes for all those parents referred to treatment as a condition of keeping or being reunified with their children.

We also discuss the issue of missing information below in reviewing the federal role, since many of the requirements to collect information are conditions of federal funding.

The issue of resources

In nearly every interview we conducted and the many reports we reviewed, the problem of inadequate resources was mentioned. Staff and supervisors told us of excessive caseloads, a lack of cars to visit children, faulty information systems, and a lack of in-depth analysis of the huge volume of information fed into the system. All these problems were attributed to a lack of resources. In some cases, funds that were voted by the Board of Supervisors for expanded DCW staffing were offset with reductions elsewhere in the agency's budget. This tactic of "give with one hand and take with the other" has undermined the credibility of Board actions affecting DCW in the eyes of many agency staff.

We concur that resources are a critical part of the equation—but there is more to it.

The other side of the resources issue, in our view, is the double-talk emanating from elected officials and the media. Simply put, it is logically inconsistent for elected officials to blame agency heads and their staffs for under-funding basic operations in ways that make agencies' missions impossible to carry out. And it is also a blame-shifting exercise of political camouflage, hiding behind finger-pointing at agency heads who do not control their own budgets.

Resources issues are also involved in the linked syndromes of pilot projects and the failure to convert most of these projects into policy. Projects are how the systems funded by the county, state, and federal governments typically respond to crisis, creating new programs that serve a small fraction of those children and families that need help. One of our interviewees called this "projectitis," and explained the term by referring to a syndrome of launching isolated projects instead of changing how agencies work together.

Resources are also critical to the continued allocation of treatment funds to a mixture of some of the best agencies in the nation and a much less effective mixture of dozens of other well-intentioned, but inefficient service providers—many of whom do not even keep adequate records on the results of their treatment. A national standard has been set forth by the federal government for family treatment programs affecting children like Isabel

Contreras. Unfortunately, the majority of treatment programs in our county that serve women with children do not meet those standards. Yet they continue to get funding from the county which originates primarily with state and federal agencies.

The treatment that has proven most effective is family treatment—two-generation programs that help mothers (and fathers) recover from their addictions and show them how to parent children born with prenatal exposure. But despite this evidence of effectiveness, most treatment programs do not use the core principles of family treatment. Such programs are more expensive to operate, but more than repay that investment with better long-term cost savings, as proven in many evaluations.

That is not an issue of scarce resources; it is an issue of mis-allocation of resources to agencies that do not meet minimal standards for effectiveness and accountability for results.

The system through the eyes of a client

In talking directly with clients of the system, a strong emphasis on personal responsibility had come through to all of these clients. They were held responsible for their prior actions, for their recovery, and for their parenting. All of that accountability and personal responsibility seems appropriate to us, and to the vast majority of the staff working in county and county-funded agencies. Many of these parents had made tragic mistakes, for whatever reasons in their own histories and biology, and those mistakes endangered the lives and well-being of their children.

But some of these clients, and some of the impressive staff members who work with them, also asked powerful questions about the accountability of the systems that are supposed to be helping them. The waiting lists, the lost files, the inconsistent rules and regulations that prevent agencies from working with each other—the clients experience all of this in ways that make them wonder why they are the only ones that should be held accountable for prior and continuing mistakes that harm the lives of children.

The federal role

County agencies that work under federal oversight and with federal funding, which includes nearly all of those with a role in children and family issues, reported to us that federal mandates and guidelines were often a barrier to carrying out their mission. For some federal requirements, there are detailed reviews, which occupy county staff for hundreds of hours. But for others—such as the requirement for a safe plan of care for every child born drug— or alcohol-affected—there is no federal oversight at all. Nor is there any federal oversight to ensure that county or state agencies are actually counting these referrals, or the referrals for developmental assessments that every 0-2 year old in the child welfare system is supposed to receive. The state doesn't count them, the county doesn't count them, and the federal government never asks whether they are counted—despite a clear congressional mandate to do so and a state plan that explicitly accepts that mandate.

Federal agencies have funded dozens of pilot projects, but have provided little support in securing longer-term funding for these projects. An experiment with flexible federal funding was mentioned positively by several county officials, but some of them added that the reporting requirements for the project were far from flexible. Some federal pilot projects require evaluations, but others don't even ask those receiving federal funding to compare the results of the project with a group that didn't receive the services covered by the new program.

A further federal dysfunction is the inability or unwillingness to follow through with those programs that are effective. Each administration "discovers" new problems, which are essentially a re-labeling of old problems. It then launches its own small-scale programs to address the "new" problem, without building on the foundations of the best programs that had been funded by prior initiatives. Often there is no ranking of federal projects against each other, even though clear criteria exist which could be used to identify the most effective programs and those that do not merit continued funding. One official told us that federal agency officials fear the reactions of members of Congress who may have projects in their district identified as ineffective.

The role of front line workers

It's easy to criticize front-line workers. Some of them are time-servers, and others are timid. Some have great difficulty making judgments about competent parenting because they've never had to struggle with a drug-exposed child.

We heard about "wrap-around teams" that come into the homes of adoptive and foster parents and tell them how to parent the difficult kids they are raising. Yet on some of those teams, there isn't a single person who ever raised a child, who ever gave birth or adopted a child, or dealt with the needs of a prenatally exposed child whom they've cared for themselves.

But then there's this: some of these workers go into homes where everyone knows that violence can break out at any time. And sometimes they go in with a police officer, and sometimes they go in by themselves, because there's a kid who may be in an unsafe place, and the worker has a commitment to do what she can to watch out for that kid.

And then they go to court, and the judge berates them for something, and they have to sit and take it because you always have to pretend the judge knows what he's talking about even when he or she hasn't got a clue what is really going on.

And then they go through budget season, and the higher-ups tell them they need to take another cut, and caseloads are going up, and someone gets the bright idea that every other Friday you shouldn't work and shouldn't get paid—but your caseload will stay the same. You try telling a pro football player who makes millions of dollars that he has to play a little offense along with defense— and he quits in a huff. But add new cases to the workload of public workers on the front lines—no problem.

So front-line workers have multi-faceted roles, but most of all, they are what that label says: on the front lines. We borrow that label from war, sadly, where the front lines are dangerous, and where so much of the real mission is carried out. And often, the carryover from war to this work is closer than we'd like.

The U.S. military has been working at the task of services integration since 1947. It has not yet achieved that state, but it works at it very hard, for obvious reasons. People die when support doesn't come in time from the other units—when air cover is late, or when the ship sails without the necessary supplies. No branch of the service can accomplish its mission without support from the others.

Civilian agencies have much further to go. Yet the professionals who work at the intersections of agencies are among the most valuable employees of federal, state, and local governments. They are "multi-lingual," able to speak IEP and IV-E, CAPTA, ASFA, and IDEA. They wade through the alphabet soup, undaunted by the chunks of floating acronyms they encounter as they move upstream, doing their work.

Yet workers told us they felt at risk, disrespected, ignored, and devalued. They told us that they repeatedly brought back to their supervisors stories and evidence of interagency barriers to working together, without any follow-up action from their supervisors or policy leaders. They said they got little credit for the innovative ways in which they had to work out informal cooperative agreements with workers in other agencies, when their agency leaders had not been able to negotiate effective formal agreements to work across agency lines. They welcomed accountability for results, as long as it was accompanied by policy-makers' accountability for the resources they needed to achieve the results.

Conclusion

Someone said to us during our interviews that when agencies and politicians act like children, the real children get hurt. We saw much to confirm that judgment.

If Isabel Contreras had not been kidnapped and had remained in the hospital where she was born, she might have eventually come in contact with at least a dozen county and other local agencies.

Those agencies include, among others, the hospital, child protective services, foster care agencies, early mental health providers, child care and early childhood education providers, drug and alcohol treatment agencies, neighborhood primary health providers, mental health agencies, the family court system, agencies that work with children with disabilities, the school system and its special education units, and family resource centers that have been set up to work with families with problems. There are also interagency bodies on child abuse and prevention of abuse and neglect that have jurisdiction in such cases. Other agencies that could have been involved before Isabel was born include the LAPD—which had arrested her mother twice—the maternal and child health agency, the local health clinic, and the managed care agency where she received prenatal care.

All of these agencies had a role, or could have had a role, in helping Isabel Contreras. Instead a pervasive pattern existed of agencies and programs ignoring other resources available to them and their clients, because it was easier in the short term to operate alone.

The bridges across agencies are like the invisible bridges inside a baby's brain—the millions of tiny synapses that become thought and mind, memory and life itself. When those bridges are down, the things that should happen don't, and children's lives shrink to become far less than they could. And that is wrong—whatever the excuse, that is wrong. It is wrong when it happens inside a child's mind, and it is wrong when it happens within the organizations that are supposed to be helping that child grow and thrive.

Our mandate was not to suggest solutions, but to try to understand the conditions that led to Isabel Contreras being born substance-exposed and to understand what might have happened if she had remained in the hospital. The easy answer is that her mother had an addiction, and that addiction caused the problems that led to Baby Isabel being placed in the hospital's intensive care unit. The more challenging answer—because it challenges each agency and elected leader in the county to commit to operating differently—is that the resources and leadership were simply not available that could have helped Baby Isabel and her mother to overcome the problems caused by her mother's addiction.

We conclude this summary with three broad areas where we believe progress could be made, based on what we were told by those we interviewed:

The county needs to get serious about three things:

- Accountability: if the Board of Supervisors, agency heads, and the CAO's office are serious about better oversight of these issues, they will establish new metrics, with monthly review of what agencies are doing together—not just each agency's separate scorecards. When the report card is about child welfare parents in the treatment system who are monitored by the court—three agencies are effectively involved with the same family, rather than having three cases that are fragmented across three agencies.
  - o Accountability also means an annual rating of each agency's performance. If you get money from the county to help kids and their parents—the county should measure how well you achieve that goal. Each dependency court judge should ask annually for a performance review of what happened to each of the parents or children referred out to service providers. It makes no sense to make profound decisions about removing children and ending parents' custody rights without determining whether the service providers who are supposed to be making reasonable efforts are reasonably effective. We will return to this issue below.

- Prenatal exposure is an interagency problem that belongs to no agency, but requires the efforts of many agencies.

The lives of as many as 21,000 births and nearly 400,000 children and youth are involved. The CAO should report monthly to the Board of Supervisors on at least four measures: women screened for prenatal use, women admitted to treatment, the treatment outcomes for those women, and the birth outcomes for all women screened. The Board should make clear that getting pregnant women into treatment is the highest priority among all clients— regardless of other federal and state priorities or mandates. Arizona and Santa Clara County have adopted such priority statements as formal policy—and this county should do the same, and then enforce it with monthly reviews of admissions and their outcomes.

We recognize that there are significant privacy issues involved in this screening. For that reason, we have suggested state legislation that requires universal prenatal screening for substance use. We are currently screening in California for more than twenty birth defects—all of which have lower incidence than prenatal exposure. To argue that it is a private matter as to what a woman puts into her body while she is pregnant requires a suspension of belief that an infant has a right to be born without physical and mental handicaps. If those handicaps are preventable by reasonable caution, the burden of proof is clear: children should be protected. Prenatal use of alcohol is the primary preventable cause of mental retardation, and no privacy argument can eliminate that reality.

At the same time, we do not believe that women using drugs in pregnancy should be prosecuted, unless they continue to do so after their baby's birth in a way that endangers the child. But we do believe that women using drugs or alcohol during pregnancy should receive a referral to family treatment followed by monitoring of their prenatal care and their birth outcomes. If they do not enroll in treatment, assuming the treatment program they are referred to knows how to respond to their addiction, then they will have made a choice, determined in part by their brain chemistry, to be sure. But that choice and that chemistry—untreated—means they are unwilling or unable to take the medicine they need, just as a diabetes patient needs to take her medicine regularly. Without it, her baby is in jeopardy and needs a safer home.

- Third, we are convinced, after reviewing recent legal cases and talking with attorneys who represent children and work on children's cases, that a new legal doctrine is needed that updates the reasonable efforts requirements of federal funding. What is needed now is a greater emphasis on reasonable *effectiveness* of services provided to parents and children. We now know enough, after decades of evaluations, to know what kinds of service are most effective. Yet that information is essentially ignored in court proceedings. A mere referral to services is today enough to satisfy "reasonable effort"—yet a majority of those referred never receive services or are referred to services that fail to meet federal and state standards of effectiveness for family treatment. If we ask parents to make all possible efforts to be able to parent their children safely, we should also ask service providers funded with public resources to make all possible efforts to provide effective services—not merely to provide reimbursable services. The law firm sponsoring this report is currently preparing a more detailed case for the doctrine of reasonable effectiveness, relying on precedents established in *Brown v Board of Education*.

Ultimately, all three of these are about the first: accountability. If elected officials persist in rhetorical politicobabble about these issues, the lives of more children will be harmed. If they use clear metrics to measure progress, screen and respond to prenatal exposure, and adopt a legal standard that holds both parents and agencies accountable, thousands of children will have better odds of leading fuller lives.

Respectfully submitted, Sam Leonard and Joshua Bronson